THE
Billionaire's
SECRET

USA TODAY BESTSELLING AUTHOR
ASHLEY ZAKRZEWSKI

Copyright © 2023 by Ashley Zakrzewski

All rights reserved.

No part of this book may be reproduced in any form or by any electronic or mechanical means, including information storage and retrieval systems, without written permission from the author, except for the use of brief quotations in a book review.

Dedication

A big thank you to my husband for being supportive in my writing endeavors and believing in everything I do. Without him, my books wouldn't be possible.

Thank you to my parents for raising me to chase my dreams and never give up! Writing can be a very secluded career and everyone around me checks in and keeps me sane.

To one of my good friends, Amy Stephens, thank you for keeping me sane. To another couple of decades of being writing besties.

1
Desmond

Two towering wrought-iron gates opened to my approach, and the luxurious engine of the SUV roared as the wheels churned the gravel down the winding driveway, stirring a thick cloud of dust. I reached the end of the driveway and cut the engine in front of the Renault Mansion. After inserting the key, the satisfying click signaled the unlocking of the door. I pushed it open, my mother's foot bobbing in a steady rhythm, her high-heeled shoe clacking against the marble tiles of our foyer. She still lived in the mansion after my father's death.

My eyebrow raised, and then I gave her a glassy stare as I shut the door, knowing since she was waiting for me, she had some gossip she couldn't wait to share. She had on a black cocktail dress and her hair was in a neat bun. Leave it to my mother to always look so damn put together. Her lips were painted a deep shade of red.

"Weren't you supposed to be going out with Gerard tonight?"

Her lips pressed together in a slight grimace. "Desmond, there's plenty of time for that. You're home early."

I put my briefcase down and loosened my tie with a sigh. "I have a date tonight and need a quick shower," I said, moving toward the stairs.

My mother, Madeline, aged overnight after my father's passing. She became even more protective of us, especially Leanne. At twenty-two, my sister was determined to make her own way in the world. She bought a club, which was mine originally, with a friend in a bad part of town. Mom always lectured her about it, warning her of the perils of working in such a place. My mother was constantly on edge, her lips pressed together like a zipper to keep it all in.

"I hardly see you or your sister. She's either at that Club Bush or she is with that Dan person. It's not safe for her to be there. Such a dangerous neighborhood. And you're always working, just like your father. Don't you ever stop to enjoy life?"

She acted like we didn't have bodyguards watching us everywhere we went. Every day something reminded me why, with every breath, we were at risk; the Renault name brought enemies with it, both foreign and domestic, and billions of dollars in wealth had to be protected.

"I got my work ethic from Father. You know that. The one thing he instilled in me was the importance of the family image and keeping the businesses running smoothly. With that immense responsibility comes many late nights. You know that better than anyone."

She gestured to a bottle of aged whiskey on the counter behind her. "Have a quick drink with me, son. You have time, right? Or does this girl you're seeing have you wrapped around her finger?" Her eyebrow arched, and her gaze held me captive.

Wow, Mom. Tell me how you really feel, why don't ya?

"You got me for fifteen minutes, and then I have to take a shower and go."

Her words were laced with frustration when she said, "What do you mean, fifteen minutes?"

I could sense my mother's unease as I followed her to the living room and hung my blazer and navy tie on the back of the settee. She stood in the center of the room, her arms crossed, her eyes darting from the corner of the room to the window.

"So, what is it? What's bothering you?"

"I met Kimberly Bennett and her little boy today." Her eyes were peering at me as I poured two glasses of whiskey.

"Okay? And?" I raise an eyebrow. *Seriously?* She wanted to talk to me about the newest hotshot business owner in town? "Ms. Bennett must have some serious backers to rent the Thornton Co. building. And she has a child. That's a well-kept secret."

"Do you know her?" she asked as I handed her the glass.

"No. We both went to one of those dreadful networking events a while ago, but we didn't speak. What was so notable about Kimberly and her little boy that you had to bring it up? Am I missing something?"

Oh God, is she going to set me up with her? That was where I drew the line. I didn't need her meddling in my love life.

"What was notable, Desmond, is that the child is a mirror image of you at that age. He has your eyes, your smile, and he tilts his head like you sometimes do. In fact, it quite startled me."

"Really, Mother, you're just being..." I stopped in my tracks. "I recall Cecily telling me about the achievements of her half sister. Cecily hoped Kimberly visited her family so she could introduce her to me."

"Wait, who is Cecily?" my mother asked.

"Kimberly is Cecily's sister. I dated her six years ago. We met at one of your fundraisers."

Cecily was shy and unassuming, not the type of woman

who normally caught my eye. But her enthusiasm and dedication to her work, supporting parents with young children from poorer backgrounds from the Bush area, held my interest.

I invited her out to dinner to find out more about her work and then took her home. Of course, I accepted her invitation to come in 'for a coffee or something.' The 'something' turned into an enjoyable three hours in her bed.

I saw her again a few more times, but the relationship fizzled out soon after the death of my father. I had to take on more responsibilities, including extensive traveling to visit Renault Tech subsidiaries. Plus, I didn't want yet another casual coupling in my life. Much of my antics calmed down after my father's passing, and I grew a reputation as a shrewd and imaginative business leader. Although the tabloids still loved to follow me and exploit me as a womanizer.

"You were seeing Cecily McCormick?" Her eyes locked on me. She always pushed her limits in my personal life, so she shouldn't be surprised she had no clue. Some things I liked to keep private.

"It was a long time ago. The relationship was very brief. I haven't seen her since. Does she still work at that nonprofit?"

Honestly, I should have kept in touch with her. She was an amazing woman and had so many noble plans to help the struggling neighborhoods. The one thing I liked about her was she couldn't care less about money. She got paid horribly, but absolutely adored what she did. Before our breakup, we discussed Renault Tech donating money so they could help even more families. Growing up, we always had money, and sometimes it was nice to be able to use that to help others. Cecily was very passionate about the community.

"Oh, did you not know? Cecily died."

My head snapped up. "She died? When? How?"

Nobody knew about us, so it made sense that I didn't get a

phone call, but there wasn't anything in the paper about it either. For someone so well known around this area, it came as a surprise.

"At least five or six years ago."

The color drained from my face. *No. It isn't possible.* I always used a condom, but I recalled one rather energetic occasion when I stayed the night at her apartment. It was two days after my father's death. The sex, an all-night session, was frenetic and intense. Cecily was very generous in her desire to comfort me, then we ran out of condoms. And maybe just one time... in the early hours of the morning when I slipped inside her from behind. *Jesus! No! It can't be.*

"How old is the child, Mom? What's his name?" My stomach was in knots, running through the timeline.

She shrugged her shoulders, gazing around the room. "He could be about five or six. What on earth is the matter? You're white as a sheet."

"That child may be mine..." The words came out of my mouth, but my hands raced to cover it. This doesn't make any sense. *Why would Cecily keep this from me?* We didn't end on bad terms, so maybe she was seeing someone else right after me, and that was why she never called. Yet, my mother's words rang through my head again. *He looks just like you.*

"Did you get Cecily McCormick pregnant?"

My fingers rushed through my hair and then landed on my hips. *It can't be.* "Mom, I swear I didn't know she was pregnant, but there is a possibility."

She grew still for a moment, touching her chin, and then the pacing began.

"Maybe we are getting ahead of ourselves. Surely, she would have told you, right?"

"Maybe. It was a long time ago, and I was a little impetuous then. But we ended on good terms... or so I thought." I buried my face in my hands. *This can't be happening.* I picked up my jacket and moved toward the door. There was no use in just sitting around here when I could go and sort things out. There was only one way to confirm or deny me being the father.

"Where are you going? What are you going to do?"

"I'm going to talk to Ms. Bennett. She will know who the father is, and then we will know for sure."

It was seven o'clock. Kimberly would still be in her office. Owners of start-ups worked all hours of the day and night to get their business established, not that Bennett Technologies looked anything like a start-up, but I was banking on my hunch about her.

There was no time to arrange for my bodyguard Ward to meet me. In the car, I called Marsha. "Hey, I've got to cancel our date tonight. I'm sorry. Something urgent has come up."

We hadn't seen each other much in the past month because of business meetings and she worked a shit ton of hours, too. Our schedules were opposite. I withhold the news of me possibly being a father so as not to worry her before it was confirmed.

"What am I going to do with you? This is one of my rare nights off."

"I'm pretty sure I know what I want to do with you. I'll make it up to you, multiple times. Promise."

"You'd better. Wanna know what I'm wearing right now?"

My cock stiffened. "My naughty girl. I'm driving, but I'll call you later."

The tires squealed off the long circle driveway in front of the mansion, heading for Bennett Technologies. She must be successful if she could already afford to rent from there. Thornton owned the building outright but occupied the top five floors and typically rented out the rest. I often glimpsed the simple yet impressive banner that blazoned her name high above the Bay. With her being back in Bayview, I had never brought up my relationship with her sister, and now I regretted that. I visualized her face from the last time. A blonde with glasses.

The parking lot was desolate with only two cars, so I pulled into a spot right outside the front doors. In a few quick strides, I was pushing the buzzer and the security guard recognized me.

"Good evening, Mr. Renault. How may I help you?"

Everyone knew me, the scion of the uber rich Renault family. Apart from my reputation with women, I was known for my astute leadership of Renault Technologies, a multinational conglomerate with significant share ownership in almost every type of business one cared to name—resorts, hotels, restaurants, and insurance. The list was endless, but excluded pharma and arms. My family deliberately avoided those two industries. We owned a jet, a yacht, race horses, several homes, a fleet of vintage vehicles, and those were just the outer and visible trappings of our wealth.

"I'd like to see Ms. Bennett if she is still here."

His forehead wrinkled. "Do you have an appointment, sir? It's late for her to be having company."

"No, I don't. Just let her know I'm here to see her."

"Yes, sir. One moment."

The reception area was open and spacious, elegant and welcoming. They framed the walls with prints, placed two plush white leather settees on either side of a large mosaic coffee table, and added large leafy plants. Whoever decorated this place didn't skimp on the small details.

"Ms. Bennett is on her way down. Please take a seat."

My body was restless, and I needed answers so I couldn't sit down. *Why hadn't anyone told me about him?* The timing was right and if he was my son, I shuddered at the thought of him not having a father around his whole life.

Within minutes an elevator door opened and an attractive blonde wearing glasses with her hair in a high ponytail stepped out dressed in a gray pencil skirt and red silk shirt, an ensemble that showed off her figure to perfection. She tapped her way toward me in black high-heeled pumps.

Oh dear God! How can anyone get any work done with that in the office?

I couldn't take my eyes off her. She was a fucking vision. I took in everything about her as my practiced eye skimmed over her body. It's hard to believe she was related to Cecily, who was quiet and understated. This one looked confident, a badass. Her very appearance was an announcement. I instinctively braced myself for the assault. She looked feisty, and this wasn't just any old conversation.

"Good evening, Mr. Renault." She smiled, but her eyes were questioning. "This is an unexpected surprise. What can I do for you?"

My mind came up with many answers to that question, but I was here on important matters and needed to stick to my guns. I had many questions and right now all I wanted was answers.

2
Kimberly

WHY WOULD Desmond Renault be in my reception area this late at night? My laser-like blue orbs appraised him. His sleek gray Italian silk suit fitted him to perfection. His tieless open-neck shirt just added to his allure. *Ahh, yes, the notorious manwhore of Bayview. Damn, the man is attractive.*

I knew of Desmond Renault, of course. *Who didn't?* But I'd never formally met him. Glimpsing him across a crowded room didn't count. Up close and personal, he was hot as hell, even more handsome than his photographs suggested. I had a thing for men sporting a scruff, but he wasn't my type. Arrogant and entitled I could do without. His reported tendency to hop in and out of the bed with different women, as regularly as he trimmed said scruff, was unappealing. *What could he want with me this time of night?*

His eyes skimmed over my body, heat rushing to my cheeks. "I'm sorry to barge in on you unannounced." Desmond looked around at the reception. "Can we talk in private?"

Bennett Technologies had no business with the Renaults so his presence was confusing.

"Yes, of course. Follow me."

My back was to him as I walked, but his eyes were drinking in my body, every inch of it. I led him to a door off the reception area and ushered him in.

"Do sit down." I gestured to one sofa and then sat opposite him, hoping the flush wasn't still visible in my cheeks.

"Ms. Bennett, my mother saw you with a young boy today. Is he your nephew?"

I bit my lip. Of all the things I expected to hear, that sure wasn't one of them. My entire day had been off-putting, so I guess it made sense to end this way. "Yes, why?"

"I don't quite know how to say this, so I'm just going to cut straight to the point. Your nephew might be my son."

My blue eyes opened wide, and then I laughed, my head rolling backward. *He can't be serious! Is he doing drugs?* There was no way William was his. My sister wouldn't have ever slept with a man like him. *Is this some kind of sick joke?*

He stared at the upsweep of my throat, and he waited for my laughter to subside.

"I didn't think I said anything funny." His demeanor went from collected to irritated.

"Are you kidding me? It is funny. You're funny. My sister didn't know anyone like you. We are talking about the same woman, right? Cecily McCormick?" I spoke in short staccato sentences, each one intended to puncture his arrogance.

"Someone like me? What does that mean?" His eyes searched mine.

"Where did you meet? I mean, you guys didn't exactly hang out in the same circles. So please tell me how you think you are William's father?"

"Don't answer a question with a question. Didn't they teach you that at Yale?"

My breathing hitched. Desmond knew I went to Yale? Did he research me before coming here?

"You, Mr. Renault, are a man-whore, a notorious womanizer, if I'm being polite. My sister is, was, a very respectable woman who was immersed in her work and didn't frequent the places to meet someone like you. And she was *so* not your type. So, tell me, what's going on? Why did you turn up here and make such a ridiculous assertion?"

Cecily never told us who the father was, but I always assumed it was because he was a married man, not Desmond fucking Renault.

"I'm a guest on your premises, and this is the first time we've met. Are you typically so insulting and judgmental about people you don't know? And what exactly is my type?"

I flushed with a little bit of guilt but not enough to apologize. *Nope. I definitely wasn't going to do that.*

His gaze went down to the opening of my shirt, its three top buttons undone. *Seriously? He can't even help himself right now from staring at my cleavage while having this conversation. He's a joke!* I shifted in my seat. He was being suggestive, a typical male tactic to throw me off my game. There was a slight curve of his lips.

"I believe you met my mother at Action for Children and she said the child with you was the spitting image of me at that age."

He can't be serious? He slept with my sister? Why wouldn't she tell me about it?

"Cecily and I were in a brief relationship nearly six years ago. It lasted about five or six months. We met at a fundraiser hosted by my mother. I didn't have knowledge of her passing or having a child. If the boy is mine, I don't know why she didn't tell me since we parted amicably."

My eyes latched on to his face. I mentally removed his

scruff and aged him down to a boy. There was some resemblance for sure. William's eyes were the same color and shape. He had Desmond's nose. But none of that said William was his son. *No way.*

I met his eyes. "You should know I'm going through the process of adopting William, my sister's child, who couldn't possibly be your son."

After five years, my mother pushed me to do a formal adoption, and now Desmond was here claiming to be his father? The timing couldn't be worse.

"Nevertheless, I want to meet... um... William and have a DNA test done. And call me Desmond, please. Mr. Renault makes me feel like I'm eighty years old."

Nope. That won't be happening. Won't be on first-name terms with you, ever.

"That won't be necessary."

"If William is my son, I have every right to see him. It's not like I stayed away on purpose... I'm not a deadbeat father."

"Hey. Hold on. This is moving way too fast. You arrive at my office offering no kind of proof of him even being yours and now you are talking about meeting him? No way. He's only five years old, and you aren't an appropriate father for him, even if you were his father."

Desmond bristled in his chair, the vein in his neck trembling. "There seems to be little point in continuing this conversation tonight. I find your tone offensive and unhelpful. Let me assure you I have no intention of disrupting William's life or being inappropriate, as you put it, around him. What does that even mean?"

Everything about Desmond Renault screamed inappropriate. The way his eyes scanned my body or the way he licked his lips as he spoke. The man couldn't even keep his eyes to himself for more than a couple minutes.

"You know what it means. Your lifestyle isn't fitting for the needs of a young child. William doesn't need you. And you won't disrupt his life? That's just hilarious." I was throwing down the gauntlet. Nothing could stop him from seeing William once he proved his paternity, but there were steps that needed to be taken. Precautions and all that. He needed to slow down.

"What did your sister say when she discovered she was pregnant? She must have given some indication about the identity of her child's father."

"Well, she certainly made no reference to you. She had all sorts of plans for their future and none of them included any man. Unfortunately, there were birth complications, and she didn't make it through the delivery."

I hated having to talk about this again. It was painful, but William deserved the very best and we could give that to him. Could Desmond? Would he be around enough? I just couldn't imagine him as a father.

"Like I said, my mother and I have been raising William. He's a happy little boy and doesn't need this kind of upheaval in his life."

He swiped his hands down his pants, fidgeting in the chair. "Look, all I want to do is find out whether William is my son."

That raised my hackles. "Where were you for the last five years? We took care of him before you, and it will continue after you." I stared at him, my eyes pinpoints of fire and fury. "William doesn't need your money. He is well provided for, I assure you."

Desmond stood up, the vein in his neck pulsating. "There really is no point in continuing this discussion. You will hear further from my lawyer."

He walked to the door and turned for one last look. "What is your nephew's full name?"

"William Lucas McCormick. Why?"

Desmond closed his eyes and inhaled deeply. "Goodbye, Kimberly."

I watched Desmond Renault exit the building and disappear into the night. He never looked back, but the way his face fell when hearing his full name scared me. Something wasn't right.

A frown took over my face as the letter Cecily left in a safety deposit box came to my mind. He was set to open it on his eighteenth birthday, but what if that letter contained proof of Desmond's paternity? I clamped my hand over my mouth. *Oh dear God. No.* We needed to open it.

I rushed back to my office and found my phone and tapped on the name of the only person who could help me through this.

"Hey, I need your help now. I'm in trouble."

"Kim, you're frightening me. What happened?" Barb asked.

"I think I've discovered who William's dad might be. I'm coming to you. There's not a second to lose. Have you lodged those adoption papers with the courts?"

"Yes, but the hearing won't be for another six weeks. Who do you think it is?"

My arm clutched my purse to my side, and I tried to maneuver the phone back to my ear, stepping into the elevator. "I'll tell you everything as soon as I get there."

3
Desmond

As soon as I got home, I dialed Alana Glacey, an ex-girlfriend now living with my best friend. The Senior Partner of Glacey Associates, Alana was not the Renault family's legal adviser, but she was the person I wanted to help me with my son.

Before meeting Kimberly tonight, I was uncertain about what I wanted to do but now it was crystal clear. How dare she insinuate I was an unfit person to raise my own child? William Lucas McCormick was indeed my son. Cecily gave our son my middle name.

She was so quick to judge me without even getting to know me first, and she should be the first person to understand that everything you read in the tabloids wasn't true. Kimberly had her fair share of articles, and not all of them painted her in a magnificent light. Yet, she couldn't even give me the benefit of the doubt before insulting me.

Obviously, she had no clue of my middle name so she couldn't put the two together, but I was his father. If Kimberly gave me more of a chance to explain tonight, then things could have gone smoother, but she was on a warpath. It didn't matter what came out of my mouth, she wouldn't have heard it.

Once the DNA test was finalized, Kimberly was guaranteed to be in my life. As my son's aunt and current legal guardian, it was impossible not to be in the same room with her. Now that I knew of his existence, he wouldn't be without a father any longer.

Alana was a beast in the courtroom and her specialty was child cases.

"Alana? Listen, I know it's late, but I just found out I have a son and need to retain your services."

She remained quiet for a moment, which I expected, because no one saw that coming.

"Yes, you heard me right. A son. Now, let's get down to business."

I explained the situation. Alana thought Ms. Bennett would be more likely to listen once the DNA test came back.

"Think about it from her perspective, Des. You walked into her place of business and sideswiped her with your paternity. Not only that, but of a child she has been raising for five years. Don't think about her as her aunt, but like his mother," Alana said with emphasis on the mother part.

"Okay, so maybe I jumped the gun by going there tonight and should have waited to talk to you. A son, Alana. I never knew I had a fucking son out there."

Words couldn't even describe the betrayal by Cecily for not telling her family about me. Was I that bad of a person she wouldn't tell me about my own flesh and blood? None of this made sense.

"Take a deep breath. Don't get yourself worked up. Let's handle this. I'll get the DNA test, and then we will go from there. Just remember, they will use everything you say against you. Her office is likely recorded, so whatever you said tonight, it's fair game."

Shit! I didn't even think about that. Although, it was mostly her insulting me the whole time, so I should be good.

"Alright, we should both get some sleep. Our wake-up times come too soon. Thanks for your help."

"My pleasure, Des. You know that."

I couldn't comprehend why Cecily withheld her pregnancy from me. Nine long months, and she still said nothing. Now I was a father, even though I hadn't had the chance to meet my little one yet. I had more money than I could ever spend, but that shouldn't impede my rights as a parent. William was my son, and my blood ran through his veins. I missed out on his first five years of life, but soon he would know me as his dad. I'd do whatever I could to make up for the time I lost.

Tears stung my eyes as it hit me—I was a *father*.

I didn't want William to think the reason for my absence was because I didn't care about him. That it was my decision not to be there. Kimberly's reaction was genuine, so Cecily didn't tell anyone about my paternity. I commended Kimberly for taking William in as her own and raising him in my absence, but once the test came back, I wanted to be in my son's life. She couldn't keep him from me. Instead of fighting me, she should give me a chance to prove what kind of father I could be.

My eyes shut and I took a deep breath, calming myself, trying to find the silver lining in today. If my mother wouldn't have meddled, then I wouldn't have known about William. Another couple of years could've went by with my son running around the same town as me without my knowledge.

"What's going on, Desmond?" she asked, most likely listening in to the conversation with Alana, not having the concept of personal space.

"You're here. Have you eaten anything?" My stomach was growling since I only had a protein bar today for breakfast.

"I canceled dinner with Gerard when you ran out of here like some demented soul. What's going on? You got me worried."

"It's okay." I put my arm around her shoulders. "Let's get something to eat and I'll explain everything."

Let's pray Kimberly came to her senses and stopped insulting my ability to be a father. Sooner or later, we would be in each other's lives whether we wanted to be or not.

4
Kimberly

MY TIRES SQUEALED to a stop in front of Barb's two-story colonial house in a tranquil neighborhood. I shouldn't be bothering her this late, but I didn't know what else to do. The air was still, and the night was peaceful, but inside, Barb was pacing back and forth, her light-blue pajamas shaking with her every movement visible through the floor-to-ceiling glass windows. When her eyes landed on me, her face softened, and she scrambled to the front door.

"Oh, honey." She bundled her arms around me. "What happened?"

Everything spilled out in quick succession. About how Desmond Renault appeared at my office. How he said he knew my sister and he may be William's father. I tried to stay calm, but I cried at how Desmond looked at me with such conviction.

Barb ripped away from me. "Come here." She guided me to a couch in the corner of the room. "Sit down and take a deep breath. Let's talk it through."

The tears ceased as I did as she said. I told her how fearful I was, how I didn't know what to do if he was William's father. I'd been the only mother he'd ever known, the one who'd been there for him since he was born.

"It's okay." Barb patted my arm. "We'll figure it out. But first, you need to calm down." She reached for the coffee table, clutched a box of tissues, and passed them to me so I could dab my eyes.

"Do you want some tea?" she asked. "I think it'll help relax you."

She went to the kitchen to make it. I took in the pictures of William and me on the walls, the bookshelves full of novels, the cozy blanket she always kept draped over her chair. The familiarity of the place wrapped around me like a hug.

When Barb came back with the tea, we sat and drank it. She was right. The warm tea started to make me sleepy.

"Right now, it's too late for me to do anything. I expect him to reach out to his lawyers tonight to request a DNA test, so I'll be hearing from someone tomorrow, I'm sure."

"What am I going to do if William is his? Can he take him from me? Will he deny my adoption request? Barb, I can't lose him. He's my everything. There must be a reason my sister didn't want him to know."

Her hand caressed my back, and she studied my eyes. "All in due time. Try to go home and get some rest. I'll contact you as soon as I've heard from his lawyers, okay?"

My body rose off the couch, and my feet shuffled to the front door. "I don't know what I would do without you."

Barb grinned, blew a kiss at me, and I left.

As the engine roared awake, I hauled out of her driveway and headed home. Hopefully, my mother Angela wasn't waiting for me because this was going to blow her mind even more than mine. With working more and more, she stepped up and had been a godsend for William and me. She took care of him while I was working because I refused to put him in daycare, not knowing who I could trust to take care of such precious cargo. After the horror stories people told me about daycare workers, I couldn't bring myself to take that chance.

After pulling into the driveway, I parked my car in the garage and fumbled for my keys in my purse. As I put the key in, the door flew open, revealing my mother's concerned face. She knew something was wrong; the blotches on my face gave it away. *Shit!*

I hesitated, not wanting to have this conversation again tonight, but she pulled me inside and shut the door, ushering me into the living room.

"What's going on?" Her voice was calm but her face was intense.

"Desmond Renault showed up at my office."

My mother's expression didn't change, but her eyes widened a little. "Desmond Renault? Why? Is he wanting to do business with you? That's wonderful. He's very well known around here."

I closed my eyes and took a deep breath, repeating myself once again. "No, Mother. That wasn't it. He says he's William's father."

My mother sat open-mouthed, staring at me with disbelief.

"Desmond Renault? You're telling me that *the* Desmond Renault is my grandson's father? Cecily made a child with Desmond Renault?" Her grip on the couch tightened, her knuckles turning white, and her face draining of color.

"Mom. Calm down. That's what he said, and repeating his name won't make him go away."

She paced across the living room, her brows knitted together. She shook her head and ran a hand through her hair. "It's just unbelievable. How did this happen?"

"Um... sex? That's usually how it happens." I shifted,

averting my gaze, not wanting any images of my sister and Desmond in bed together.

"Don't be facetious, Kimberly. How long have you known about this?"

I groaned. "I just found out tonight, although I didn't believe it at first."

Her gaze intensified. "And you do now?"

"I think it's a strong possibility. All the times I pestered Cece to reveal the identity. No matter how much we pleaded, she was tight-lipped and that frustrated me to no end. Sometimes I wondered whether he was a married man and that's why she didn't tell us."

"Why did he wait so long?" My mother's voice shook.

"Cece met Desmond at one of those glitzy charity dinners hosted by Renault Technologies." His brown eyes, expensive suit, and air of sophistication mesmerized my sister. "It was short-lived according to him. She never told him she was pregnant."

"So, how did he know there was a child?"

"His mother saw me today at the AFC with William, and when she got home, she told Desmond how much William favored him. So he came to my office tonight. He knew Cece was my half sister."

"What are we going to do, Kimberly? You're only weeks away from finalizing the adoption."

She doesn't need to remind me because I was already freaking out over here. "On my way home, I dropped by Barb's. I'm afraid I wasn't welcoming to Mr. Renault. She told me that the Renaults were major players in the area and that I should prepare for some tough days ahead. They also hold considerable influence in this city."

Mom's eyes remained fixed on mine.

"That letter Cece left in her safety deposit box for William may tell us the name. Barb thinks it would be a good idea for us to read it, and in William's best interest to do so, too. We should go down there first thing in the morning."

"Yes, okay. But can he stop the adoption?"

William had a stable home with us, and God knew what he was going to get if he went to live with Desmond. A different woman every night to call mommy. *Definitely fucking not.* I would fight this to the ends of the earth to keep William safe and guarded.

"He would have to provide proof of paternity and Barb thinks a judge would decide what was in William's best interest, given all the circumstances. Maybe we can head Desmond off by giving him full access to William."

My mother was going to continue this conversation until I was blue in the face, but after the long day I had, my bed was the only place I wanted to be. Plus, I was sick of saying his name. He had me so riled and there was nothing more I could do tonight.

"Look, Mom. I'm beat. It's been a long day which ended badly. Let's get some sleep and deal with this in the morning."

Mom smiled. "How about you have a relaxing bath, and I'll bring you some comfort in a cup," she said with a twinkle in her eye.

"Yes, extra creamy with extra marshmallows."

"Coming right up, baby."

Mother and I stepped through the revolving door into the bank, the air assaulting us with the smell of stale cigarettes and cleaning supplies. The tellers stared at us and my heartbeat quickened as I swallowed the lump in my throat. We made our way to the back of the bank, where the manager's office was. He looked up as we entered, his gaze cold and unwelcoming.

"Can I help you?" His voice was gruff and unfriendly.

"I need to access my sister's safety deposit box. Cecily McCormick."

He stared before sighing and getting up from his chair. "Come with me." He unlocked a side door and led us into the vault.

It was ominous, and I inhaled a faint smell of lemon lime cleaning supplies. They lined the walls with rows and rows of metal boxes of different sizes, each one with its own key. The manager stopped in front of one box and embedded a key in the lock. He swiveled it, and there was a loud click as the mechanism opened. He stepped aside and gestured for us to take it.

I tiptoed forward and reached into the box, my hands quivering. Inside, I found a thick envelope with William's name written on the front. I plucked it out and hugged it to my chest.

"Thank you."

The manager acknowledged me and waited outside for us to pass him before closing the vault. Mother and I shuffled back to the front of the bank, the envelope tucked in my purse. A sense of relief washed over me as we stepped back into the sunshine. We did it. Hopefully, this letter would tell us who William's father was, and that it wasn't Desmond Renault.

Back at home, I put the envelope on the coffee table and gawked at my mother. "Are you ready?"

She nodded.

I sat on the couch, opened the envelope, and began reading. My heart pounded as I scanned through the letter and recognized the name. My mother's hand landed on my shoulder, offering support as she was reading it as well.

"What do we do now?"

Mother exhaled and hugged me tight. "We make preparations."

I nodded, my mind spiraling with all the outcomes. The future felt uncertain, but I knew one thing—I would not lose William to a womanizing asshole like Desmond Renault.

5
Desmond

A FEW MINUTES BEFORE SEVEN, I arrived at Bennett Technologies and the receptionist guided me to the same room as the previous night. My eyes widened, and my pulse quickened as she stepped into the room. She was breathtaking in a pale-blue sleeveless dress, which accentuated her petite frame with diamond-shaped cutouts at her chest and waist, not exactly appropriate business attire but I had never been one to complain. I straightened my posture and rose to my feet. Her assistant wasn't very forthcoming on the phone to mine about this meeting. "Good evening. I didn't expect to see you again so soon."

"Mr. Renault, please sit." She took her place on the opposite couch. "I want to apologize for my unseemly behavior yesterday. It was a shock and I didn't respond well."

Yeah, that is an understatement. It still irked me how she painted me as a womanizing villain and believed everything she read about me in the tabloids. Maybe she finally came to her senses.

"I was a little abrupt in my approach. They said you have something to show me?"

Kimberly reached across the low table and handed me a white envelope. I took it and frowned. The name written on it was William Lucas McCormick. *What in the world is this?*

I held a puzzled expression. The handwriting was familiar from when Cecily used to leave me cute notes when she left before I woke up. It brought tears to my eyes. We weren't serious, but she was a wonderful person.

"Go ahead, open it." She encouraged me.

My eyes trailed to the opened envelope, knowing Kimberly already read it. My chest rose and fell before I took the piece of paper out and folded it open on my lap. *Should I even be reading this?* Cecily wrote this for our son, and it felt like an intrusion.

"I shouldn't be reading this."

"Believe me, you want to. It answers our questions, and you should know."

I was going into this blind, not knowing what it contained. After one last look at Kimberly, I prepared myself for the worst.

My Dearest Darling William,
You're growing big and strong in my tummy right now and should be born in just a few weeks. Your auntie Kim and nana Angela are so excited to meet you. One of the happiest days of my life was when I found out about you. I've always wanted to be a mama, and I can't wait to hold you in my arms.
There are some things that you won't quite understand, and for that I'm saving this for your eighteenth birthday. If things have gone according to plan, you still don't know who your father is, and I'm sorry for that, but I thought it was the best option for you to have a normal life.
Your father is Desmond Lucas Renault, and he lives in Bayview.

He might be living somewhere else now with a big happy family, but he will take you in with open arms.
I fell in love with your dad the very first time we met. As you will be, he is very handsome. Desmond is kind and generous to those he loves and will do anything for his family. He will love you, son. If I'm right, you will have his beautiful brown eyes and a smile that lights up the room. I hope you end up with the best parts of both of us.
I'm sure you will both be upset about this, but we can discuss it when you're ready. Your father didn't abandon me or you. Let me make that clear. He doesn't know you are his. If he did, then he would be a big part of both our lives. He isn't the type of man to shy away from responsibility, that I know.
There are reasons why I decided not to tell him, and I'll explain once you've read this letter. Your dad and I lived very different lives, but the time we spent together was very special and we parted as friends.
I love you so very much and only want the best for you. If you are ready to meet him, I will help you every step of the way. Your father might have a family by now, but he'll embrace you as his son.
Please come and find me when you've read this letter so we can talk.
With all my love,
Mom

Kimberly's eyes were on me, and she was trying to invade my thoughts. I tried my best to keep my facial expression blank, but inside I was unraveling. Why did she want to keep my son from me until his eighteenth birthday? She said she loved me? So many things were swirling around in my head, and tears stung my eyes as I fought them back. *He is my son.* I knew after hearing his full name, but this cemented it. It was in writing.

Holy shit, I'm a father. Reading this, knowing that she was gone and I could never ask her why, it hurt.

"I'm sorry. I didn't expect this. Will you excuse me for a few minutes?"

I put the letter on the table, leaving the room. When I got out of her office, I stumbled backward against the wall, my breath catching in my throat, then slid down the wall and my body crumpled to the floor. I buried my head in my hands as the tears spilled over. The words in Cecily's letter looped through my mind. Held captive in a homemade prison of guilt and regret, I replayed our relationship over and over. A fool for not realizing she was pregnant when we said goodbye all those years ago. How could she love me, yet keep me from knowing about our son? All these years, he was living in the same city and I never knew. *Why would she not tell me? Tell her family?*

The stubble scratched my palms as I ran my hands over my face. With a heavy sigh, I trudged back inside. Kimberly still sat on the couch, scrolling through her phone. She smiled and I couldn't help but return it even though my heart was shattered into pieces.

"Are you okay?" Her voice was breaking. I couldn't imagine what was going through her head right now. She read the same letter as me.

"Yes. Thank you for sharing this with me. You didn't have to."

She nodded, her gaze locked on the envelope in her trembling hands. I could tell she had her own reasons for wanting to show me the letter. Kimberly couldn't deny that I was his father now. That was the reason for our meeting today.

I fell silent and my throat tightened as I tried to find the words to ask, "Where do we go from here?"

A heavy pause filled the air before she suggested, "We

should talk about that. Do you want to get out of here and grab a bite to eat?"

"Rain check? I'd be poor company right now." My eyes pleaded and I drew in a slow breath to hold back the emotion that threatened to spill out.

"I've got an apartment upstairs, with a mini-fridge stocked with wine and other refreshments. You could do with a glass of Pinot Grigio or something even stronger right about now. What do ya say, Desmond?"

What the hell is she doing? Why didn't she just let me go home?

"You have an apartment here?" How simple that must be to have your residence within the building you work.

"Yes, it's nice to have since I spend many hours here. Sometimes I get so sucked into things I don't realize it's already midnight. Is that a yes?"

I took a minute to mull it over. This was the first gesture to being civil from Kimberly, and even though I would rather be anywhere else than here right now, whether I liked it or not, she was the guardian of my son. I needed to get in her good graces. "Yes, I'd like that. You just called me Desmond for the first time, so you've decided I'm not the rogue you thought, huh?"

She laughed. "Yes, I've changed my mind about you, only slightly though, since Cece said some nice things."

"She was so proud of you," I told her. "She bragged about your early entry to Yale and your business start-up in Boston, hoping you would return to Bayview so that she could introduce us."

"Well, that didn't happen, did it?"

That came out more sharply than she intended, I think, but I couldn't blame her. Here I was, the guy that wasn't there all those months through her sister's pregnancy, not when she died, and not afterward. There was some resentment.

Kimberly stood. "Shall we?" She led the way to the elevator, and I walked forward to call the transporter. Nothing happened. Then Kimberly pressed her thumb on the same pad on the wall I touched and the elevator doors opened.

"You're high tech here. I'm impressed," I said as we stepped inside.

She chuckled. "It only works on the elevator for Bennett Tech floors. Everyone else still lives in the twentieth century when it comes to elevators."

I liked her laugh. My eyes rested fleetingly on her vermillion lips. "I'll have to get you to update Renault Tech."

"I'm your girl; anytime you're ready, just let me know." She flushed. "I didn't mean I'm your girl, girl, I meant..."

My fingertips brushed her arm. "I know what you meant."

6
Kimberly

A CURRENT OF energy shot through me at his touch, and my skin buzzed alive with a hundred tiny bumps. I looked at his hand, smooth and tan, against my pale arm. Even in the warmth of the elevator, a chill passed through me as I tried to distance myself from his proximity. I was aware of his every movement, my breath coming quicker until the elevator doors opened and my cheeks grew red.

Desmond Renault paused, his icy brown eyes burning with desire. His presence was intoxicating. Temptation coursed through my veins, a desire to give in to the magnetic feeling of sinning. Whoever created Desmond Renault personified temptation. I turned as we walked out of the elevator and an alluring smirk played on his lips, daring me to come closer. I bit on my lower lip to stymie my desire.

My thighs quivered. I was desperate to keep him from seeing the effect he had on me, so I closed my eyes and turned my back to him, hiding the heated flush on my cheeks. *What the hell is wrong with me?* Oh God, I turned into one of those women who threw themselves before him. In the darkness behind my eyelids, I imagined the sinful things that must follow such an electrifying moment. *I will not succumb to his magnetic pull, dammit!*

Desmond's lips curved into a wide smile and his eyes widened as he took in the luxuriousness of my apartment. Creamy, leather furnishings offset the rich, mahogany walls. Crystal chandeliers sparkled from the high ceilings, and vibrant works of art hung on the walls.

I gestured toward the living room. "There's some wine in the fridge and glasses in the kitchen cabinet. Oh, and there's scotch too. I'm going to order some Thai takeout and then take a quick shower."

He nodded, taking in the surroundings.

I made my way across the living room, stifling a groan. My feet were heavy, almost as if lead encased them, but I pushed myself forward and stumbled into my bedroom. I kicked off my heels as I entered with a loud exhale. Hell, I was panting like some out-of-shape sprinter who just ran a four-minute mile. My hands shook as I tugged off my dress and underwear, then threw them on the bed before collapsing against the door.

The frigid water flew from the showerhead, striking my skin with a vengeance. I cringed and pressed my forehead to the cool tiles, wishing I could wash away the hollow longing in my heart. I hadn't been intimate with anyone since Justin moved two months ago. He had once been my Disney prince, but the elusive spark that could have ignited into a fiery love affair never materialized. A deep ache swelled in my chest. Justin and I weren't exclusive, or at least we never said so, but we shared a bed when he was in town. More of a *friends with benefits* situation. I wished I loved him, but that special something just wasn't there.

My fingers were following the water down my body, looking for the spot that beckoned for touch. A wave of pleasure came over me as my head fell back. The delicious sensation of my fingers moving circles gave me the release I so desperately needed.

I scrubbed my body with a washcloth, letting the water wash it away, and then grabbed the towel waiting for me and dried off. Desmond was alone in my apartment, and that gave me anxiety. I slipped into my sweatpants and t-shirt.

In my living space, Desmond was admiring the décor. His eyes took in the huge open plan living area with an expanse of floor-to-ceiling windows. My kitchen area was deep red and ultra-modern. But what seemed to catch his eye was the stunning Cherry Baby Grand, which sat in pride beside one window but shielded from the rays of the sun by a Chinese screen with a cherry blossom design.

"This is an amazing space," he told me after I coughed so he would know I was back in the room. "Do you play?" He gestured toward the piano.

"Do you think it's just for show?"

Why do I always have to be so damn confrontational? Or is it just with him?

"It's just a pleasant surprise, that's all. My mother required lessons when I was younger, but I haven't played in years."

I softened my tone as I said, "I like to play, but that doesn't mean I'm good. It calms the part of my brain that gets frazzled from spending too much time in front of a computer screen."

I stretched my legs out on the deep comfortable sofa opposite him, appearing relaxed and uninhibited. He poured a glass of chilled Chardonnay for me. When his eyes went straight to my breasts, I looked down. I didn't put my bra back on. *Fuck.*

He wrenched his eyes away as soon as I cleared my throat. If he didn't want me to think he was a womanizer, the least he could do was go an hour without staring at my ass or breasts. The funny thing is, I was wearing red and white polka-dot lounging pants and a white t-shirt, yet he was still staring. My hair, loose and damp, tumbled around my shoulders.

"I've ordered our food. The restaurant is just down the road. They know me, so we should have food in about fifteen to twenty minutes."

"So you live here?"

"No. It's more of a crash pad if I'm working late or have drunk too much to drive home. Friends often use it if they're visiting. I'd die if I had to live in the Bay twenty-four seven. William, Angela—that's my mom—and I live in Sunnyside."

"Close to the mountains," he said. "It's beautiful up there in the spring and fall. We have a house up there. Leanne and I loved spending time there when we were younger. I still go when I can find the time."

I knew where he meant, at the foothills of the mountain. The properties there were hardly wooden hangouts but massive homes. "I love it there, too. I've wanted to live there since I was a child. Mom struggled to raise two girls with no man, and things were tight for us growing up. So it's nice to enjoy a different life."

"You were successful from a very young age." His eyes raked over me.

"Are you asking how old I am?" A chuckle escaped my throat.

"A gentleman would never ask a lady her age."

"Are you a gentleman?"

"I'm not sure a man-whore and a notorious womanizer can be a gentleman," Desmond said, but with a wink.

How does this man make my lady bits beg for his touch? What is it that makes him so fucking irresistible?

"Maybe one day I'll tell you my life story, including my age. And perhaps you've changed, and I was just being a tad bitchy."

"I'm not ready to forgive you yet." His lips curved, and there was a feral look in his eyes like he knew my release just minutes ago was thanks to his touch.

"What must I do to earn your forgiveness?" I asked.

Shit. Am I flirting with him?

Desmond took a sip of his wine while gazing at me. "I'll think about that and let you know."

My whole body was vibrating with the magnetism of this man. I held his gaze, drawn in by those mesmerizing eyes. "Fine. I hope you're not withholding your forgiveness to punish me."

Yes. I am flirting with him.

"That's what I'm doing." He smirked.

And he is flirting with me.

I gazed at him over the rim of my glass and lingered on every aspect of his facial features, his square jaw, the dimple when he smiled. The shape and contour of his lips, his brown eyes. He was a handsome devil. Cece fell in love with him, and I could understand why. How would it be to be the focus of his attention? A little shiver went down my spine.

"Tell me about William," he said.

Thank God! Yes, let's change the subject!

"Yeah, let's talk about that. You can see him whenever you want. It's just a matter of agreeing what works for both of us with our schedules."

Desmond narrowed his eyes. "It still befuddles me. I want to approach this with a clear mind after we have both taken into consideration what is in the best interest of my son."

Okay. I don't like where this is going. "That's fine. While we eat, perhaps I should tell you a little about William, but I would like to hear your ideas for how we take this forward."

"I've asked my lawyer, Alana Glacey, to contact you about doing a DNA test, proving I'm William's biological father.

Although, that's a moot point given the letter, but that was before."

"Of course, I expected that."

"I guess once the DNA test results come back, the courts will require my consent to the adoption."

Fuck. Barbara already warned me about that. "Yes, I believe so," I responded with a heavy heart. "I hope you won't raise any objections."

He sidestepped the implicit question. "Do you have a date for finalizing the adoption?"

"Six weeks."

Desmond twitched. "I hope you'll push that back, now that I'm in the picture."

I knew it. "Why? Do you foresee a problem?"

He wouldn't waltz in here and deny my adoption request, would he? After everything I did for his son, for William. Surely, he was kidding.

"I would like to get to know my son before I sign him away. He should know I'm his father; my mother and sister Leanne would like to meet him too."

"Okay, let's just slow down here. You're on a high-speed train. First, I'm not asking you to sign him away. Angela and I are William's family, not random strangers. He's been with us from birth and right now, we're the only family he knows."

"I know that. My words came out badly. I just meant I'd like to spend some quality time with him and let William get used to the idea that he has a dad and a larger family alongside you and Angela before we enter any formal agreement."

Desmond lacks emotional intelligence. Not surprising for a man-whore.

"Fine. Why don't you come to our house for the first few visits so William can get comfortable with you before introducing him to your family? I don't want to freak him out. This is all very new."

I was in survival mode. Maybe this would keep Desmond occupied long enough for me to figure out what to do next. Barb had to stop him from taking away William. He might not come right out and say it, but he wanted William to be with him, not me.

"Yes, of course. You're right. We should take it slowly."

"Would you like to come over this weekend? Saturday afternoon. I'd like to tell William you're a friend of mine for the first visit."

"That sounds fine. Should I bring him a gift? What sorts of things does he like?"

"He's an avid reader, and he likes dinosaurs and robots—nothing over the top. We want him to appreciate what he has."

Desmond grinned.

"Ah, there's our food," I said after the elevator opened and the security guy handed me the bag. "Thanks."

I'm starving.

"Lots of delicious stuff here. I chose for you," I told Desmond, pulling out the containers and setting them on the counter.

"That's fine. I love everything Thai."

"Great. While we eat, I can show you the photo album of William. I'll arrange for a copy to be made for you."

He grinned. "Thank you. Leanne and my mother can't wait to meet him."

His mention of Leanne, William's other aunt, gave me a jolt. Everything changed in just twenty-four hours. Desmond changed my reality, and the uncertainty of the future scared me.

We laughed and chatted at the dining table, taking bites in between flipping through the album. Desmond loved the cute stories that went along with all the pictures from our family vacations. A couple of times I swear he looked distraught. It never occurred to me that maybe this was showing me just how much of William's life he hadn't been a part of, and that wasn't my intention. As much as he infuriated me, he wanted to be in his life, and I would not deny him access to his son. His presence was enjoyable when the focus was on William, and he seemed to be getting more comfortable with the idea of being a parent. This ride we were on should be interesting if nothing else.

Once we got to the end of the album, we were both yawning, our bellies full, and the clock read midnight. He looked at the mess on the table, then he stuffed everything back into the bag it came in. Most men wouldn't have thought to clean up after themselves.

"Well, thank you for showing me that and for dinner."

My eyes caught sight of the slight bulge in his pants. *What are you doing?* "Yes, of course. We both have had a rough couple of days."

At the door, he held his hand out toward me. "I look forward to seeing you on Saturday."

"The elevator will take you to the main floor," I said, pushing the button and then swiping my finger. "So just let yourself out. Good night."

I watched Desmond as the elevator doors shut, his eyes still locked on me. *Did he feel that magnetic pull, too?*

Since it was so late, I called my mother to check on William.

"How did it go?" Angela asked.

"Not where I expected it to go. He suggested I push back the adoption."

"We're William's family too. He may be his father, but he's only just came forward."

"I'm going to fight this with everything I've got. By the way, he's coming to see William on Saturday. We'll just say he's a friend of mine. I don't want to drop the whole father thing on him yet. How is he, anyway?"

"He left for the Land of Nod ages ago."

I chuckled. "Night, Mom. See you tomorrow."

"Night, baby girl."

I was restless and not quite ready for sleep yet. My mind was churning. I couldn't get Desmond Renault out of my head. There was one thing that helped me ease my mind a bit. I went back into my living area and sat at the piano. A little Mozart. My nimble fingers caressed the keys as my favorite "Wiegenlied" piano solo floated through the apartment. It was one of the many classical lullabies I played for William when he was a baby.

The thought of losing one of the two people dearest to my heart broke me, and I cursed the day my path crossed Madeline Renault's. Fate had an unmerciful way of upending people's lives when we least expected it.

The tears flowed as I continued to play. I was crying for everything—the pain and horror, the grief. My life was about to fall apart again, and I could do nothing to stop it.

Cece loved Desmond! *Unimaginable. She* wanted him to know his son but left it up to William to make that choice, but only when he was of age. *Why?* I believed Cece wanted to protect both William and Desmond, two people she loved. That was just like my sister, selfless.

My sister would not have wanted the life Desmond offered. It was likely that if she would have told Desmond, Madeline would have forced them to get married, and his lifestyle would have killed her.

I understood my sister's reasons for not telling Desmond,

but I was the one facing the consequences of Desmond discovering William before he came of age.

Well, I was going to honor her wishes to the best of my ability. I will fight tooth and nail for my nephew, to give him a normal life, away from the glare of cameras and any fallout from his father's notorious lifestyle.

First thing in the morning, I would contact my guy to get ammunition. Desmond Renault was sure to have some dirt in his past.

7

Desmond

I RAISED my sweaty palm to the Bennett's mahogany door and knocked. Beads of perspiration rolled down my forehead, but I wiped them away with my sleeve. After a few moments, shuffling feet and a muffled exchange came from behind the door. Then it swung open and a petite woman with graying hair and a warm smile appeared. "Hi, I'm Angela. Do come in."

After everything, I didn't expect such a warm welcome. This woman seemed to be much happier than Kimberly. *Thank God.*

"Nice to meet you." My heart fluttered in my chest as I handed her the largest bunch of tulips and hydrangeas I could find in the flower shop nearby. "These are for you."

"Thank you. They're lovely. Come. Kimberly and William are in here." She opened the door and ushered me into a room where her daughter and grandson were sitting on the floor in the middle of a gigantic wooden puzzle. Kimberly was fitting pieces together while William was taking apart a section he already completed. My eyes widened as I looked around before settling on my son, who focused on the task before him with a mischievous grin.

Oh my God, he looks like me. My heart dropped. His face, while still so small, had my nose and cheekbones. His eyes and hair were the same as mine. Time stopped as his little hands moved the puzzle pieces around. How long until his little hand would be holding mine? He looked up from his puzzle and our eyes met.

This moment would be secured in my heart forever. The little boy smiled, and the reality was starting to sink in. That was my son. William Lucas McCormick. I didn't expect to have children for at least another five years. Marsha and I weren't that serious because of our hectic schedules, and I wasn't the type of person to forget protection. Yet, Cecily had given me the best gift of all.

"Hi, Desmond," Kimberly greeted. "Come and join us."

Angela blazed a quick smile before turning and walking away, clutching the bouquet to her chest. "I'm going to leave you guys be and get these beautiful flowers into some water." As she opened the door to leave, she glanced back over her shoulder and winked before slipping out of sight.

"William, this is my friend Desmond. I told you he was coming to visit today."

He jumped up from the floor, ran over, and looked up with wide eyes as he asked, "Do you like dinosaur puzzles?" His hands were clasped behind his back as he swayed.

I smiled and crouched down. "I love them, but I'm not very good."

His face lit with enthusiasm, and he beckoned me to follow. I settled on the floor beside him, my legs tucked beneath me. He animatedly showed me the puzzle, the light dancing in his eyes. "Here."

He handed me a small triangular piece of wood and

gestured to the corresponding gap in the jigsaw puzzle. I implanted it, and when it fit, William let out a loud cheer and beamed at me. From the corner of my eye, I could see Kimberly watching us.

"Do you want to do some more?" William asked, his eyes shining.

I smiled and ruffled his hair. "Yes, of course I do. And when we're finished, we will open the surprise I brought you." I gestured toward the wrapped gift on the table.

William's eyes went wide as he turned to look at me. "You did?"

I gave him a playful smile and said, "Yes, but we will open it only after we finish putting together the dinosaurs." His face lit with joy, and he nodded. "Okay!"

"William, I'm gonna leave you with Desmond for a minute, okay? I want to help Nana Angie with her flowers. Is that okay?" His face lit with a toothy grin, and he nodded. "Yes. I'll show Desmond how to finish." He bounced from foot to foot, already eager to see what was inside.

I looked at Kimberly with a grateful smile, and she winked before disappearing around the corner. The Bennett women gave us boys a chance to bond undisturbed for a good half hour, but their curiosity got the better of them and they strolled back into the room to find William beaming once again.

William was piloting the tiny robot, zooming it all over the room with an eager expression. Angela approached him and asked if he wanted to help her bake cookies. He perked up, his eyes lighting up. "You can help too," he said, grabbing my hand and leading me toward the kitchen.

Angela Bennett's kitchen was alive with laughter and chatter as William's eyes sparkled with mischievous delight. Kimberly glanced at me, her face beaming, before looking back at William. I watched him as he dipped his small finger to snatch a small bit of cookie dough.

Kimberly studied her watch and grumbled. Four hours passed in minutes. Hopefully all of our get-togethers would go this smoothly.

"Come on, time to clean up the puzzle in the living room, take a bath, and then a bedtime story."

William picked up the puzzle and put it in the big box in the corner, then she handed him a fluffy towel for his bath.

"See ya in the morning, Nana Angie," he said as Angela bent down to hug and kiss her grandson.

Then William's little arms wrapped around my knees, and he looked up with shy, curious eyes. A surge of emotion overcame my body as I bent and scooped up my son in my arms. William held my gaze and ran a tiny finger along the side of my face. In that moment, my heart swelled with love for the child I created with Cecily McCormick.

Kimberly said, "Do you have something to say to Desmond?"

His eyes, wide with awe, peered at me. "Thank you for my robot."

I smiled and ruffled William's hair. "You'll have to give him a name."

He nodded, still gazing at the sleek metallic figure in his hands. "Will you come and play again, Desmond?"

Startled at the question, I looked away as my voice trembled, glancing at Kimberly and then Angela, who met my gaze. I finally croaked out, "If Nana Angie and Kimberly invite me again."

William wriggled in my arms and stretched his arms out toward Kimberly. She smiled and reached for him, taking him from me, then he buried his face in her neck and snuggled close.

"Good night, William," I whispered as she carried him away.

"Good night," he replied before they disappeared around the corner.

I took a step away, ready to leave, but Angela caught my arm. Her eyes were pleading and her voice trembled. "I'm sorry for wanting more of your time, especially when seeing you and William together reminds me of Cecily. I know I'm being selfish, but stay a little longer?" She gave me a hopeful, yet sad smile.

I hesitated for a moment before giving her arm a reassuring squeeze. "Of course, Angela. I'm happy to stay."

My posture deteriorated as I dragged my feet across the dining room floor. I chose a chair, clearing my throat gently to break through the thick tension that filled the room.

"I don't want to pry, but I'd like to know about you and Cecily. She never talked about you. Kimberly said you met at one of your mother's fundraisers."

"Yes." My voice was low and full of regret for our short time together. She was a kindhearted woman with a quick wit and a bright smile, who was always eager to learn and take on new challenges. My chest tightened at the love Cecily had for me, even if she hadn't said it out loud. "We weren't together but about six months. It wasn't anything serious, but her letter suggests otherwise. I'm so very sorry for your loss, Angela."

"So, you didn't love her?"

"She was one of the most genuine people I've met, but I wasn't in love with her." I knew it might hurt her, but I couldn't lie. Love wasn't something that appeared overnight. I could be myself with her, but it never got that deep. We both led different lifestyles and she wasn't the type to crave being in the spotlight. If anything, she was the opposite.

Kimberly stepped into the room, her hands on her hips.

Her tone was sharp as she addressed Angela. "Come on. You're not being fair to Desmond."

"I just wanted to know whether he had feelings for her."

"Let's drop it, okay? What happened between Desmond and Cece is in the past and not our business. We should focus on the adoption."

I groaned, knowing the conversation was going in an unfavorable direction. She was asking too much of me right now. *How can she even think about adoption when his father is standing right here?* I crossed my arms over my chest, both as a means of self-comfort and to put some distance between us. Kimberly wasn't going to like my answer, but if I pissed her off, she could keep William away from me, and I couldn't take that chance.

"So, are you going to block me from adopting William?" she asked.

The air between us was thick with tension and my palms grew sweaty. I tried to maintain a neutral expression, but the two Bennett women studied me. Angela's eyes avoided mine, while Kimberly's bored into mine, her lips pressed into a thin line. The challenge in her gaze caused a lump in my throat as I struggled to think of a response that wouldn't be too confrontational. She waited for me to break the silence with something that would either prove her right or reveal a chink in my armor.

The room spun. I only met William today, yet here I was being asked to make a life-altering decision. Couldn't she give me some time? Was it appropriate for her to even consider adopting him now that I was in the picture? "Kimberly, I'm being pulled into a whirlpool. This whole situation came out of nowhere, and like you, I'm still trying to come to terms with it. I'm not ready to answer that question yet," I replied, her eyes searching mine. "I think I need some time to get to know William better."

"Do you mean you're not ready to decide yet, or that you won't agree to the adoption?" she asked, her face etched with concern.

She was pushing me. Kimberly wanted me to slip up. I stood and crossed my arms, my posture screaming defiance. "You always do this," I accused. My face softened as I moved closer, lifting my arms in an open gesture. "You insist on pushing me into a corner every time, when we need to make sure we're on the same page."

She looked away, avoiding my gaze. "No, I don't. I just want to understand your intent here."

"I know you and Angela are William's blood and you have raised him, but I'm his biological father and I'm not prepared to sign him away. It's not my fault I didn't know about his existence. You can't expect me to have all the answers already."

Kimberly's mouth twisted as if tasting something sour. She planted her feet on the ground and spoke in a voice as icy as New York City in December. "There's that phrase again—'sign him away.' You've used it before. He's not a piece of land, Desmond, or something inanimate you sign away. There are needs, feelings, emotions involved. Do these words mean anything to you, or are you completely emotionally illiterate?"

My jaw clenched, and my hands curled into fists as I stared at her. Every time I tried to be amicable, she found a way to push me to my limits. "Why do you have to come at me like this each time we see each other? Here I am, trying to be there for my son, and you are making me feel like an imposter. It's hard enough, okay? I don't need you riding me too."

She didn't even flinch. Her voice was even but laced with venom as she zeroed in on the jugular. "Would you have married Cece if she told you she was pregnant?"

"How am I supposed to answer that?" I crossed my arms, trying to calm myself before walking out that door.

"Okay, how about this? Why do you think Cece wanted to keep William hidden from you until he was an adult?"

I paused, unsure of what to say. There was no answer for that. I'd been wondering about that too. My shoulders flattened, the weight of the situation pressing on me. When I spoke, my voice sounded hollow. "Cecily isn't here and the decision for what's best for William is up to a judge. They will do it based on what's best for him—not you or me. That's all I want. Whether that's with me or you guys. Stop making me out to be the bad guy. All I want is to be there for my son, since I haven't been able to for the last five years. Can't you understand how devastating it is to know my son has gone without knowing his father?"

Her mouth dropped. "A judge? You're going to take this to court?"

Anger radiated from my pores, and I glared at her with a look of betrayal. She wasn't listening to me. She was too focused on this adoption, and right now, that should be the furthest thing from her mind. "It's clear you've set yourself up as my judge, jury, and executioner. You've decided I'm not fit to be a father. Well, there's only one way to settle this: let a judge decide." I paused, and the tension in the room was palpable.

"It seems like Cece thought the same thing; otherwise, she would've told you about her pregnancy and not planned to keep him away from you for eighteen years."

My shoulders tightened and my head drooped as I felt the familiar weight of guilt and disappointment come crashing down. She didn't understand what it had been like to discover I had a son, or the regret for not being in his life all these years. My fingernails bit into my palms, and I held back the urge to lash out. It would do me no good for them to see my other side.

Nothing could have prepared me for this conversation tonight. How dumb was I to think that I could come here and meet my son without her conning me into talking about the adoption? Maybe she doesn't have William's best interest in mind. Because anyone in their right mind would know that a child shouldn't be without their father, especially when they wanted to be in their life.

Angela threw her arms in the air. "You two, this has to stop!" She turned to me, and I looked away, avoiding her gaze.

"I think I should go now." Kimberly might hate it, and there wasn't anything I could do to change that, but her mother didn't seem to hold the same view She needed to be kept on my good side, because when Kimberly and I couldn't agree on a single thing, maybe she could talk to her daughter.

"No, you can't leave like this." Angela stepped closer and put a soothing hand on my arm. "We sit and discuss this like adults."

"I'll give anything to work this out amicably, but as you can see, Kimberly and I do not see eye to eye. I think it's best if we take a step back and let the lawyers handle this."

"Fine. Let's do that, but I'm giving you fair warning, Desmond Renault. You're going to have one hell of a fight on your hands," Kimberly spat out, her eyes blazing with rage. She shifted her weight on her feet.

"Angela," I said, turning toward her, standing in the doorway, my voice calm and measured. "Thank you for welcoming me into your home and giving me the opportunity to spend time with my son."

Angela creased her brows. "I hope you will come again soon. William likes you."

I searched her face for an unspoken message, but all I saw was her exhaustion. "My discovery of William has turned your plans upside down. I don't want to fight with you and I hope you'll keep to our verbal agreement so I can spend time with William."

"Yes, of course," Kimberly said. "I'm not the Wicked Witch of the West, but I'd prefer if you planned with Angela. Why don't you exchange numbers? That way you coordinate easier."

Angela handed me her phone, and I programmed my number in and then sent a text so I'd have hers. She didn't seem to want to leave us alone anymore as I walked to the front door, which I understood after such a heated argument.

"I suppose I'll see you in court, as they say."

My brow furrowed and I shook my head. "It doesn't have to go that way."

"I think it does because it's quite clear to me you have no intention of letting me adopt William. Anyway, whether you agree to it or not, we'll still have to go to court."

I put a hand on her shoulder, trying to show her I wasn't the guy she thought. "Good night, Kimberly."

My steps were heavy as I trudged down the driveway, my gaze still set on the porch where she stood. A part of me yearned to go back, but I continued on, my mind filled, hoping maybe she'd get to know me. I was not the same playboy figure the tabloids made me out to be.

8
Kimberly

I OBSERVED DESMOND WALK AWAY. The warmth of his hand was still on my shoulder. Desmond Renault had a magnetism which both captivated me and made me want to resist him. He pissed me off and thrilled me at the same damn time. How the hell was I supposed to have him around me for the rest of my life? If he stopped the adoption, William and I would see each other every day, because he was my baby. We had a routine and Desmond didn't know half of what it took to be a parent. There was a difference between being a father and being a dad.

I didn't hate him, but for him to just walk into our lives unannounced with the news of him being William's father and then now talking about provisions for his car. *We got this!* We have been doing it for the last six years.

He doesn't know about his piano lessons every other Wednesday, and his soccer practice on Sundays at four. No matter what was happening at work, Angela or I made sure he got to his practices. But would Desmond? Would he put William first? I wasn't diminishing the guy because we were both CEOs, but my work would never be more important to me than my family. Could he say the same?

Angela came up behind and I was still standing at the door with it open, tears streaming down my cheeks. "Come on inside and tell me what's going on between you two."

I followed her to the couch, wiping the streaks away, and sat. "What do you mean? There's nothing going on. He just makes me so angry." I peered away from my mother, picking at a piece of lint on the couch, avoiding eye contact. She didn't need to know about everything else. Things were complicated already, and the sexual tension between us could not be thicker.

"Is it just about William?" my mother asked, her voice quiet. I kept my eyes averted.

"It's obvious that Desmond doesn't want me to adopt William." I shifted back in my seat and folded my arms. "You don't think I'm interested in Desmond Renault, do you? I assure you, I'm not."

Mom took in a slow breath before responding. "I understand. It must be hard for Desmond to accept giving up his son. And I quite like him. Can you imagine how it must feel to have someone else have your child? William is his flesh and blood, too. Put yourself in his place. This is coming from me, the woman who has been there every day for William, but Desmond is his father, and he has just as much right to have him as we do."

"I don't want to stand in Desmond's way of having access to William while we still have custody of him." My eyes fixed on the paperwork in front of me. "He's looking for an excuse to fight for full custody in the courts."

My mother sighed and picked up her drink. "It looks like the decision isn't up to us then, so we should prepare ourselves for the worst. Although, he doesn't seem like the type of guy who would keep William from us."

My voice was tight. "Mom, Desmond has a history of womanizing and partying. I don't want William near that lifestyle."

"Don't be so hard on him." Her brow creased as she pushed up her reading glasses from the edge of her nose. "It seems like such a long time since Desmond did something like that—it must have been when his father passed. He's grown a lot since then, and I haven't seen any bad stories about him in ages."

"Jesus, what are you? The president of the Desmond Renault fan club? Do you want him to take William away from us? Because once he has custody, we have no say in anything. Well, are you on his side or mine?"

"First off, you need to learn how to talk to your mother because I do not deserve this, and second, you are coming off very negative. You are so focused on how it would change your life, when you should be excited that William has a father. One who wants to spend time with him. Once he finds out, he is going to want to spend every waking moment with him and could you blame him?"

I bit my lip and tapped my foot, waiting for her to stop speaking. Maybe I was being a little selfish, but it was in William's best interest. The Renaults were well known for their wealth and extravagant lifestyle. He wouldn't ever have any privacy, get handed everything, and that was not how Cecily would want him growing up.

"The more unkind you are toward him, the more he will resist you." She placed a calming hand on my shoulder to emphasize her point.

My shoulders slumped in exhaustion as I swayed to my feet. These last few days were a blur and I didn't want to say his fucking name one more time. He needed to go back to his own life, a different woman every night, and leave us the fuck alone. My voice was dull. "I just want to draw a hot bath and go to bed. Is that alright?"

A wave of disappointment washed over her. "We can discuss this more later, but you need to at least eat something. You've been running around all day."

"I'm fine, Mom. Don't worry about me. I'm not hungry."

Angela shrugged before getting up to heat some leftovers in the microwave. She grabbed a bottle of scotch from the top shelf of the cabinet and said she was going to watch a movie.

"Alright, I'm heading up. Good night."

My head was pounding as I filled the tub. I poured in two lavender bath bombs, and as soon as they touched the boiling surface, a soothing scent wafted throughout the room. It was a smell I grew to love during my brief stint as a spa attendant in college. It was always the same scent, soft and subtle, and it calmed me.

My nephew was the one constant in my life, and after everything happened in Boston, he was the only thing I looked forward to every day when I got home from work. Cecily trusted us to take care of him, and I couldn't let her down. Maybe, I was being too harsh to Desmond, but he needed to change to be a good role model for his son. I wished things were different.

I shifted in the tub and closed my eyes, letting the water's warmth penetrate my body. The water was filled with bubbles, their softness cushioning me from the hard porcelain surface. I couldn't shake the argument I had with Desmond earlier.

It was a heated one, full of accusations and threats, and it ended with me exhausted. The six weeks until the adoption would go by at a slow place, and I wasn't sure if I was strong enough. No matter what, the judge would make the final decision and either way, he would continue to be in my life. Holidays and birthdays would be celebrated with Desmond, and for some reason, I was literally gagging at the mere thought.

The tightness in my chest only grew as I shuffled in the water, trying to focus on something else. I searched around the bathroom, taking in all the details—the shelves of toiletries and the fluffy white towels. Everything was so peaceful, like its own little bubble, removed from the chaos of the outside world.

But even in this haven, the disagreement and the hurtful words occupied my thoughts. I was baffled, unable to make sense of my conflicting emotions. One moment I had the urge to strangle him, the next I yearned to kiss him.

The warmth of the water soaked in as I closed my eyes. The exhaustion of the day drained out of me until my thoughts were empty. Desmond Renault was a despicable man that made my blood boil, but he also invaded my dreams at night. *God help me!*

9

Desmond

The parking garage was dark and suffocating with the harsh smell of exhaust hanging in the air. I had been in the same place since I arrived half an hour ago, the only sound the rhythmic thumping of my anxious heart. Despite the chill of the night, I was sweating, not to mention it was getting harder to keep my eyes open without them burning. My hands trembled as I held on to the steering wheel. The day would never end, from the stressful demands of work to the bitter argument with Kimberly. It was worse than pulling fucking teeth.

There was one other place I needed to go tonight. Marsha hadn't seen me since I received the news about being a father, but I hadn't forgotten about her. I shouldn't worry myself since we weren't serious, but I could use a little bit of a distraction and a release tonight.

After calming down, I dragged myself out of the car and shuffled to the elevator. My weariness grew heavier with each step. The elevator creaked and groaned as it rose to the tenth floor. Hopefully, she wouldn't be able to see my anger with a forced smile on my face.

The elevator ride took forever as it crept up the shaft. The doors opened, and I stepped out into the hallway on the tenth floor, taking a deep breath and walking to apartment 1023. I ran my fingers through my hair, trying to make myself more presentable, then knocked.

"Hey," she said, her voice tinged with concern as she opened the door wider and took in my disheveled appearance. She was searching my eyes for answers. When I pulled her into a hug, her slight frame collapsed into mine, as if seeking solace from my arms. She was exactly what I needed after these tiresome few days.

She touched my face with the back of her hand and drew it downward. "Baby, what's wrong?"

I moved her away and took her hand. "Let's sit. I have something to tell you," I whispered. She nodded, and we walked to the sofa, sitting side by side.

I took both her hands and looked into her wide, round eyes, the color of rich caramel. "I have a son, Marsha," I whispered. "His name is William, and I got to meet him today."

Her mouth fell open and a flush of red hit her cheeks. "You have a child?" she said, disbelief dripping from her words.

I nodded, averting my gaze as she withdrew her hands from mine and drew her arms across her chest in a protective embrace. "Why are you only now telling me about this?"

"Because I just found out," I replied, my throat thick with regret. Marsha wanted to have kids eventually, I knew that, but she had always said she didn't want to be a stepparent. I had never judged her for that, but that was the reality we were in now. If we stayed together, and eventually got serious, she would become his stepmom. We might not make it a few more months, but she had to know.

"That makes little sense, Desmond."

My shoulders dropped, and my chest caved in. "I was

seeing someone about six years ago, but it never blossomed into something serious on my side. It lasted for about six months, then we went our separate ways. She got pregnant and never told me."

"And what? She wants you to take responsibility now?"

I bit my lip, trying not to get defensive of Cecily. "She died in childbirth. Our son, William, lives with his aunt and grandmother now. Look, it's a long story, but I can't stand by and not be in his life."

Did she expect me to just walk away from my child? I might be many things, but a deadbeat father wasn't one of them. If I had known about William, my entire life would be different.

"So, what are you going to do?" Marsha wiped tears from her cheeks and shoved her hair out of her eyes.

"My lawyer is dealing with it," I said, my voice softening. "It will go to court and there's bound to be more publicity around the whole thing."

She held a pinched expression. "How does this affect our relationship?"

My forehead creased with confusion. If she didn't want to continue this, that was understandable, but she needed to clear and certain. "Why should it?"

Marsha rubbed her hands together and stared at the floor. "I want more out of this relationship than you do. With a child in the mix, I don't think I'll be able to get that from you. I'm sure I'll see even less of you now."

Her voice trembled as she spoke, and my eyes widened when she finished. I searched her face, then asked, "Marsha, what are you saying? Are you using this as an excuse to push me away?"

"I don't want to push you away." Her voice was soft and

full of emotion. "I care about you and I'm committed to this relationship more than you are."

This was where our intentions differed. She had never mentioned wanting to be serious, even though I wasn't seeing anyone else, but neither of us could provide stability right now. I cupped her face in my hands and brushed a few strands of hair out of her eyes. "Oh, Marsha, come here." I pulled her into me and claimed her trembling lips with mine. She sighed in my embrace and wrapped her arms around my neck as we kissed with passionate desperation. We were both breathing heavily when we pulled away.

I picked her up by her ass and walked into the bedroom. After everything today, I needed to lose myself in the softness of a woman. Kimberly Bennett riled me, and I needed to banish her.

She anchored her hand on my belt, then I slipped a finger beneath her thong. It was like she knew I was going to show up tonight, so she wore a simple wrap dress that was easily removed. I ran my hands over her chest and stomach. Marsha closed her eyes to focus on the sensations. I threw my free hand around her back and my grip became possessive.

"Right now, I need you." The heat of her body was against mine. The aching need for a woman's softness burned in my chest. I had let my anger over Kimberly Bennett consume me and sought a physical distraction, believing it was the only way to get rid of it.

Once Marsha fell asleep after her euphoric satisfaction, I headed home. Very seldom did I sleep over at her place. Tonight, our conversation took a turn, and we would need to discuss it further, because she claimed she wanted more from me, but that was the first time she had ever mentioned it. I didn't like being caught off guard.

My mother paced the living room as I stepped into the foyer. Her forehead creased with worry. How long had she been waiting for me?

"How did it go? What's he like?"

I gave her all the details. The evening went well, and William seemed to like me, which was important. Sooner or later, we would reveal me being his father, but he needed to be comfortable around me first. Kimberly and I could agree on that.

Her face softened and she smiled. "He sounds like a kind, intelligent boy."

"You'll like him, but I'm afraid Kimberly and I will be going to court soon."

Madeline attempted to give me a comforting smile, her lips pursed and her eyes tight with worry. "Don't worry, darling, we have good lawyers," she said. "Sadler will knock this on its head in no time."

I crossed my arms over my chest. "Sadler isn't who I'm using. I've already hired Alana Glacey. We've talked about this."

Madeline pursed her lips and looked away. "Alana is an excellent lawyer, but Sadlers have been the family lawyers for decades and are much more experienced."

"You'll have to trust me on this. Alana is who I need. In fact, she's perfect."

The surrounding air was heavy, and I avoided her gaze as I made a beeline for the walkway that would take me to my wing of the mansion.

After my email was typed and sent to Alana, I opened the contacts list on my phone, pressed Mark, and waited for an answer.

"Desmond?" his voice crackled over the line.

"Sorry to call you so late," I said, "but I need some information."

"Alright." Mark sighed. "What is it?"

"I need some information on Kimberly Bennett," I said, my jaw tight and teeth gritted.

"I know who she is, Desmond, but I don't think..."

"I wouldn't be asking if it wasn't important."

"Does this have anything to do with our venture? Is she involved in it somehow? I hope not."

"No, not related at all," I replied. "You haven't been in touch about the deal in a while. Are we finished? Have you got what you need? I've got a lot of things to attend to and I would like to clear this up."

"We're not in a place to wrap up yet. We're not done. You know the outcome we want."

This had been going on for too long. "Mark, I need my life back."

"Is she your latest conquest?"

My hands were shaking. Mark should stay the fuck out my business. He needed to just do his job and that was it. "No, I'd rather not say right now why I want information.

Will you help me or not? I hate fucking calling you."

"Alright, okay. Leave it to me. I'll see what I find out and get back to you."

The phone was heavy in my hand and I hung up. I despised the man on the other end of the line, but I only had a few more months, and then our business would be done with.

Kimberly Bennett was proving to be a major obstacle, but there were still hints at her vulnerability that made me long to protect her. It wasn't until that moment that it occurred to me—she was part of my family now and I had a responsibility toward her.

Damn that woman. She was a royal pain in the ass, but I couldn't shift the images of her out of my mind. They were images of her naked body beneath mine, writhing under my touch, her back arching as my fingers slipped inside her.

10

Kimberly

AN ENVELOPE WAS DELIVERED with my name scrawled across the front in bold black ink to Bennett Technologies. When Bartholomew, my longtime executive assistant, brought it to my office, it was obvious this was the response from my contact. I tore open the top and extracted the folder inside, flipping through the dozen pages. My eyes scanned over legal and financial documents as I tried to make sense of the information.

This was a complete breach of privacy, and many individuals didn't realize how easy it was to get hands on their financial information, but Desmond wasn't stupid. He was expecting this. When I saw the word murder, my hand clutched my chest. I held the dossier heavily in my hands as I told Bartholomew I was going to my apartment for a while and not to disturb me. Disbelief and a sense of dread surged through me as I made my way to the elevator.

I fumbled with my phone until I got his number pressed in, and then I held my breath while it rang. "What the hell?" I said when he picked up. "Are you sure?" Some of the information within this dossier was heart-wrenching and this kind of information couldn't be taken lightly.

"There's no doubt," he said with a deep sigh. "It wasn't an accident that killed Damien Renault; it was murder. Someone sabotaged the *Gambit*."

The words coming straight from his mouth made my chest tighten. Who would want to kill Damien Renault? My mind rushed to William. With the knowledge of Desmond being his father, did this mean he was in danger?

"Does the family know?"

"No, and they don't need to."

Silence stretched between us as I contemplated the tragedy of Damien's death and the information that these papers contained. The *Gambit* was their family boat, yacht, whatever it was, it was huge. Everyone knew about Damien Renault, and the day he died it was everywhere. *Why would someone want to kill him, though?* This information just didn't make any sense. I should have read the entire dossier before I called him because my eyes began scrolling through again to see Michael's name.

"Michael Morse killed Damien Renault and his family doesn't know that?" I asked, my voice rising an octave. Something just wasn't right. They were best friends and well known in Bayview. Somehow, though, money had a way of ruining relationships and lives. Did Michael get greedy? Was Damien too much of a competitor that he needed to flush the market?

"Look, what are you going to do with this? You need to be careful."

"Where is Morse now? He hasn't been around since I came back to Bayview."

"Did you hear what I said? You're stepping into dangerous territory."

I went straight to the couch, sat down, and placed the papers beside me, trying to soak this all in. Yes, I heard him, but something... wasn't making sense. There was more to this story than what was in these papers, and I would find out with or without Zachary's help. "Why did Michael kill Damien Renault? The two families were good friends. There must be something missing..."

"Read the damn report, Kimberly. Damien was going to out Michael for money laundering. The Feds were onto it and Michael did a disappearing act after Damien's death."

The only thing swirling around in my mind was Desmond. Did he know about his father's death? That Michael was responsible?

"Did Michael want Renault Tech to take part in money laundering?"

"I'm going to say this one more time. Step away from this. If I get access to this information about Desmond's family, which is not in the public domain, you too can be exposed. You don't know who else is involved. It's likely they keep a watch on Desmond because he is or was having a sexual relationship with Svetlana Gorev, who is linked to the Russian mob. Svetlana used to work at Renault Tech and there's a rumor she was Damien's mistress," Zachary Warner added.

What in the actual fuck? No way I heard that right.

"Damien Renault was cheating on his wife with Gorev and when he dies, she moves on to his son? That's disgusting."

There was the proof of being a womanizer again... *Desmond, come on. Prove me wrong.*

"I don't have all the facts, so I can't comment. But apart from that, there's no criminality in Desmond's background, only adolescent stuff, youthful hijinks. He and his friend Johnny Morse spent a night in police cells as teenagers for drunken behavior in public."

"Yeah, well, I'd expect that, but there's nothing about his

sex life. I expected some scandal. Maybe a sex tape or something scandalous."

Zachary chuckled. "What's going on? You seem out for blood. Everything documented about Renault and his family is in that dossier."

I stopped pacing back and forth. I must have skipped that bit about Desmond and this Gorev woman, but it could prove useful. And did Desmond know about his father and Svetlana, but went with her, anyway?

"Is Desmond at risk? Is he still being watched?"

"He could be on a dormant list because their relationship seemed to have cooled off. It all went quiet a while back, but whenever he goes to Russia, he will be under surveillance. If National Security suspects he is susceptible to blackmail, then he will be under constant watch."

"Is his home and office bugged?"

"That I couldn't say. If it's a live operation, very few people would have access to that information including me."

The fact that Zachary was able to obtain this information horrified me. What else could he get his hands on? Were there people out there with my information? About my time being held prisoner? "The Feds assured me that my records would be sealed if I agreed to work for them for five years. There's only two left and I'm off the hook. You fixed that, remember?"

"Yeah, but I'm retired now, Kimberly, and anything can happen for many reasons. Look, you know where to find me. For God's sake, be careful and don't leave that stuff lying around. In fact, if I were you, I'd burn it."

"Thanks, Zachary."

I walked into my bedroom and pushed a well-hidden switch. What looked like a solid wall rolled back to reveal a safe. After punching some numbers on the keypad, the safe opened, and I placed the dossier inside with all the other things I wished to keep from prying eyes.

I felt deflated. What would I even do with this information? It wasn't what I expected and apart from Gorev and the Russian mob, it was useless for my needs. Revealing the true circumstances of Damien Renault's death would only open old wounds for Desmond, his mother, and sister. It would be much worse if they discovered that a close friend murdered their husband and father. And I didn't want to do that. But didn't they have a right to know?

Should I warn Desmond he was under surveillance every time he went to Russia and perhaps even in his own home? Then he would want to know where I got the information.

I clasped my hands, trying to talk through this, biting my lip, as I weighed the pros and cons of various courses of action. I might not like Desmond Renault right now, but when it came to William, I had to protect him, and this information didn't just affect the Renaults, it now affected my family too.

11

Desmond

William perched on the stone steps, his legs swinging. A few steps behind him stood Angela, her gray hair swept up in a ponytail. My gaze shifted to the door, searching for Kimberly, but the doorstep remained empty. My heart sank as I stifled a sigh.

William's face was beaming as I stepped out of the SUV. His small feet carried him as fast as they could across the gravel, calling my name with glee. He leaped into my arms and I caught him. He looked up at me with bright eyes, placing his tiny hands on either side of my face. The familiar flutter in my heart started as I looked into his eyes, wondering what our day would bring. "I've missed you."

His face flushed with excitement, and Angela stood with a proud, beaming grin. With a mischievous twinkle in my eye, I held William at arm's length and said, "We're going to do something different today."

His eyes widened and he looked back at Angela. "What? Oh, tell me!"

"I want to take you and Nana Angie fishing."

"Yeah!" William yelled, bouncing up and down and clapping his hands. "Can we, Nana Angie? Please!"

Angela smiled, but her cheeks flushed. "I don't know how to fish. I've never been before."

"Never too late to learn. Or too young," I said, smiling at William.

"Where are we going?" William asked.

"We're going to drive up into the mountains."

"Are there any bears up there?" he said and then started making growling noises.

"No, William, you know that. We've been up to the mountains before." William nodded, grinning at me with a glint in his eyes.

I chuckled as my son was being mischievous. "Come on, I have everything we need." Angela and William rushed to the car, and I opened the front seat passenger door for her. I put William in the back and fastened his seat belt.

True to my word, the Renaults' wooden lodge contained three additional sets of fishing tackle and outfits. I hoped Kimberly might join us.

Luke Ward was waiting at the lodge. He was the Renaults' head of security before Damien died and was even more protective of the family since. He had recently become my biggest confidant.

"This is my friend, Ward." I extended my arm in his direction. "Ward, this is Angela and William."

Ward greeted Angela and shook hands, then bent to greet William. "Hello, little man. I'm pleased to meet you because Desmond told me you are his good friend."

"Desmond is my friend, but I would like it if he could be my daddy too."

My eyes widened, and Ward's brow furrowed as he

glanced back and forth between us. Angela's face was unreadable. We all knew he was my son, but William didn't.

"Can you be my daddy, Desmond?"

My throat closed. With everything going on with Kimberly and me, as much as I wanted to tell him, it was in my best interest not to step on her toes.

Angela came to my rescue. "Why don't we do some fishing? The fishes are waiting. Let's get our gear on and when we get home, you talk to Desmond about being your daddy."

"That's right, buddy. Why don't we have a talk about it later?"

"Okay. Come on, Nana Angie. Let's get ready for the fishes. Are you coming fishing with us, Mr. Ward?"

"Well, I'm coming with you, but my job is to make sure Desmond doesn't fall in the water."

William laughed. "Don't be silly. Daddies don't fall in the water."

"Well then, I'll make sure you don't fall in."

William gave Ward a sweet smile. He tugged at my hand. "Let's go. I want to see the fish."

"You go with Ward. He'll help you put on your fishing gear. I want to talk to Nana Angie for a minute."

Ward took the hint and led the little boy away.

I turned. "Where did that come from? Thanks for coming to my rescue, by the way. I didn't expect it to be so simple or happen so soon, but I don't want to do this without Kimberly."

"That's how children are. He likes you and he doesn't have a daddy. I think the fact he has started big boy school has prompted it. The children are much more vocal; he goes on playdates and sees other children with both their parents at home. He's more aware now that he doesn't have a father."

I missed his first steps, first word, and first day of school. No matter what, Kimberly wasn't taking any more firsts away from me. Now that I knew William was mine, they would have to kill me to keep me away.

"Justin Thornton used to kind of fill the male role that all boys need, but he hasn't been around for a while."

My ears pricked up. "Justin Thornton? Are they seeing each other?"

"They were until Justin moved. I know he comes back here, but Kimberly never talks about her love life. Although all I've heard her say lately is she doesn't have time for serious stuff. That woman focuses too much on William, which I'm not talking down on that, but she deserves to be happy too."

My jaw tensed. What in the world did she see in that guy? He seemed so... vanilla. And she didn't strike me as that type. She was too sassy and dominant. Justin didn't seem like the type to be able to satisfy all her needs.

"I'm relieved you and your family will be in his life. Up to now, all he's had is me and Kimberly. Little boys need their fathers."

This was why I liked Angela. She wasn't trying to keep William from me, not that Kimberly was, but she wanted to adopt him. And what did that say about me as a father? Letting another woman adopt him when I was standing right here, begging for the chance to prove to her I could a good father to William?

"I wish Kimberly would see it like that." I sighed. My mind was still teeming with that little tidbit that Angela revealed about Kimberly and Thornton.

"Give her time. She'll come around. She adores that little boy. It's not your fault, so don't blame yourself. She waited for almost five years before filing for legal adoption. You came once she finally had the heart to do it."

Whatever happened, one of us was going to be hurt.

"So, did Kimberly and him ever get serious? Did my son get

attached to him?" My jaw clenched, thinking about him getting to spend time with my son, doing things with him like taking him to the park or zoo.

"No, I don't think it was ever like a commitment type of thing. You know what I mean."

So it was more of a *friends with benefits* type thing? It made a little sense as to why she had her business in the Thornton Building. I had never been too keen on Justin Thornton. The man was a tad arrogant. It surprised me that someone like that would be Kimberly's type. If I were honest, a slither of jealousy raced through me.

"We better join Ward and William before they catch all the fish. Why don't you change and I'll find them? We passed the stream on the way up. Just follow the road and you'll see us."

I took my gear and left.

Thirty minutes later, we were all by the water, the sun shining overhead and the breeze stirring up a gentle ripple in the lake. William was already hooked. His eyes were wide as he cast his line into the water, his small hands gripping the rod as he waited for a bite. Angela was just as eager as William to catch something.

Ward was keeping a watchful eye on us all as we fished. He was standing a few yards away, scanning the area with a vigilant eye. I told him to take it easy, but he said his job was to protect and he couldn't do that sitting down fishing too.

We had been at it for a while, and no one caught anything when Angela shouted, "I've got one!" She reeled in her line and on the end was a small fish, its scales glinting in the sun. She beamed as she showed it off, and William's eyes lit up.

A few minutes later, William shouted out, "I've got one too!" He reeled in his line, revealing a larger fish than the one Angela caught.

Ward gave him a pat on the back after we all cheered and applauded him. We admired the fish for a few minutes, and then I reminded William that the fish go back into the water, and he agreed. William let it go and it swam off into the depths.

The rest of the afternoon was spent fishing, and by the time the sun set, William caught three more fish.

As we packed up our things and walked back to the house, a sense of satisfaction that only comes from a day spent out in nature washed over me.

As Ward drove us back to the Bennetts' home, William fell asleep against my side. Becoming a father was scary, but I would do everything I could for my son. We would be spending many more days fishing together.

Until the next time...

12
Kimberly

WHEN DESMOND DROPPED William and Angela off, I went to the door. Desmond came out of the vehicle to greet me. William was clamoring to be let out and Angie went to his aid. William jumped out of the SUV and raced to me. "Kimberly, we went fishing for fish with Ward and I want Desmond to be my daddy."

I caught the boy up in my arms, buried my face in his hair, and kissed him. I looked from Desmond to my mother and back again.

"Kimberly, got a sec?" Desmond asked.

I looked at William and kissed his cheek. "Did you have a good time, baby?" He nodded. "Did you catch a fish?"

"Yes, I catched a fish. Desmond helped me. And Nana Angie catched one too. But we had to let them swim away after we catched them."

"After you caught them, William, not catched."

"After I caught them," William repeated, grinning. He motioned Desmond over and pulled him close. William put one arm around Desmond's neck and the other around Kimberly's. "Nana Angie, will you take a picture?"

"Yes, of course, darling." Angela took out her phone. "Can you smile, Kimberly?"

I gave a grimace. She clicked the camera a few times. "There, it's done. Come on now. We need to get you something to eat. Come with me."

William wriggled down to the ground supported by Desmond and me. "Are you coming, Desmond?"

"I want to talk to Kimberly, buddy, then I gotta go home because it's late, but I'll see you soon and we'll talk. Okay?"

"Okay." He grabbed Desmond around the legs and hugged them. His dad picked him up and carried him into the house.

I remained outside waiting for him, my face like thunder.

"What the hell is going on, Desmond?" I tore into him when he returned. "When did you decide to tell William you're his father?"

How dare Desmond just walk into our lives and think he can do whatever he damn well pleased with no consultation? My blue eyes launched scorching rays at him.

He stared at me and contained a smile. "Why are you so angry with me, Kimberly?" His voice was soft.

"Answer the question. Why did you not even have the courtesy to inform me you planned to tell William you were his dad?"

"I planned nothing, except to take my boy fishing. I hoped you would join us. And I didn't tell him I was his father. When we arrived at the lodge, William informed my friend that he'd like it if I were his daddy. It came out of the blue and I was as shocked as Angela and Luke when he said it. Angela came to my rescue. I told William we'd talk about it later. I didn't want to say anything to him until you could be present too."

What kid just goes around asking random men to be their daddy?

"I swear that's how it happened. Ask Angela. She was there. I wouldn't lie to you about something like that."

I glanced toward the house. My mother and I would have it out later.

"Look, there's something I need to say. Will you come and sit in the vehicle with me?"

"What now? You submitted your custody claim?"

"Please. Just come sit with me for a few minutes."

I strode to the dark-green Chevy Trailblazer, opened the door, got inside, and slammed it shut. I folded my arms and stared straight ahead.

"You and I should make time to tell him together. I want to name him in my will. I admit I'd prefer if he lived with me, but I don't wish to just take William away from you and Angela. Let the transition happen naturally over time, giving William as much space as he needs to get to know my family."

Bile rose from my stomach into my chest.

"Alana Glacey tells me it's more than likely we'll have a custody hearing on the original date set for the adoption," Desmond continued. "I hope we won't go to court. You and Angela will have as much time with William as you want and we make that formal."

There was a sharp intake of breath. "This is what I feared. You would want to make William's life the circus that yours is."

"Kimberly, that's not fair. It was inevitable once I discovered my son that I'd want to see William and have him be in my life. I'm his sole parent now, and I'm sure Cecily would want that to happen. I'm also the CEO of a multinational company. My life is far from a circus, and I'm questioning why you persist in projecting an image of me as some wild, rampaging sex maniac."

Maybe because you ARE.

"No, this wasn't inevitable. You should just have left him alone, given who you are. And I've told you, I'm going to fight for William. I will honor Cece's wishes."

"We've been here before. I won't get into this debate with you repeatedly. Every time I try to move us forward, you yank my chain."

"You want to move us forward in only one direction. Yours." My voice was hard and accusatory. "Some newshound will ferret out this information. Thank God my sister won't be here to deal with the vilification."

"You're being so unfair. You've opposed me from the get-go. I'm surprised that you allowed me to even see my son without a court order."

"Why don't you just leave things as they are, Desmond? You should be the one spending time with William whenever you wish, but he lives with me and Angela. Once it's known you have an illegitimate child, William's life won't be the same."

All I could picture was paparazzi following me and him everywhere after the news broke. William wouldn't have any privacy.

"I'm sorry. Once we go to court, it'll become public knowledge. I'll take every step to protect my son, and you and Angela."

"How will you achieve that? You're not sorry; you planned this all along. And you're not that straight-up guy you'd like the world to believe. What dark secrets are you keeping?"

I bit my lip to stop from blurting out that the authorities were keeping tabs on him whenever he goes to Russia because of his previous—or was it current—liaison with Svetlana Gorev, who was linked to the Russian mafia. Were they using him to get a foothold in Bayview?

"What are you talking about? Where is this coming from? Is this part of your plan to smear my family's name so you get to keep my son? Really? Is that who you are?"

I pummeled Desmond's chest as tears ran down my cheeks. "I hate you and your whole damn family. I'm sorry William was with me when I met your mother." My voice rose an octave with every word spoken.

Desmond pulled me into his arms and held me. "Shhh. I'm sorry. It will be okay. Don't cry. We'll work it out." He stroked my hair.

My arms crept around his neck and my face pressed into the skin around his Adam's apple. I breathed in a hint of woodsy and spicy mingled with his natural masculine scent. He felt solid, like a rock I could hold on to. His lips pressed onto my forehead. I raised my head and fumbled for his lips.

He tightened his arms around me. He kept his body passive, but his mouth yielded to the pressure from my lips.

I pushed him away, opened the vehicle door, and jumped out. What in the world was that? I ran into the house and shut the door without a backward glance.

Now it was time for the truth. I didn't believe a word of the story he told me because it made little sense. William wouldn't come up with the idea to ask him to be his dad on his own.

"What happened today? Desmond tried to explain it, but I don't believe William would come out with that with no prompting?"

"Well, he did. He told Desmond's friend he'd like it if Desmond was his daddy."

"Out of the blue? Are you sure about that, or did you put him up to it?"

"We can't avoid the inevitable. We need to face this and deal with it like adults. I wish we were not in a tussle with Desmond over William, but we are. I think the best solution, given where we are, is for you and Desmond to agree on joint custody."

"No, that's not happening. I won't let William's life be disjointed and pushed from here to there. Children need to be settled in one place. I won't let him be torn apart like that. He's much too young. Desmond will not agree to joint custody. He wants William to live with him."

Maybe I was being overdramatic, but he lost his mother, and now suddenly, Desmond came into his life and wanted him to move in with him? He was too young to be shifted around between houses. Instead, he should have a stable residence where he spent a majority of his time, and it made sense that it would be with my mother and me. After all, we were the ones who raised him.

"Do you think he'd be happy living with a stiff and starched-up Madeline in that mausoleum? It gives me the creeps. It's like something out of an Edgar Allan Poe novel. William will live with us full-time, and Desmond can see him whenever he wants. That's the outcome I'm pushing for. Desmond isn't the squeaky clean guy you think he is."

"What are you talking about? Do you know something?"

I stared at my mother. "It doesn't matter. All I know is that the life he leads is not one I want for William."

"Come on, I know you. You know something. You better tell me what's going on."

"Desmond has a girlfriend. I've seen them together. They've been in the papers. She's a detective."

"So? What has that to do with anything? Isn't he allowed to have a girlfriend?"

"Well, he also has a mistress in Russia whom he sees when he goes there and God knows how many other women around the world. He's not a fit person to have custody of your grandson, Cece's son, and my nephew! Suppose Cece knew this and that's why she wanted to keep William away from him. If we agree to even joint custody, we'd be betraying her."

There must be a reason she wanted to keep his paternity a secret. Something more to the situation that hadn't come to light yet.

"Oh, baby, you've got it all wrong. It's Damien who had an affair with a Russian girl who worked as his assistant. Svetlana, I think her name was. Can't remember her other name."

My eyes widened. "You know about that?"

"Damien's affairs have been the subject of Bayview gossip for years. Madeline held her head high, but I don't know how she put up with it. After Damien's death, Madeline gave a short shrift to Miss Svetlana. She was sent back to Russia in the blink of an eye."

"But not soon enough to stop Desmond hooking up with her, and for all I know, he still is. I need you on my side on this. We have to stick together."

"I'm on your side, but what about what William wants and needs? You should have seen them today. Desmond and William, I mean. They were just adorable together and I think William already loves his dad. It's so natural. It's as if William knows he shares Desmond's genes."

I looked daggers at her. "You've been encouraging this, haven't you? I should've never let Desmond meet him."

"It was your choice. You decided to stay away when Desmond was around. If I didn't know better, I'd say you have feelings for him. Look, baby, William has been talking about daddies and asking why he doesn't have one. He wanted to know if his daddy was in heaven with his mommy. What could I say? I tried to explain, not very well, why he didn't have a daddy. He asked me if Desmond would like to be his dad. There. Now you know." She threw her hands in the air.

Why was my mother working against me? William didn't

need to know that right now. Now Desmond was going to tell him, and there was nothing I could do. Especially with her nephew asking him to be his daddy. Tears formed.

"I think this has gone on long enough and you need to face facts. You and Desmond need to sit with William and tell him before the court hearing. Do you understand? Desmond told me today he doesn't want to do it without you being present."

I sobbed. This whole thing was sapping my strength. I needed to keep my resolve strong.

"Just talk to Desmond, baby, and listen. Listen without alienating him. But for now, let's get you to bed."

I slept the whole night.

The next morning, I needed to push through this so I picked up my phone. It was just six in the morning. I tapped on the Desmond phone icon.

"Hey," he answered. "Kimberly? Is everything okay?"

"We need to talk."

"Okay. What did you have in mind?"

"I'd like to see where you live, meet your mother again, and sister if she's around. But the important thing is that you and I talk alone."

"How about breakfast?" he asked.

"I just want to talk."

"Why don't you come to the Mansion? My mom and Leanne will be here. Will you bring William? They are both dying to meet him, especially Leanne."

"No, not today. This is about you and me getting on the same page. Come here later and we will talk to William. Perhaps you'd like to put him to bed and read him a story."

"I'd like that. I'll see you later."

"Yes. Bye."

I lay in bed thinking about what I needed to do today. I'd prefer not to visit the Renault Mansion, not to see Desmond or his mother, but I had to. Yesterday he'd taken the first small step in my direction. He was willing, if given custody, to let the transition happen naturally, but wanted more.

There was a good reason I wanted to meet at the Renault Mansion. I'd have to leave early enough to drop by my office and pick up my tech. There was no way William was going into that mausoleum, even for a visit, before I checked it out. If Desmond was being bugged, I needed to know.

I was glad Justin would be in town for a few days and I would see him tonight, because I needed some tension lifted as soon as possible.

When I arrived at the Renault Mansion, the gray granite walls of the exterior looked forbidding. It screamed institution more than a home. They sculpted everything in perfect symmetrical lines, but it looked cold and austere. It was a far cry from the riotous and colorful flowers and shrubs with overflowing hanging baskets that fronted the home Angela and I shared with William.

Desmond opened the door and greeted me with a kiss on the cheek. I gave him a quick once-over. Even in jeans and a t-shirt, he looked good. *Hot* was the word.

He stepped aside to let me in. "This is my mother, you already know her, and my sister, Leanne."

They ushered me into a large honey oak paneled space, a stunning marble fireplace recessed into one wall. Above it hung a large framed painting of the four members of the Renault family, lit by a downlight. A montage of photographs and an enormous vase of flowers, the fragrance from which filled the room, adorned an antique oak pedestal table. A pair of plush armchairs flanked it. The staircase blended with the décor and curved its way to the upper floors. The entire room was lit by the natural light that streamed in from windows high above my head. I loved beautiful things, and this room ticked all the boxes. In contrast to the exterior, my first impression of the interior of the Renault Mansion was one of warmth and welcome, overlaid by the exquisite elegance of understated wealth.

"Welcome to our home. I'm so happy to see you again," a coiffured and groomed Madeline Renault greeted.

"Hello, please call me Kimberly." I smiled at the older woman, who inclined her head.

"And you must call me Madeline. How is William? Such a delightful little boy. He looks so much like Desmond when he was that age. It quite startled me when I first met you both."

I gave Madeline Renault a tight little smile. If only she knew how much I rue that day.

"William is fine, Madeline. He had a great time fishing with Desmond yesterday."

"I'm looking forward to seeing him again. Perhaps you'll let him spend a little time here with us soon."

Desmond caught Leanne's eye and a silent communication passed between the siblings. Before I could respond to Madeline, two arms engulfed me in a close embrace.

"Hi, I'm so glad you're here. I've been looking forward to meeting you and William. I'm Leanne, but you knew that. We are sister-aunts and must get to know each other."

I couldn't help smiling at the natural and enthusiastic welcome from Desmond's sister. I liked her already.

Leanne and I linked arms as she led me to a beautiful lounge with views of the mansion grounds. "Come and sit. Here is some freshly brewed coffee."

"You have a beautiful home, Mrs. Renau... Madeline. The mansion looks austere, imposing and a little grim from the outside," I commented in my customary forthright way, "but it's lovely, and homely, inside."

Desmond's lips twitched. I was going to be quite a challenge for his mother. If he only knew the half of it.

"Thank you, dear," Madeline responded. "The mansion has been home to three generations of Renaults and we look forward to welcoming William as part of the fourth generation."

Desmond cleared his throat, causing Madeline to glance at him and catch the almost imperceptible movement of his head. The message was clear: *don't go there, Mom.*

This was a different side of Desmond, and I happened to like it. He seemed protective of me, but I didn't know why. Just because he was William's father didn't change anything.

The perfect hostess, Madeline Renault recovered the situation by changing the subject.

"Desmond tells me you went to Yale, and earlier than most, which means you're a pretty sharp young woman. What is your unique selling point at Bennett Technologies?"

"Mom!" Leanne exclaimed, just before Desmond intervened. "Chill. She isn't here for an interrogation. She should do the grilling before she allows William to visit our grim mausoleum." Leanne put her cup down and took mine. "I'm sure you'd like to see the rest of the house. Come, I'll show you."

Desmond made a move to get up, but Leanne waved her arm at him, a gesture that told him to stay where he was. "No, not you, Des. You've already spent time with Kimberly. I'm going to show her around. I'll bring her back in about half an hour, okay, big brother?"

"Fine. But only half an hour," he warned. "We need to talk."

Great. The perfect opportunity to bug hunt. Priorities were Desmond's bedroom and his study. The former might be more difficult, but maybe not. I'd just have to see what was possible on this visit.

13

Desmond

Forty-five minutes later, Kimberly followed me down a winding path lined with tall, fragrant flowers until we reached an old wooden summerhouse tucked away in a corner of the manicured grounds. We stepped inside, and I took a seat on the cushioned bench while she shut the door behind us, the weight of her request for privacy bearing on me as we talked.

"I'm listening," I said, my tone skeptical after our heated exchange the other day. "Have you changed your mind about my proposal?"

She hesitated and shifted her gaze away from mine. "My response to the two parts of your question is 'Maybe' and 'No.'"

I raised an eyebrow. "I'm confused."

"'Maybe' I've changed my mind, and 'no,' I'm not willing to accept your proposal."

I frowned, my brown eyes troubled. "I'm still lost. Break it down for me?"

She pressed her lips together. "Let's put the brakes on this conversation. Angela said I should give you a chance to explain, so let's see if you can clear up any misunderstandings without things getting ugly."

Or without you kissing me before running off in a huff. I'm still trying to figure that one out.

My imagination went back to that kiss yesterday.

"You've walked away twice. So now what?"

"Go ahead, state your wants and needs and anything that is nonnegotiable. I'll make a response and let's see where we go from there," I said.

"So just to be clear. We have physical joint custody where William lives with both of us on agreed terms, or one of us has legal custody, which is just about consultation on major events in his life. Right?"

"Yes, but I'm not happy with either of those," I told her.

"And you prefer not to go to court but want to shake hands on a verbal agreement."

"Yes. I'd prefer to work things out between us. The lawyers will draw up a legal document, but you can trust me. As I said yesterday, I want to give William all the time he needs to get to know me and my family."

"How long is a piece of string? How long will you give William to get to know you and your family and who decides when he's had long enough? What criteria will you use to measure that?"

That was a good question, but how could I know the answer right this second? All we could do was hope that when the time came, we could all be adults and do what was best for him.

"William is still very young. You see why he'd be better off with Angela and me? He'd be able to grow for a while longer out of the glare of the spotlight, which he will be in as your son. He has routine and stability, which is so important for young children. His mother is all around him in our home. He is happy. Please don't uproot him. Spend as much time with him as you want. You, Madeline, and Leanne are still his family. Desmond, please, I'm begging you to consider this. And I don't beg, but for William's sake."

Did she think I couldn't provide a stable, loving home? She was making a ton of money and was a hotshot right now in the area, so it wasn't just me that would be in the spotlight and getting into tabloids. Why did she treat me differently? This was all leading back to my past when I would sleep around, and I tried to explain I wasn't like that anymore, but nothing would get past that thick skull of hers.

"That's a powerful argument, and under normal circumstances, there's a lot going for it. But I'm determined to create all those things for William, and he'll still have you and Angela in his life. You've overlooked one crucial thing. To emphasize the point you made yesterday, how long do you think it will take before it comes out I'm William's father, especially as we've agreed to tell him? And that's nonnegotiable for me. Little people talk. One way or another, it will come out. I want to get ahead of that and will be better able to shield and protect him. How disconcerting it must be for you and Angela to discover that William has a father who wants to be in his life. Be the parent he doesn't have. You talk about emotions and feelings, but you've not considered one thing."

"And what is that?" she asked.

"I cannot forget what I know. At first sight, I fell in love with my son. I'm that little boy's dad, Kimberly. The relationship between parent and child is so precious, and I didn't choose to be out of his life. Now I know him. He cannot be in and out of my life for the next thirteen years. I don't want to split his life into regimented segments. Neither do you. He has a say in what happens. I'm not asking, and this is the concession

I'm making, that we allow a process whereby William himself is involved in how this happens."

Both of us wanted what was best for him, and offering to do it at his pace would take away the pressure of doing it too early or uprooting him from the life he already built.

"I'm willing for it to be an organic process, evolving according to William's rhythms. As a baby in his mother's womb, he didn't have a choice. One was made for him. Cecily had her reasons for that decision. I told you I didn't want to just take William away from you and Angela. Now it's my turn to beg. Please don't let a third party get involved in this decision. Please, Kimberly, allow me that."

I stared at her, trying to gauge what must be going on in that head of hers, but she was so damn hard to read.

"That's quite a speech, but we're no further forward. The bottom line is, you want William to live with you and will do everything in your power to achieve that. He is young and impressionable, and I cannot trust you. You're still thinking only about your needs. So I guess we will see each other in court. I'll stand a better chance there once I've made my case against you."

She'd been amicable, less defensive, and even teased me a little. I dropped my guard and she switched on me.

"Then you leave me no choice. My petition for custody will go forward. It's clear that you have every intention of vilifying my name. You've suggested as much. You're right, we are no further forward and there's no room for negotiation. Your position has not changed since day one."

"I won't negotiate about what's in William's best interest."

"So, you claim the high ground and make me the villain?" I scoffed, standing straight up with force.

"Yes, I am, and you are," she said, getting up to leave.

I pulled her into my arms, and then my lips were on hers.

My tongue probed, demanding a response. Her eyes closed and her hands rested against my chest as she yielded, opening up and letting me take control. It was a hard, bruising, almost punishing kiss.

I unraveled her ponytail and my fingers threaded through her hair, holding her head in place while my lips sought more from her. When her knees buckled, my arm tightened around her waist, holding her flush against my taut, unyielding body. She gripped my upper arms as the kiss deepened. It was only when an involuntary moan escaped from her that her logical brain kicked in.

She tore her lips away from mine. She stumbled back and could have fallen if I hadn't held on to her. Her breath came out in rasps and her chest heaved. My eyes bored into hers. We held an indefinable expression. She moved her body away and her blue eyes blazed back at me.

"Why did you do that?" She wiped her lips and tossed her hair over her shoulder.

"I was just finishing what you started last night."

"Don't you have a girlfriend?" she asked.

"Did you know that before you kissed me?"

"Oh! You're insufferable and arrogant!" She stormed toward the door of the summerhouse. "Don't bother," she said as I followed her. "I'll see myself out. Please say goodbye to Madeline and Leanne for me. Be at the house by six tonight to tell William. Goodbye."

I watched her cross the lawn to the front of the mansion where she parked her car. I stayed in the summerhouse until my erection subsided.

14
Kimberly

I STEPPED out into the heat, my head spinning from his kiss. My heart was pounding, unsure whether to be elated at the physical attraction or to remain strong for the sake of everything else. I challenged him and won the battle. But even through my victory, I was exhausted as I started my car and drove away from our confrontation. My fight had to be reserved for William. No matter how the fuck that man made me feel, nothing could come of it.

Why couldn't Desmond understand that the best place for his son right now was with us? The only place he ever known for his entire life. My stomach knotted as I mulled over his body language. Every time except today when I asked if he would agree to me adopting William, he avoided my gaze, shifted, and mumbled something I couldn't decipher. Twice now he ducked the direct question.

There was a reason Cecily wanted to hide Desmond's paternity until William turned eighteen, and he was rattled by that. His lifestyle was not fitting for him to raise a child, but Zachary's dossier did not further my cause. All I had was conjecture, and that wouldn't hold up anywhere. I tried to bluff him, but then Desmond accused me of wanting to harm his family. That upset me because I wasn't the villain here. Anyone from the outside could see that. Desmond and I were just two people who wanted different things for William and court was the only place that would listen to both sides and decide on what was best for him, with no biases.

But now there was significant movement on his part. He'd gone from giving time to letting William get used to his family yesterday, to letting William decide who he wanted to live with today. I was confident William would choose to live with Desmond in a heartbeat. My heart broke knowing that, but it was true.

Selfishly, I hated the fact Desmond and William got along so well. My relationship with my nephew had always been great, and he knew I would be there for him no matter what, but that didn't change the fact that to him, I wasn't his mother. Thinking about sitting down and telling him Desmond was his father churned my stomach because he would never want to leave his father's side. Especially after losing his mother.

There was also a good chance that the court would give me and Angela physical custody. The only fly in the ointment was his point about security when William was the heir to the massive Renault family fortune. I'd have to get my head around that one. I was certain that my tech was better than anything he could line up on security.

After getting home, I went to my bedroom to change. Angela and William were moving about downstairs. The last scenario flooded my mind: Desmond's lips on mine and the response evoked in my body. *Why does my body react this way?*

As it was, I'd driven home with soaking wet panties. Even now, my body still flushed at the memory of that kiss. Under different circumstances, in another time and place, I would've straddled him and ridden him hard and fast right there on the floor of the summerhouse. I was no shrinking violet with sex. I had not been fully satisfied with Chad and the other man I slept with before. I hoped he would rot in hell. Right now, I'd turned into a shameless hussy, hot for Desmond, which reminded me I needed a shower.

The warmth of his kiss still lingering on my lips. *Not a chance*. I strode to the bathroom, desperate to rid myself of the sensations he stirred in me. Flicking on the light switch, I dropped my clothes on the floor and stepped into the steaming shower. The boiling water cascaded over my skin, untangling my coiled muscles as I stood there, trying to make sense of what just happened.

I closed my eyes, letting my fingertips linger along the slope of my collarbones, the dip of my waist, and the gentle swell of my hips. My hands moved lower, exploring my body, finding every inch of softness and warmth that Desmond would never have the pleasure of experiencing. My low groans reverberated off the walls, my consciousness fading away. Every muscle in my body quivered with delight.

The hot water cascaded over me, and it cooled ever so slightly. My thoughts floated away, and I opened my eyes to the steam-filled bathroom, feeling the chill air on my wet skin. With a deep breath, I stepped out of the shower, reaching for the thick towel from the rack and wrapping it around my body.

Refreshed, I got dressed and made my way downstairs to William and Angela. I wanted to know where they'd been, and I wanted to hug my baby. My nephew helped to restore my sanity after my traumatizing brush with the FBI, and the devastating grief after Cece's death. I would do whatever it took to protect him and keep that vow I made to Cece. Angela and William were my rocks, and William was at the core of that. He helped to keep my demons at bay.

Angela would want all the details about my visit to the Renault Mansion. I could hear my mom's 'I told you so' when she heard about the significant movement Desmond made in our direction. I would not tell her how I'd maneuvered Desmond, but it had to be done. There was no other way. I believed he would keep to his word.

While waiting for Desmond to arrive, I called Barbara to update her..

"Hey, how did it go today?"

"Better than I expected. We talked, he yielded some ground, and I took advantage."

"What does that mean? I hope you know what you're doing. I think we have a pretty strong case for you and Angela to get joint custody, and I don't want you to do anything to jeopardize that. I know you don't like the idea while William is so young, but what are your options?"

"I didn't think I had any until yesterday. William is so little, Barb. He's my baby. I have to protect him, for Cece's sake. Yes, Desmond is his dad, but he is also a virtual stranger. It would break my heart to see him trudging off every other weekend, or whatever, with a backpack like some little orphan without a permanent home."

She scoffed. "Now you're being dramatic. You told me Desmond wanted to give William time to get to know his family, so what's changed?"

"That was yesterday. Today, Desmond said he will let the process evolve with no time limit on when William would go live with him." Left up to me, if that ever happened, then William would be in his teens, when a boy needs a father's guiding hand. "I want to put it on a firm legal footing rather than on the friendly handshake basis that Desmond favors. The only way to achieve that is through the courts, but Desmond doesn't want the courts involved and I don't trust that. The concession he made must be part of something upheld in law, not on some kind of informal agreement."

Barbara was too quiet. "I see your reasoning, but we have to keep this real. Joint custody is the best to hope for. Unless Desmond is a felon or you prove him unsuited to raise his own child, you may not even get legal custody."

My hands were twitching now, irritated from everything going on in my life right now. "You've explained it to me in black and white. Why do you think I had to do what I did? I don't trust him. He just wants to get what he wants, and then he'll screw me. That's what men do, and he'll be no exception."

"If you don't trust him, why do you think he'll keep his word after *you've* screwed him? Our best hope is Judge Gina Samson, coupled by how reasonable you appear to her. She is very child-centered and will always consider the child's point of view. I think our case for joint custody is pretty strong."

I would rather do anything else than worry myself over this court hearing. Desmond didn't understand what William meant to me, and even though he was his father, how could he expect for him to just move in with him? Especially with the new information from the dossier?

"In short, you want to have your cake and eat it too, right? Heads, you win. Tails, he loses. All sorts of clichés abound here."

"I suppose you could put it like that."

"No, Kim, it *is* like that. And I'm telling you now, the Rottweiler will advise Desmond against making that agreement with you and will advise him to go for sole custody. I bet Desmond has already been on the phone telling her how you tried to sandbag him. I wish you'd told me of your plan."

"Who's the Rottweiler?"

"Alana Glacey, but in court she's silky with it. Her specialty is children—abused children, trafficked children, those abducted and taken abroad, and custody cases like yours. That's why Desmond chose her to represent him and not the Renaults' usual stuffy old family firm. She is giving him some powerful coaching. Does Angela know what you're doing?"

"No. She would try to talk me out of it."

"I am too."

"Barb, I believe Desmond is genuine. He loves William more than he wants to win. He'll keep his word."

When did I become this woman? The type to keep a father away from his child? Desmond was trying to do right by his son. No matter what, I needed to be more receptive to him. We would be in each other's lives for decades to come, and there was no use in fighting every time we were in the same damn room.

"This sort of case, where a young child is involved, is closed to the public, but it's bound to leak, Kim, given who the Renaults are. I suspect that's the only reason Desmond wants to avoid going to court."

"It's my job to protect William. He's the only one I'm concerned about. There's a chance that Angela and I will get full custody, and that's a chance I have to take. The judge won't discount the first five years of William's life and the stability we have given him, compared to Desmond. I have to go for it."

"Just be careful. The last thing you should do is attack Desmond. And this is not about him but about Sammy's approach to parents who try to tarnish the other. Don't make Desmond the villain here. He isn't."

"I'm sticking to Cece's wishes. She'd expect me to do that. The letter she left William is evidence she wished to shield him from the Renaults, isn't it?"

"We can't know what was in Cece's mind when she decided. And the judge won't care about that letter, only what could be proven in the present time."

"That's what Desmond said."

"That's what the judge will say. The hearing is in three weeks, and we need to rehearse your presentation. Sammy likes to hear from the applicants and not from their lawyers. So both Alana Glacey and I will be there to support you guys, but not to speak, unless invited to do so by the judge. So you need to make certain to produce solid evidence of anything that shows Desmond isn't able to provide a stable and loving home for William before the hearing and give full disclosure to the other side."

Fuck. I can't do that. I couldn't even discuss the information I had in the dossier with Barb. If I tried to use any of the information in the dossier, it could very well backfire. It was better to stick to my original plan. Heads, I won. Tails, he lost.

"Are you still there? Is the voice in your head saying, listen to your lawyer? *Do. Not. Do. This.* Somewhere along the line, since Desmond stopped the adoption, you seem to have lost the balance of your mind. Right now, there are very valid reasons your petition for joint custody is being entertained. Let the concession go, don't push it, or it could backfire on you. And what about your relationship with Desmond, your nephew's father, going forward?"

"I believe Desmond is genuine. Whatever happens—okay, even if he gets sole custody—he's not going to just take William away. You said yourself, we have a strong case. All I'm getting is certainty and don't have to live on the edge all the time."

"I'm both your lawyer and your friend, and I'm telling you what you're doing is downright unethical. You're trading on Desmond's love for William to get what you want. It's not right, and it's not like you. What's going on?"

"Can we have this conversation another time? Desmond will be here in about five minutes and I need to get ready. We're telling William tonight."

"Okay, but you and I need to have this conversation soon."

"I'll call you tomorrow."

What Barbara said unsettled me, but I didn't have time to think about it now. Desmond was pulling into the driveway.

The doorbell rang and Angela and William greeted him. He was early, it was only five thirty p.m.

I took some deep breaths to compose myself before going downstairs to join them. The sooner we got it over with, the better. Justin was in town and I was looking forward to some sexy time. A welcomed distraction from all the bullshit that had become my life as of recently, especially Desmond Renault.

15
Desmond

My hands trembled against the steering wheel as I drove to William's house. I was nervous and scared. I did not know how to approach the conversation or what to say to explain why he had gone his whole life without knowing I was his father. Fear and dread coursed through me as I practiced different scenarios on my way over.

My mom and Leanne peppered me with questions after Kimberly left. I fumbled for answers, my face getting hot and my heart pounding faster with each attempted response. I tried to keep my emotions in check, but it was hard to remain composed; the frustration of being unable to answer their questions made my blood boil.

Ms. Bennett tried to sandbag me. My blood boiled just thinking about it. If I had known she would try to sabotage me like this, I never would have let her in the door. Her words were barbed and cutting, and I was certain she was trying to trip me up in any way she could. She proved herself to be a formidable opponent, and I could almost see her plotting ways to thwart my every move.

She grabbed my concession, then shut the damn door in my face. Was there something else driving her? It couldn't just be her love for my son unless I was a total monster. Now, Ms. Bennett, the gloves were off.

I refused to discuss the matter any further and instead concentrated on William. She didn't trust me. *Earth to Kimberly, all I care about is my fucking son.* So from this point forward, all my time will be spent getting to know William and preparing for court. If she wanted to play hardball, she hadn't met my lawyer.

Earlier, while still angry, I toyed with the idea of using whatever was in that manila envelope in my safe to my advantage, but I was reluctant to do so. I knew why. I'd told Alana about it and she said I'd have to disclose all the information to the judge, Kimberly, and her lawyer.

The FBI was something I knew about. They were bastards. Once they had their hook in, they twisted it to extract the last ounce of cooperation until they got everything they wanted. If they had something on her, it was bound to be something that would hurt her, and she was my son's aunt, dammit. I couldn't expose her. The damn woman got under my skin from the very first day I met her. I wanted Kimberly Bennett, and it drove me insane.

My relationship with Marsha couldn't go on. I'd have to end it. Even if things weren't serious between us, or at least on my side, I needed to let her go and give her a chance at finding the happiness she deserved with a man who wanted the whole picture. Plus, it wasn't fair for me to be thinking more about Kimberly than her. And right now, she never left my mind.

I sighed, got out of the SUV, and rang the doorbell.

Angela greeted me and ushered me inside. "I hope you'll stay for dinner. Kimberly won't be here, and I'd love some company."

Where was she going? "That would be lovely, Angela. Thank you."

"Hello," Kimberly said, looking me straight in the eye.

"Hi," I responded. My eyes searched hers, wanting to get beneath just a hint of defiance I detected in her blue gaze. She wore a mid-thigh tight-fitting red dress and black heels that I knew she didn't wear to work, so she must be going on a date. I bit my lip, trying to get my want at bay, especially in front of her mother. If we were alone, I might just grab her and slowly unzip the dress down her back, my fingertips slowly sending shivers down her spine, while I kissed her lavender-scented neck. Whoever she was going to see, he was obviously a very lucky man tonight.

Angela winked at me. We were both staring at each other and we had been caught.

"Well, I'll leave you babies to have a good time. I'm going to prepare dinner," Angela informed.

William climbed into my lap. "Are we going to talk about my daddy now? Kimberly said so. I want you to be."

My heart might break. He seemed so vulnerable and innocent. "Yes, we are, buddy. Kimberly and I want to tell you a secret."

William's eyes were shining. He looked from one to the other. "I like secrets. When I tell Nana Angie a secret, I whisper in her ear."

I looked at Kimberly. It wasn't as easy. She read me and took over.

"William, do you remember what Nana Angie said about Desmond being your daddy?"

"Nana Angie said to ask Desmond if he wants to be my daddy." He grinned. "Will you be my daddy, Desmond?"

"Shall I tell you something, William? I'm your real daddy.

You're my little boy because mommy and I made you, but mommy kept it a secret."

"You know my mommy?" His brown eyes stared at me.

"Yes, I do. We made you together, and we love you very much." William looked over at Kimberly, seeking confirmation. She smiled and nodded. He looked my way. "Mommy is in heaven with the angels and she is very happy. Nana Angie told me."

"Yes, she is." I pulled my son close and kissed his forehead. I knew my eyes were glistening with tears and I didn't care. This was a precious moment. So it was that simple for another human being to claim your heart. I looked over at Kimberly and mouthed 'thank you.'

"Can I have sleepovers with you in your house? Kimberly and Nana Angie let me have sleepovers with my friends and my friends have sleepovers in my house."

"Yes, William, sleepovers with me and you'll meet my mommy who is your nana as well, and you have another aunty. Her name is Leanne. You have two aunties now."

"We'll talk more about it tomorrow, okay? It's your bath time now."

William clung to me. "Will you come too, Daddy?"

"Yes, I'm coming." I stood with William in my arms and followed Kimberly upstairs.

Kimberly left once she and I put William to bed. Angela and I were sitting around the kitchen island, having a meal.

"How did it go? I gave the three of you some space."

"Angela, honestly, this is the best night of my entire life. I felt like a dad tonight and it's the best feeling ever. Thank you for preparing William. I know you did and I'm so grateful."

"I love my grandson, and I see how much he already loves you. I'm so happy for you both."

"Kimberly was wonderful. She was so gracious and

supportive, even though we don't quite see eye to eye on how to go forward."

"What happened at the mansion today? Kimberly told me about the generous concession you made. You're a good man. William is lucky to have you. But something else happened. I know my daughter. She said it was nothing, but I know her."

So, you don't know. She didn't tell you. That figures.

"Kimberly doesn't trust me. She insists we go to court. Given the Renault name, it's bound to leak out, and I wanted to control the narrative, protect William, my mother, and sister for as long as I could. And of course, the two of you will be affected. We don't have to go to court. We could get the lawyers to draw up a legal document."

"Did you say any of that to her?"

"She raised the publicity issue in the first place, in Cecily's name being vilified. It came up again yesterday, but her distrust of me is stronger than her better judgment. As for the legal document, we didn't get to that because it's obvious Kimberly is hoping she will be awarded sole custody. That's what she wants. I'm sorry, Angela, but it won't work. Our conversations always disintegrate and I'm done talking. If she wants to go to court, so be it."

"Kimberly has a problem with trusting men because of her father. He let her down. They were very close. One day he was there and the next he was gone. I also think something happened to her in Boston, but she won't talk about it. I think it had to do with her boyfriend. He disappeared, and she came back to Bayview when William was about two."

Does that explain why she is always so confrontational and aggressive toward me? Does she think I might leave William? I wish I knew more about what went on in that head of hers.

"She had these dreadful nightmares when she first arrived back home. I think William gave her the strength to pull through and put her life together again," Angela explained. "She loves that little boy as if he were her own son. Don't give up on her. Make her listen."

What happened to her in Boston? Is that the information in the manila envelope in my safe?

"I think you'll be much better at that than I will. Your daughter seems to have a natural antipathy toward me. We were making progress yesterday, but she turned and we were back to our normal state. In opposition and not agreeing."

Angela patted his arm. "Don't worry, it will work out. Things always do, in their own time. Would you like some more wine?" Angela asked. "There's another bottle in the fridge."

"No, I'm good. I gotta get home." I smiled.

"It's a shame Kimberly had to go into the office. She does that sometimes on a Sunday night if she has stuff to catch up on before her week begins. She works too hard."

I was relieved that Angela's words indicated Kimberly wasn't on a date, but I didn't know if her daughter just didn't tell her. That dress was not appropriate for work, so my better judgment said it was more than that. Goddammit, why should I care if she had a date or not? *Who are you fooling, Renault. You would mind if she had a date. You do mind that she has a relationship with Thornton.*

"Did you see the framed photograph of the three of you alongside his mom's in William's room?" Angela was asking.

I smiled. "Yes, I saw that."

"It was printed and framed before you got home yesterday, I'd bet. He has another copy in his school bag, ready to show his friends. Oh my God, Desmond!" Angela clapped a hand over her mouth.

"What, Angela? What is it?"

"You realize William will go to school tomorrow and tell everyone about his daddy? You know that, don't you? He will tell his teacher and his entire class he has a dad. By the end of the day, half of Bayview will know that Desmond Renault is William McCormick's father. I think you'll need to authenticate that by making an appearance."

I slapped my forehead. "Of course, why didn't I think of that? Little people talk. A member of my family only has to sneeze in public and it makes the headlines. I'll have to prepare a formal announcement in time for the papers before it appears as a torrid headline in some tabloid scoop."

"I could remove the photograph from his school bag and ask him to keep it a secret for now."

"No, we can't do that. It has to come out, eventually. We'll just have to deal with it. Excuse me for a minute. I need to make a couple of quick calls."

I stepped out into the hallway and called Julie, my executive assistant.

"Is everything okay?"

"I'm so sorry to disturb you on a Sunday evening."

"It's okay. My husband knows that's the price he has to pay for the megabucks you pay me." She chuckled.

"I'm glad you have such an understanding husband. The PR team should meet me at the office at seven tomorrow. A sensitive personal announcement must hit the print and broadcast media by tomorrow afternoon."

"Okay, boss, consider it done. I'll only get back to you if there's a problem."

"Thanks, and please clear my calendar for the day. If anything is an absolute must, talk to me about it in the morning. See you tomorrow."

I leaned back on the doorjamb and closed my eyes, took a few deep breaths, and imagined the lurid headlines.

Angela was watching me. "Desmond? Is everything okay?"

"Angela, am I doing the right thing? Can you imagine what

the headlines will say? And it will wash over you and Kimberly. Newspeople and their cameras will be swarming all over your place and at William's school."

"It's done already. You've told William, and that's as it should be. I'm a bit of a fatalist and think this is inevitable. William is still young. Can you imagine how he'd feel to be described as Desmond Renault's illegitimate son at eighteen? Because that's how the headlines will describe him whenever it comes out. Right now, that little boy needs a father. You know, Desmond, however damaged a man may be, 'dad' is that universal image ingrained in a child's psyche. The experience of an absent father scarred both my daughters. I don't want that for William. Fathers are not always how we'd wish them to be, and lives can be messy sometimes, but in the eyes of their children, they are important. You can't avoid this, Desmond, and you can't predict the future from here. Deal with what you know now. So just do what you have to."

"William has a sage for a grandmother," I said, smiling at her. I stepped away again to make another call to a family friend, Eric Dormund, Editor of *Bayview Times*.

"Desmond? What's up? I hope Madeline and Leanne are okay. I haven't seen Madeline for some time."

"They're both fine, Eric."

"You know this is a Sunday, Desmond, the day on which God rested."

I chuckled. "I stirred your journalistic juices."

"No, not yet. What sensational piece of gossip do you have for me?"

"I need an interview with your best."

"What's going on? Are you sure everything is okay?"

"Yes, it's just a personal matter which I'm sure will hit the press this week and you know what the tabloids do with the Renault name. I want to get in first."

"Tell me more?"

"Not on the phone."

"Okay, I'll drop by your office at about nine tomorrow. Will that work?"

"Great, I'll see you then."

I turned to Angela. "You and William should come and stay at the mansion for a few days. It's less exposed than your home. We'll see where we go from there."

"Kimberly will be against that," Angela said.

Of course she will be, and that makes it even more fun.

16
Kimberly

I HANDED A DRIPPING wet and giggling William to Desmond, who had been leaning against the bathroom door holding a towel, watching them. Desmond wrapped up William and held him securely in his arms, then took him into his bedroom and dried him.

I lay on the bed beside William, as I did most nights to read his bedtime story, thinking Desmond would sit on the edge of the bed and listen. But no, William would have none of it. He insisted Desmond lie on the other side of him. Desmond and I read the book together, speaking in the voices of the various animals appearing in the story, while William snuggled between the two of us, first touching my face, then Desmond's.

It was an occasion to be recorded for posterity because it was a first for the three of us, a unique experience. The little boy was in his element. He was excited and animated. His daddy was here, and he wanted to chatter. The Sandman took over, and we lulled William into sleep.

We lay beside him for a while before I signaled to Desmond we could leave. The moment was too intimate for my liking, and I was in a hurry to get away to see Justin. He could help take care of the tension in my lady bits. Desmond thanked me for being there and helping him through it all. It was so much easier with me around.

As I drove into the Bay, the scenes were on replay. They touched my heart. Angela was right. There was a special connection between William and Desmond. In a brief time, my nephew bonded with Desmond in a way he never had with Justin, whom he'd known for much longer. William neither clung to Justin as he did with Desmond, nor asked if Justin could be his dad. Perhaps, as Angela suggested, Renault genes recognized family. I had little doubt the most likely reason was down to Angela's prompting of William. Desmond Renault appeared to have the makings of a great dad, but I was still skeptical.

After making it to the Thornton Building, I let myself into the apartment, and Justin was waiting for me.

"Hey." He took me into his arms and gave me a quick kiss. "You look beat. Rough weekend?"

Yeah. You could say that. Spent most of it fighting Desmond Renault.

"Kimberly, are you okay? Do you want to eat out?"

"No. Let's stay in. I put a couple of fresh pizzas in the fridge earlier today. You get the wine; I will put them in the oven. I could do with a glass or three."

"That bad, huh?" He chuckled and did what he was told. He filled two glasses and waited for me to join him on the settee.

"How's the custody battle going? Still can't get on board with the idea that your sister had a child with Desmond Renault. Have you told William who his father is yet? How is the little guy? I hope I get to see him while I'm here."

"William is great. I don't want to talk about that other stuff.

Not tonight. I've had a week full of it. Let's just have a quiet evening. Tell me how you're doing. I haven't seen Barry and Iris for a while, and I have little time to visit right now."

I rested my head on his shoulder while we discussed what he was working on at CRYO. He sought my opinion. This was the best aspect of my relationship with Justin. We talked the same language around work, especially cybernetics. Much later, my phone rang. Justin groaned. "Don't answer that."

"I have to. It could be about William." When Desmond's name appeared, my finger pushed the ignore icon.

"Who was that?" Justin asked.

"No one important." I turned to him and sought his lips again. He picked me up and carried me into the bedroom.

Things got heated fast and our clothes were off in a matter of seconds. God, I've missed him. My body was begging for some attention. He propped my foot on his shoulder as he got on his knees to give me some love first. My hand ran through his hair, and the closer I got to orgasm, the more he would stare up at me. He loved to watch me as I came. As I threw my head back, his name came out of my mouth. But not Justin's.

"You've got to be fucking kidding me!" he said, removing my foot from his shoulder and wiping his mouth.

"Justin. I'm so sorry. It means nothing."

"Like hell it doesn't. I came to spend time with you, whom I haven't seen for several weeks, and you call me by another man's name. What am I supposed to think, Kimberly? Desmond Renault, of all people."

"We were doing the *friends with benefits* thing... you never told me it was more. Justin, I promise you. It isn't like that."

"What is it like, Kimberly? Are you screwing him?"

"Of course not. Let me explain."

"Explain? What is there to explain? He's a handsome,

eligible guy, a billionaire several times over, and is your nephew's father. Has he been here, in your bed?"

"No. Of course not. Well, not in my bed..."

Justin stood up and put his clothes on.

"Where are you going? Would you just listen? Give me a chance to explain."

"There's nothing to explain, Kimberly. Was it him on the phone earlier?"

My eyes beseeched him. He stared at me with a confused and hurt expression. He walked into the living area, took his things, and let himself out of the apartment.

I threw my hands in the air. It was like some damn comedy of errors. I didn't know whether to laugh or cry. It filled my inner world with pain, fear, and anger. There were only three people in the world whose response I could trust and rely on. My mom for her constant support and love. William brought me joy and unconditional love. Barb was dependable and always there. I needed my best friend.

"Kim?"

The sound of sniffles and muted sobs went through the phone.

"What's wrong? Are you okay?"

"Come here?" I asked, my voice wavering.

"Are you at the apartment?"

"Yes."

Something horrible happened, and she was the only person I could talk to about it. How fucking embarrassing was this day going to be?

"Tell security to let me in. I'm on my way."

Something was wrong with me, and it all started when Desmond walked into my office building. Why couldn't I get him out of my head? His lips? His hands running through my hair and gripping my hips? *Fuck!*

Less than half an hour later, Barbara was knocking on my apartment door. I let her in, my eyes a blotchy mascara-smudged mess. I broke seeing her face, knowing that she was the only one who wouldn't give me shit about what happened.

"Kim, what's wrong?"

The worry in her voice was unmistakable. I wrung my hands as tears began rolling down my cheeks again. "It's Justin, he's gone. We were in the middle of... you know, and it was getting more and more intense and..."

"What? Do I need to be here as your lawyer or as your friend? Did he do something to you?"

"Barb, I fucking called him Desmond." The words tumbled out of my mouth. Her expression shifted to one of terror. My face went pale and my stomach churned as I stared at Barb, desperate for answers. "He just walked out and now he won't answer my calls. I screwed up bad. Why is this happening to me?"

An icy chill ran down my spine. I understood Justin's confusion and hurt, and I wished the ground would open and swallow me whole. That damaged what little trust he had. All this crap going back and forth between Desmond and me was fucking with my head, and now the only man that I've been semi close to since Chad just walked out on me.

Desmond Renault is ruining my life.

Barb steered me to the couch and lowered me onto the cool cushioned seat. She scrutinized my face for a long moment, her mouth hanging open as if searching for the right words. My cheeks burned with shame and the filthiness of my latest indiscretion. I thought of him while in the throes of pleasure with another man. How could I have done such a thing?

"Listen, something is going on and you haven't been telling me everything as a friend. Not a lawyer. So spill because there is only one reason you would be moaning his name..." I told her what happened in the summerhouse up to where I called Justin by Desmond's name. "You went to the mansion to persuade Desmond to see your point of view and you let him kiss you?"

"Well, I didn't let him... I..." My voice trailed off.

"But you kissed him back."

I let out a vast sigh and clamped my lips together.

"It's just lust, Barb. Pure, unadulterated lust. He has this magnetism that just pulls you in. Whenever he's near me, flames flare up in my loins. It's despicable."

"You're such a hypocrite. Are you talking about the same guy you said..."

"Okay, okay. I know what I said. No need to remind me."

I knew it was crazy, but what was happening was real. My body had a mind of its own, and no matter how much I tried to fight it, I was drawn to Desmond. He made me so angry and yet I wanted to feel his touch.

"You're attracted to the man you want to defeat in court? This is insane, and what the heck did Desmond think he was doing? Under different circumstances, I'd tell you to pin him, fuck his brains out, and get it out of your system. But you need to back away."

I threw my hands in the air. "You'll get no argument from me. Court case or not, I'll never become one of Desmond Renault's bed wenches."

She shot me a look. "Well, your mouth told Justin otherwise, so get that handled. Get your head on straight because you don't have long before you're in front of the judge."

"Everything is so messed up. What I need right now is to rehearse my presentation, so make some time."

Barbara chuckled. "You'll be fine. Have you considered what I said earlier?"

"If you mean about being unethical, yes, I have. But I haven't changed my mind. I'm only locking down what

Desmond offered of his own free will. What happens when he has his own children?"

"Kimberly, Desmond Renault lives and works in Bayview, where his company is based. His family has been here for generations, and William *is* his own child. As your friend, why are you fighting him so hard on this?"

Tears streamed down my cheeks again, thinking about not getting to see William every day and drop him off at school. Not getting to read him a bedtime story every night. I couldn't lose him. Desmond might be a good father, but why did that mean that he had to live with him?

"William McCormick Senior and Mom weren't married. When she got pregnant, he left her. He went off and married another woman and never looked back. Cecily was just left behind. Then he died. Mom never told Cece any of this. She grew up thinking her dad was a great guy who died of disease. Then there's my dad."

Neither my sister nor I had a dominant father figure around, and I just wanted William to be raised right, and for the longest time, I never thought his father would ever turn up. We filed for legal adoption of William, and then Desmond showed up.

"Desmond made William happy today. I'm glad about that, and Desmond spends all the time he wants with William, but I still have to protect him. I need sole custody, Barb. Even if there is a slight possibility, I have to go to court."

We argued back and forth until, exhausted, we both fell asleep on my bed.

17

Desmond

I sat at my desk, my breathing the only sound in the room, besides the pen tapping against my desk. It wouldn't be much longer before the team arrived, and I sent a text to Kimberly to meet me here, but she hadn't responded. Alana was keeping her eyes out for any news, and I told her to tell my best friend Johnny about William before it came out in the media.

When his name appeared across my screen, I sighed. He was going to be pissed I hadn't told him myself.

"Hey, buddy, would you like to tell me what the hell is going on? Why didn't you tell me? Even my girlfriend keeps secrets from me."

"I think it's called attorney-client privilege, Johnny."

"To hell with that, Des. We are family. What do you need, buddy?"

"I don't know. I'm treading water at the moment, trying to keep the deluge at bay, but I suspect we will be flooded out this week sometime."

"Well, let me know if you think of anything. And we'll need a serious talk about this youthful misdemeanor of yours.

Who is this woman? Do I know her? Alana won't even tell me her name."

"My text message was very cryptic. Not on the phone. She is deceased. Give me a day or so and we will catch up."

"Yeah. You and Marsha should come to dinner. Take care, buddy."

I disconnect the line. Yeah, Marsha. I would have to deal with that sooner rather than later. Might as well set it up now. Sometimes I forgot Marsha was my girlfriend, since we didn't see each other much.

"Hey, babe." Her voice sounded sleepy. Not surprising.

"Hey. Did I wake you?"

"Had a late night. Where are you? Want to come play hooky for an hour? I'm wearing your favorite teddy. Work will wait."

"I'm already at work. It's going to come out about William today or by tomorrow morning at the latest. I have to get ahead of it."

She didn't even hesitate in her response. "Well, how about lunchtime? I don't have to be back at the precinct until late afternoon. I miss you. I need to see you."

The biggest problem here was her not seeming at all interested in my son. Not one phone call to see how things were going. As a father, I required her to be just as invested as I was. She wanted more out of this relationship, but her actions didn't say that.

"I think that would work. I'll have to check with Julie. My entire schedule has been rearranged today. I'll call you."

"Are you okay? Are we okay?"

"Let's talk about us later. I have to go, Marsha."

"Okay. I love you, Desmond."

My eyes were closed. "I'll call you when I'm through."

What in the hell was that about? She loved me? Was this

her way of getting me to stick around? We had both been so distant. I didn't love her. *Shit.* Yet another woman's heart I had to break.

And of course, my assistant walked in to let me know the PR team was in the conference room and ready to start. I took a deep breath, knowing that after this announcement, not only would my life change, but so would William's, Kimberly's, and Angela's lives.

I walked past her, heading straight into the conference room. Instead of beating around the bush, I got right to the point of why I brought them in. The four members of the PR team had nothing but disbelief on their faces when I told them as succinctly as possible about William Lucas McCormick. My phone rang and Kimberly's name scrolled across the screen.

"Hey, everything okay? I tried to call you last night. Did you get my text?"

"Yes, and I've spoken to Angela. She told me what was happening. I'm approaching Renault Tech's reception now."

"Wait right there. I'm coming to get you."

Telling them was the first step. It was no longer a secret. Yet, that posed some risks, and security would be important from now on.

"Tammy, draft something short and simple. A couple of sentences will do. Three at most. I have a visitor. She'll be joining us," I told the team as I rushed toward the elevator.

"Good morning!"

She gave me a look. "Angela told me what was going on, and I'm here to tell you there's no need to panic."

I frowned. "What do you mean?"

"William will not say anything at school today."

How can she know that?

"He isn't? But Angela said William will tell his teacher and classmates about me as soon as he goes to school today. That sounds like what a kid his age would do."

"But not my nephew. He knows how to keep secrets."

The elevator door opened on the executive floor and I ushered her into my office. I invited her to sit and sat down opposite her.

"Kimberly, what are you saying? I don't understand."

"Do you remember how you started the conversation with William yesterday? You said we wanted to tell him a secret. Then you told him his mommy wanted to keep it a secret that you were his dad. Great touch, by the way. Were you telling him the truth, or was it a Freudian slip? You do know what a Freudian slip is?"

"I'll ignore that last part, Ms. Bennett. So, you're saying William would have taken what I said literally, and he won't say anything about me being his dad?"

"Exactly."

Well, hot damn, my choice of words proved useful.

"But we can't take that chance. There's too much at stake."

If it got out before we were prepared, things could go sideways, and I didn't want William to have to worry about paparazzi swarming around him walking out of school.

"I'd bet my bottom dollar William won't say a word until he checked it out with me or Angela. But I agree, the stakes are high and we'll have to do it before the hearing, anyway. So since we're here, let's just get it done."

I nodded. She looked beautiful as always with her trademark ponytail, glasses, reddish-pink lipstick, and high heels.

"My PR team is in the boardroom. We should join them. They are working on a press statement. I want to keep it short and to the point. I'll introduce you as William's aunt."

"Do I have a name?" She side-eyed me.

"Of course. Everyone knows the newest badass business owner in town."

She smiled at me for the first time in forever.

"Is that how I'm described, or is it just your name for me?"

I gave her a grin. "What do you think?"

She shrugged. "As long as they don't think I'm one of your women."

Is she flirting with me? God, I can't ever get a read on her.

"The way you glare at me, no one in their right minds would think that. I like my women to hang on my every word and look at me."

She snorted. "Okay, let's get this over and done with."

"Wait, one more thing. I intend to keep Cecily's name out of it and yours."

"Bad idea, Desmond. It's bound to come out at some point and I don't want it to look as if we're hiding anything and have to face all that noise again. I say we go full frontal."

I tilted my head. "Okay, you have a point. Come on, let's go."

I ushered her into the boardroom, my hand touching the small of her back. She moved away.

"Hey, everyone, this is Kimberly Bennett. I'm sure you know her as the CEO of Bennett Technologies. She is also my son's aunt."

Everyone greeted Kimberly, and I held out a chair for her to sit.

"Okay, do we have a short, two-sentence announcement?" I asked.

"How about this?" said Tammy Dresden, the head of PR. Two sentences appeared on the screen on the wall.

Kimberly read and considered the words. "I'd like to add something."

"Of course," I said. "The floor is yours."

"It needs a reference to my sister's passing, and my name should be added so that both sides of William's family are seen to be standing together on this. I'd also like to remove William's last name. The press will find out soon enough, but at least we should set the tone for respecting his privacy."

Everyone nodded. "Of course, Ms. Bennett," Tammy Dresden said. "That is an improvement and makes it more authentic."

Within minutes, a new version of the statement appeared on the screen:

Desmond Renault, the CEO of Renault Technologies, has confirmed he has a five-year-old son named William, whose mother died several years ago. The boy has been living with his mother's family. His maternal aunt, Kimberly Bennett, CEO of Bennett Technologies, and Mr. Renault both ask that you respect the family's privacy in view of William's tender age.

"Great job, guys. That about does it. Short and to the point. I don't think we need anything more," I said, looking at Kimberly.

"As soon as this hits the press, you will be inundated at your respective homes and they will try to snatch a photograph of William," said the head of the PR department.

"Thanks, Tammy. We'll just have to deal with the fallout. Place an embargo on it for six tonight and get it out to the usual suspects."

"Oh, Ms. Bennett, one last thing," Tammy Dresden said. "We expect most calls to come to Renault Tech, but you should expect some as well."

"Any calls to the mansion will be directed back to Renault Tech. You're welcome to do the same if it would make your life easier," I added.

"Thanks. I didn't think of that."

My heart fluttered because soon enough the entire world would know I had a son. I could go out and shout it from the rooftops if I wanted.

"Good. You should tell your board members as well. I still have that thankless task to perform, but I'll wait until after the embargo hour and will make one conference call."

This should be interesting, since Justin was on her board.

"Thank you everyone for coming in so early," I told the team. "I appreciate it."

I turned to her. "Kimberly, would you step into my office for a few minutes?"

She nodded and followed me out.

Once we were back in my office, I offered her some coffee.

"Oh yes, please, I never say no to caffeine in the morning."

Before I could reach the door, my executive assistant appeared with coffee, fruit, and muffins on a tray.

"Thanks, Julie. You really earn those megabucks. Always thinking ahead."

Julie smiled back.

"Please schedule a conference call to the board members," I said, "but directed to the mansion anytime between five thirty and six thirty this evening. Let me have the name of anyone not on the call."

"Certainly, Desmond."

Gerard Strongman, my CFO and potential stepfather, already knew about William, and I would tell him about the press statement as soon as I was done with Ms. Bennett.

"Have you had breakfast yet?"

"Only coffee this morning, so this looks wonderful."

"Help yourself," I said.

I poured us a cup of coffee and sat opposite her. Except for lipstick, she seemed to have little to no makeup on. Her skin was flawless.

"You're staring, Desmond."

"I'm just always trying to get a read on you, but you're a complicated woman."

"Do you want to get me?" She flushed as the words left her lips.

I smiled. There it was again. That delightful blush. Just beautiful. No cleavage this time for my eyes to linger on, though, but the styling of the bold two-tone dress revealed well-toned arms and a long neckline.

"Yes, I do. You're the only mother my son knows. Last night, you were super supportive of the relationship between me and William. Thank you for that."

"Does that surprise you?"

"Yes, it does, since you've left me in no doubt that you think I'm unsuitable father material."

"I don't want to stop you being a father to William. I just want him to stay with Angela and me until he is much older."

"I think we've said all there is to say about that. You don't trust me. You're a smart woman. You knew I'd do nothing to harm William, including removing him from you and Angela. So you pushed and pushed until I opened the door."

"All is fair in love and war. No hard feelings, right?" she said, averting my gaze.

"None, but remember you said that."

"Is that a threat?"

"No, not at all." My brown eyes pinned her and my voice softened. "More of a promise."

She swallowed. "So, tell me, how else do I amaze you?"

"Take today. I expected you to roar into my office, six guns blazing, but there you were being helpful and charming."

She gave me her sweetest smile. "I'll tell you what I'm not

sweet and light about, Desmond. The idea that we should stay at Renault Mansion. Angela told me she and William are staying with you for a few days for security reasons. You do not know what I do, don't you? My security will trump yours any day."

There is that firebird I know. Tell me how you really feel.

"Your walls will keep the ordinary camera lenses away and you think your security will protect William. But there's very little you can do to keep the super paps out. So we'll just have to get used to it."

"No one is asking you to live there, Kimberly. As austere and grim as you find my home, the invitation is open and you'll be welcomed anytime. If I know my mother, she's already prepared a room for you."

"Nope. That won't be happening, Desmond. I'll spend as much time as possible with William. I hope that's okay with you, but that's it. And I said that inside the mansion was homely."

William's first night with me would be less stressful with her around, and she would understand that it was best for my son. She had her reservations about me, but this wasn't about me.

"At least for the first night if you stayed over, it would help him settle down if he knew you were staying."

She peered at me. "Since when did you become a child psychologist?"

"I just want William to be happy and comfortable in my home. One day it will be his."

She shrugged. "I need to get to my office to prepare for tomorrow's onslaught."

"Do you have time for a quick lunch later? I could come your direction," I suggested.

She peered at me like she was taking me in. I was dressed in dark blue jeans and a Henley of the same color, not intending to have an ordinary business day today.

"I'm sorry, Desmond. There's no time today. I must go." She stood up, walked to the door, and opened it.

Something was going on. She was different today. Not as much of a firecracker as she usually was in my presence. Noted.

I watched the jiggle of her ass as I followed her to the elevator. "Well, will you come to dinner at the mansion later and you can put William to bed? Whether you stay is up to you."

"Yes."

"Good. I'll see you whenever you get there. I'm going to get William from school today with Angela."

Kimberly stopped and turned back to me. "Are you serious? *The* Desmond Renault is going to stand outside of William's school? Why would you do that?"

"I'm not going to stand outside the school. Angela and I will be driven by Luke. I'll be in the back of the vehicle with darkened windows. No one will see me. It'll be fine, Kimberly. Don't make a big thing of it."

She turned on her heel. "No need to come with me. I'll see myself out."

Her tone told me not to push it, even though my mind envisioned me pushing her against the elevator wall and slipping my hand in between the material of her panties and her slick skin.

Just then, my executive assistant claimed my attention. "Desmond, Eric Dormund has arrived for the interview."

When I looked around, Kimberly was gone.

18
Kimberly

I HURRIED AWAY from Renault Tech. Being in Desmond Renault's presence disturbed me. It had mortified me to cling to him in his truck that evening after he'd taken William fishing. Then there was the kiss in the summerhouse. Now I was fantasizing about him if I'd called out his name while with Justin. What was wrong with me?

I enjoyed our sparring just now, with just a little flirting, I admitted. The truth was, I enjoyed being around him, but wanted to avoid him at the same time. It was confusing, distracting, and yes, he excited me. Desmond Renault spelled danger, and I was playing too close to the fire.

Barb was right. I needed to back away. Except now I was going right into the lion's den. But Desmond was right. I had to stay with William at least for this first night. Apart from anything else, it might give me the opportunity to make a better sweep of the mansion. I hadn't been successful before. Leanne hung on to me the entire time, and the mansion was vast.

I'd have to find some pretext for going into Desmond's bedroom. Nothing came to mind, but I'd think of something. If

Angela was taking William straight to the mansion after school, then I needed to get there as soon as possible after that.

I hurried to the hotel where Justin might stay since he was no longer staying at my apartment. I had to make him understand that he'd gotten it all wrong. It was just that with all this custody and court business, Desmond Renault was in my head.

Yes, I might fantasize about him, but I wasn't sleeping with him, nor would I. I didn't want to lose Justin. I needed a friend, even one without benefits. He provided a shield for me.

If I stopped, I would admit more than I cared to, but I was too preoccupied to analyze what my feelings were for Justin. As I'd expected, Justin was registered at the hotel, but he was not there now. I left a note for him.

Back at my office, Jonas and Bartholomew were waiting for me. They were speechless when I told them about William and Desmond and the pending press statement.

"There will be calls from the press which should be directed to the Renault Technologies PR department. The person there is Tammy Dresden. Just refer callers to Renault Tech. They will deal with everything."

"Yes, boss." He grinned. "So, you'll be parenting William with the most gorgeous man in Bayview, in the whole state."

"How about in the whole country, Jonas, or even the world? Does your husband know you have a crush on Desmond Renault?"

"Now that you mention it, I better tell him." He grinned.

"Go, both of you. I have work to do," I said, wanting to curtail any further discussion or speculation about Desmond, William, and myself.

"Oh, Jonas, wait. I need to talk about trackers with you."

"What do you need, boss?"

"Jonas, I'm not your boss; you're now my partner. Get used to the idea."

"Kimberly, you'll always be my boss. So, what about trackers?"

"I need something simple and unobtrusive that I iron into all of William's clothes, even socks, underwear, and shoes."

"Wow, that's a bit over the top, isn't it?"

"Not when you're the heir to a family fortune worth billions."

Jonas whistled. "It's a whole new world."

"Yep."

No matter what happened at the court hearing, Cece entrusted me to take care of William and with that came a sense of overwhelming responsibility to protect him. Desmond was proving to be a good father and was constantly thinking about William and his best interests. Staying at the mansion wasn't the worst idea he ever had. As far as physical security, he had us beat. With the press statement going out tonight, we should receive the worst of it.

Now that everyone was going to know that William was Desmond's son, there were precautions I wanted to take, just in case. Trackers in his clothing would help me feel better. No matter what happened or who he was with, Desmond and I would have his location.

With the knowledge from the dossier, Michael turned on his best friend, Desmond's dad, and that scared me. It proved that so many people would do whatever it took to get their hands on the Renaults' fortune.

Cecily wanted to protect William from dealing with these issues at such a young age, or at least that was what I assumed. Desmond was his father, though, and since paternity had been verified, I couldn't keep them apart. Who was I to deny a father time with his son?

I loved my sister—hell, I missed her a fuck ton—but if she

were here, I supposed seeing Desmond and William together would have changed her mind.

Desmond: So... will you be staying tonight? My mother literally will not stop calling me to double-check... We haven't had guests at the mansion in years and she wants everything to be perfect and welcoming.

Madeline Renault caring about other people's feelings? Holy shit, I never thought I'd see the day.

Me: Most likely not. I'll leave after William falls asleep. Tell her not to go overboard. He's not going to care about what thread count the sheets are.

Madeline Renault was insufferable and I couldn't believe I would have to deal with her for the rest of my life.

19

Desmond

I GAVE myself a strict forty-five minutes to spend with Marsha before I had to leave to pick up my son. I wished it would be enough, as I knew it would be painful to tell her I couldn't continue seeing her. Despite Marsha being an incredible person, it was getting harder and harder to ignore the subtle hints of neediness. Although it killed me inside, if I wanted to focus all my energy on my son, then Marsha and I wouldn't work out.

"I won't be long, Ward," I notified my friend and driver.

Our eyes met in the rearview mirror. Ward nodded.

"Hey," she greeted me, opening the door. "I see it's dress down Monday at Renault Tech," she quipped.

"Yeah, I did very little formal business today."

She moved toward me to get a kiss. I gave her a quick peck on the lips. "What's wrong, Desmond?"

"Come, sit with me."

She led me to the couch and sat on my lap. Yeah, this wasn't going to go well. "Look, Marsha, it's been quite a difficult time for me. Everything is going a million miles an hour and there aren't enough hours in the day."

"Since you discovered your son, you mean?" She moved off my lap and sat on the couch.

"Yes."

"I know you have to give this a lot of attention and it shouldn't affect us, but it has. Our schedules are already opposite and now that you've got this going on, I see you once a month."

She wasn't daring me to choose between her and my son, was she? That was dangerous because she wouldn't like the answer.

"It's more than that, Marsha. For the next while, I need to get to know William and spend time with him. I'm the only parent he has and I want to make up for that five-year absence. It's not fair to ask you to wait around while I make up for lost time with my son."

"Is that your way of saying you want to end it? Just say it, Desmond. If that's what you want, just say it. Don't string me along."

I bent my head. This was downright uncomfortable. But she was right. We came to a natural parting of the ways.

"I think it would be for the best, Marsha." She got up, walked to the door, opened it, and held it open while staring at me. I walked toward her. "Please, Marsha, let's not end it like this."

"How do you want to end it, Desmond? Do you want me to beg you not to dump me, or should I wail and cling to you? Just go because I don't want to do either of those things."

I stood still, looking at her.

"Please leave."

I laid a hand on her shoulder. She shrugged it off. "Marsha, please, I don't want to leave like this."

"If you don't leave now, I'll start screaming and someone will call the police, which would be ironic, since I'm the police. Please just go. Now I'm begging you."

I moved out into the hallway. Marsha's door shut behind me. Sobbing came from behind her door. I stepped back toward the door and raised my hand to knock but dropped it to my side again.

I found the last twenty minutes quite difficult, and it was best not to step in again. As I made my way out of the building, my phone rang.

"Hey, Alana."

"Des, I have some news. I've just received a call from the judge's clerk. Gina Samson wants to meet with William."

"What? Why? No, he's too young."

"That is the procedure in Family Court, if deemed necessary. There is a children's center right next door to the court. Sammy will see him there. It will be very informal and friendly. I've been through this many times."

"Will Kimberly go with him?"

"No. Sammy won't have either of the petitioners there. It will be Angela Bennett, unless you object. When a date has been agreed on, I'll let you know. It will be before the hearing."

Angela and I had a good relationship, and she liked me. She wasn't insufferable like Kimberly. If anything, she was happy William had a father in his life.

"I have no objections to Angela, but I'm not happy about the whole thing. Also, can we change my petition from seeking sole custody to joint?"

"What's going on, Des? I'd advise against it. You know she is going for sole custody. Didn't you want William to live with you?"

"I've come to an arrangement with Kimberly Bennett."

"Desmond, that's not a good idea. Are you talking about a legally documented agreement?"

"You must trust me on this, Alana. I've given it a lot of thought and I know what I'm doing."

"Well, you need to explain it to me because your final petition is being submitted this week."

"I'll find some time to come by, maybe tomorrow, but you're not going to change my mind, Alana. I have to go. I'm picking William up from school."

"Just make sure you get your butt over to my office."

"I'll be there. Bye."

The talk with Kimberly in my office earlier helped to make my mind up. She loved my son very much and wanted to protect him, even from me. Angela said enough to alert me about her trust issues with men, and it provided some insight into her responses. It had a lot to do with my role as a father to someone she loved.

I'd played hardball with her from day one and she bested me. All her fight and protection instincts came to the forefront. But I'd seen a softer, gentler, even playful side to her today. I was certain she even flirted with me a little. Well, I was going to disarm her. I was going to play soft ball. I wanted to challenge Kimberly Bennett.

20
Kimberly

MADELINE WAS the first to approach William, while Leanne's hands palmed her face.

"Hello, Angela, I'm Madeline. It's a pleasure to meet you. Welcome to our home. This is my daughter, Leanne, and this is Hanna, who lives with us and takes care of the family." Madeline bent to William. "Hello, young man, do you remember me?"

William shook his head. He had a tight grip on Desmond's hand.

"I'm your daddy's mommy. You can call me Gramma Madeline."

William looked at his dad. "I told you about your other nana," Desmond said to his son. The little boy nodded. "So Gramma Madeline is your other nana."

William stared at Madeline and allowed her to give him a kiss on his cheek. Leanne stepped forward and knelt down in front of the little boy. "Hello, William, I'm Leanne, your auntie." She gave him a big hug. "I'm so happy to meet you."

"All the family is here." There was a moment's silence as everyone digested the phrasing used by Madeline Renault.

"Hello, Madeline," I responded. "Thank you for inviting us to stay. I'm not sure it's necessary, but Desmond persuaded my mother."

"Desmond is just concerned about his family's safety, and you are all most welcome. I'm so glad you're here."

Madeline should stop referring to *my* family as part of the Renault family. I supposed William was, but I was not, nor my mother.

"Desmond, why don't you show everyone to their rooms? Angela, when you're ready, come and join us in the kitchen. Hanna has prepared milk and cookies for William, unless you prefer him to wait for his meal. You must tell me about his daily routine."

"Thank you," Angela said. "William usually has a small snack after school. Some milk and cookies will be perfect."

Leanne, of course, monopolized my nephew and William seemed drawn to her, too. The two of them disappeared to explore the mansion grounds and to find the tree house that was first Desmond's and then Leanne's. Madeline insisted they kept it in good repair for her grandchildren. Madeline expressed her longing for young ones to be running around the mansion again. She expected Desmond to have made her a grandmother by now, so it overjoyed her to discover William.

Desmond dealt with his conference call to his board members to inform them of the deluge that was coming tomorrow following the announcement. The call meant Desmond missed bath time, but he joined us for the story. I timed his conference call for about fifteen minutes, max. I gave myself ten minutes to check out his room for bugs—more than enough time. Though why would anyone want to bug his bedroom?

My first impression was how large his bedroom was and its neatness. There was not even a tie slung over a chair. Desmond Renault was a neat freak. I checked all the likely places—lights, picture frames, beneath any ledges. I found nothing. His study was the most likely location. I might give that a once-over later after everyone went to bed.

I sneaked a peek into his dressing room. There were at least a dozen silk suits going from grays to dark blues to black, plus evening wear. He had more shoes than I did. His drawers were also color coded and laid out just as neatly. *Wow, he is definitely a neat freak.*

I checked out the bathroom. It was enormous with a glass surround shower and a sunken jacuzzi bath. The tiling was marble in avocado, green, and cream. Everything was pleasing to the eye. How the other half lived. Like the rest of the mansion, it was simple but high quality—nothing opulent or overdone.

We had to follow the same ritual as before. Tonight, William was extra chatty. He told us all about his adventures with Auntie Leanne in the tree house.

"Daddy, Auntie Leanne said the tree house was mine now. Can my friends come see it?"

Desmond and I glanced at each other. I gave him a slight nod. This is how the identity of William's dad would be revealed to everyone.

"Only if you are a good boy and go to sleep."

"Okay, Daddy." William closed his eyes. "I told Maurice I was going to a sleepover at my daddy's house. He said I didn't have a daddy. I want to show Maurice my tree house," the little boy revealed.

Desmond glanced in my direction at my intake of breath before he kissed his son. "Well, he should be the first to come and play in your tree house."

The boy nodded. "Good night, Daddy. Good night, Kimberly."

I kissed my nephew. "Good night, baby. Sleep tight." Within minutes, the little boy was fast asleep, exhausted by the day's adventures.

"Can we talk?" Desmond asked.

Nodding, I got off the bed, making sure not to disturb the sleeping kiddo.

"Let's go downstairs to my study," he whispered.

Once we were seated, Desmond asked about the judge wanting to meet William.

"Yeah. Barbara told me today. Angela will take him one afternoon. He'll leave school a little earlier."

"And you're fine with it?" he asked.

"I'm not sure I could stop it. Barbara assures me that this is perfectly normal, especially for this judge. Why? Do you have a problem with it?"

This was something we could agree on. William was too young to know what was best for him, but the judge still wanted to meet with him, and there wasn't anything either of us could do about that.

"I can see why it is necessary for older children."

"Don't worry, William is not easily spooked. It'll be fine. He is the central person in this and he has an opinion. You've heard how talkative he is."

"I've asked Luke to arrange a permanent security escort for William and Angela whenever they go out, and before you object..."

"I'm not going to object. When I said you would be a disruptive influence, I meant it. It's tiresome, and it's what he doesn't need."

He groaned. This was going to turn into another fight. It wasn't my fault he was in the eyes of the tabloids. And no matter what, he can't disagree. Cameras would be shoved in his face.

Security detail, though, I wouldn't object to because I've read that dossier and knew how desperate some people could be. After the manner of Damien Renault's death, security was essential.

"It doesn't have to be disruptive. William and Angela won't even be aware. The grounds of the mansion are monitored constantly. Did you see any evidence when we were in the summerhouse, for example?"

We stared at each other, both remembering what happened in the summerhouse.

I flushed. "I didn't see anyone because I wasn't looking for anyone."

Desmond smiled. "Ward's team are among the best in the world. They are ex-Army, Marines, Special Forces. I vetted each one because I'm entrusting the life of my family to them. You won't know this, but Leanne spends a lot of time in the Bush with her boyfriend."

My eyes widened. "You let your sister stay in the Bush?"

"She is an adult. I can't dictate where and with whom she lives, although I'll admit I tried, but I can keep her safe. Most of the time, she doesn't even know her bodyguard is around. She is part owner of a nightclub on the edge of the Bush, which was originally my club, but Johnny Morse bought fifty percent when my father died, then Leanne took over my half. Also, I've asked Luke to arrange protection for your home in Sunnyside."

"Fine. As long as I don't see them."

I was exhausted and the energy for objecting was gone. But then my mind started turning, and all this talk about security made me question whether Desmond had knowledge of the true cause of his father's death.

"By the way," Desmond said, "I've instructed my lawyer to

change my petition from seeking sole custody to sharing custody with you and Angela."

He watched me closely. An unidentifiable expression flitted across my face and was gone. "Why?"

He stared at me for a long while. "I don't believe any judge on this earth would grant you sole custody of my son without just cause. And there is none. It would seem perfectly fair to anyone, and even lenient on my part, to seek joint custody, and I'll state my reasons in my final petition."

Why is he being like this? Now suddenly he is changing his mind. There has to be an ulterior motive. A hidden agenda.

"I'm holding you to the explicit condition in our conversation in the summerhouse. We both agree William's well-being and his needs are paramount. There are no fixed dates and times when I see William. It is left to his personal preference, even if you're awarded sole custody. Deal?"

"Yes, that's what we agreed." I stared at him, trying to contain my excitement.

"Two other things," he said. "I'd like William to take my name. I'm not replacing Cecily's. I'm suggesting he's formally known as William McCormick Renault."

Things were slowly changing.

"The second thing is, I'm opening a bank account in William's name into which I'll pay five thousand dollars each month, with you and or Angela as signatories, but I'll need you to come to the bank with me to sign the documents, or I can bring them to you if that's easier."

"There's really no need for that. William's needs are adequately taken care of."

His net worth might be a gazillion times more than mine, but we didn't need his money. Neither did William. Cecily did not want her son to be spoiled. She wanted him to grow up like we did, working hard for our success. Unfortunately, growing up with the Renault name meant everything would be handed to him.

"I'm not going to fight you on this. William may not need it, or you, but I do. I'm William's father and not only is it my obligation, but I want to take care of my boy. Would you deny me that?"

I sighed. "Okay, as you wish. If I don't agree, Angela will, so what does it matter?"

"Good. Thank you." He smiled at me. "I believe it's time for dinner. Are you staying over?"

"Actually, yes. I'm exhausted." I looked at my clothing because I didn't pack a bag, but at this point, I didn't care. The worry came from him changing his mind. Was he admitting defeat? I would talk to Barbara in the morning. Did it give my petition for sole custody more or less chance of success?

21

Desmond

MY QUARTERS in the mansion comprised the entire west wing, but apart from my 'entertainment and party suite,' as Johnny called it in bygone days, I hardly ever used the lower half of my six-room apartment on two floors. I toyed with moving out of the mansion into a loft apartment overlooking the Bay, but since my father's death, that idea dropped out of sight. I couldn't leave my mother alone in this large house. Since Damien's death, I installed layers of security around my family.

Tonight, Kimberly and William occupied the two rooms on the other side of the hallway to my bedroom, with William directly opposite. I left my door slightly ajar in case William woke, found himself in a strange place, and became distressed. Kimberly was next door to William.

Mindful of my son's presence in my home for the first time, I dozed rather than allow myself to fall into a deep sleep. When I heard a muffled sound in the middle of the night, I knew something was wrong. I was out of my bed in seconds, grabbed my robe, and hurried to William's room. I opened the door to find my son asleep and looking very peaceful.

I stood watching my boy sleep for a while. It was strange how fate worked. If someone described this scene to me six weeks ago, I would have snorted in derision. I was now a father and my heart swelled with pride. I would protect my child with my life.

I stepped out into the hallway when the sound came again. Someone was obviously in distress. I stepped down the hallway and stopped at Kimberly's door. I listened. It was quiet at first, then I heard a distinct whimpering in her voice. *"No. Leave me alone."*

I eased her door open and looked into her room. She was lying on her back, but in the dim room I could see little else. The form in the bed thrashed about, arms flailing. *"No. No. I'm not going. I don't want to go. Leave me alone."*

I moved swiftly across to her bed and placed a firm hand on her shoulder. "Kimberly, wake up. Wake up, Kimberly."

As soon as I touched her, her body stiffened, and she sobbed. *"Please, please don't do this. No more, please."*

I sat on the bed then, switched on the light, and pulled her into my arms. "It's me, Desmond. Wake up. You're dreaming." Her eyes flew open, and she looked unseeingly at me. "It's okay. It was just a dream." She clung to me. Sobs shook her body. I held her, stroking her hair. Her head was resting against my chest and her arms were around my waist.

I held her and soothed her for a while, only relaxing when she'd fallen asleep again. I kissed her hair. The warmth and scent of her body tantalized me. Every muscle, sinew, and pore in my body responded to the little blonde I held in my arms. What would I not give to stay with her? I banished it from my mind before it took me elsewhere.

I gently laid her back and covered her. I stood looking at her for some time before returning to my room.

That was some bad dream. Who was she talking to? I

stayed awake thinking about Kimberly Bennett and what might have gone on in her life. Angela said she had nightmares when she returned from Boston. Did her boyfriend do something to her?

I left my bed and headed downstairs. Halfway, I stopped and returned to my room. Whatever was in that envelope, Kimberly should be the one to tell me. We have come a long way since the beginning and I wanted nothing to hinder that. It doesn't matter what that envelope said because she was William's closest thing to a mother, and as his father, it was my job to ensure his well-being.

One day, after she proved her notions about me were wrong and I wasn't a playboy sex-crazed maniac, maybe she would come clean and tell me where the nightmares derived from.

There were so many things Kimberly and I didn't know about each other, but did that matter? We're connected now. At some point, we would need to become a united front for my son's sake.

22
Kimberly

I woke the next morning thirsty and with a thick head. My nightmares were back again. The last time I dreamed of him was over a year ago, once Bennett Technologies was founded.

Chad and I planned to relaunch our little start-up back in Bayview. But before we could, Chad got drunk on his own PR, always thinking he was smarter than everyone else and he could use my code to further his own ambitions. He'd gone up in a puff of smoke and taken me with him.

Angela told me, on my return from Boston, I shouted for someone to leave me alone and said I didn't want to go somewhere. Memories of the six most horrendous weeks in my life returned to haunt me in my dreams. My thought process halted. *Oh my God!* Desmond came into my room. He held me while I sobbed.

I hadn't told anyone about that time—not Barbara, not my mom. No one. I suddenly felt exposed. As soon as possible, I had to leave the mansion.

Oh my God! I overslept, and that never happened. I sent a

text to Jonas and planned on calling Barb on the way to the office. By the time I arrived downstairs, breakfast was almost over. Desmond insisted they left me to sleep. Only he knew why I needed an extra hour or two.

"Good morning, everyone," I said. "I'm so sorry I overslept."

Madeline was the first to greet me. "Good morning. It's alright. You and Angela are not strangers or guests. You're family and Desmond insisted we let you sleep."

I gave Desmond a fierce look, but he responded with a warm smile.

"Good morning, baby," Angela said, rising from the table. "I'm glad you got a little extra sleep this morning. You deserve it. You're just in time to say goodbye to William. We're about to leave."

William jumped off his chair and rushed to meet me. "I made some pancakes with Hanna. Look, we left you some."

"Thank you, baby. Did you sleep well?"

William nodded. "Auntie Leanne said I can decorate my room, and she is going to help me."

"That's good, baby. You must tell me all about it when you're home from school." I looked across at Desmond again, this time with a question mark on my face.

Everyone trouped to the outer room, where Ward was waiting.

"Use the back exit out of the mansion, Ward. We have visitors today."

"I'm on it. Everything has been taken care of."

I was out of sync with what was going on. We wrapped William in a shower of hugs and kisses as everyone said goodbye to him. By the grin on his face, the little boy was enjoying being the center of attention. He let go of Angela's hand, ran to me, and hugged my legs. I scooped him up and buried my face in his neck. "Have a nice day today, baby. I love you."

"I love you," he responded. "Bye, Desmond. Bye, Auntie Leanne. Bye, Gramma Madeline."

"Bye, William," they all chorused.

"Are you coming to my school to get me again, Daddy?" William glanced back at Desmond over his shoulder.

"Yes, William, I am. See you later, buddy," Desmond said as the little entourage of three headed toward the back of the mansion.

"William is going to decorate his room?" I asked.

"His room is plain," Leanne responded. "I wanted to jazz it up with cool boy things, but Des said to let him choose what he wanted. So, we're going shopping on Saturday so he can choose motifs and books and things he wants in his room. I hope that's okay."

Life appears to have taken wings overnight. "It's fine, Leanne. I was confused. We have nothing planned for Saturday, so it's okay."

"I'm so sorry. I should have checked with you first." She turned to her brother. "Des, I didn't mean to... it's just... I'm so excited to have a nephew, I just wanted him to feel..."

"It's okay, Lea. No harm done." He put an arm around his sister's shoulders and gave her a squeeze. "Just remember to check with Kimberly or Angela first next time."

Desmond changed the focus of the conversation. "We're all over the news media this morning—papers, TV, radio. There are photographers and reporters outside the mansion, but it's not as bad as I expected. There are a couple of tabloid horror headlines—'Desmond Renault's Love Child,' 'The Renault's Illegitimate Heir.' I expected worse. Let's hope it's a one-day wonder and will be off the front pages tomorrow, but we should still expect to be hounded by photographers for a while."

"The *Bayview Times* has done a great piece about The Renault Foundation and the various improvements and causes it supports in the Bay," Madeline said. "They've even interviewed a couple of residents about the benefits the improvements have brought to their lives. Right at the end, there's a very sober couple of paragraphs about the family's desire to shelter William until now, restating our wish for the media to respect the privacy of a young child."

"Do you know who did that piece, Desmond? It just says '*Bayview Times* Correspondents.' It's excellent."

Desmond responded, "Yes, I did an interview with Eric yesterday. He sends you his best wishes, by the way."

"It's an excellent piece. I'll have to take him to lunch. We haven't seen each other for some time."

Desmond eyes locked on me. "Are you okay?"

"Yes, I'm fine. I hope you're right, that it's a one-day sensation and we can all get on with our lives."

"I've had a report from my guys. There's been some activity around your house, but most people left when it became clear no one was at home; however, I expect one or two will hang around, trying to get a shot of William. Kimberly, we'll have to..."

"Yes, I know," I interrupted him. "We'll have to put up with your guards."

Desmond's lips twitched. "As I've said, you won't ever see my bodyguards. They are there to protect your home. It's not a big deal. Come, let me show you." He led me to the window. "You see that guy ahead? What is he doing?"

"It looks like he's replanting a flower bed. I guess he's your gardener."

"He is a landscape gardener. When his ten-year service in Iraq and Afghanistan ended, I gave him a job. What about that guy at the wall to the left of him?"

"Okay, okay, I get it. They're not gun-toting heavies." *Still doesn't mean I have to like it.*

"But both would be in this room in less than a minute, neutralize an intruder, and secure the family. That is if an intruder could get into the grounds."

Fuck. That was an insane level of security. He must know how his father died. But he always looked so relaxed. There was nothing anxious or on high alert about his behavior. There was something about Desmond Renault I underestimated. He was known as a playboy, but there was a steeliness at his core. Maybe he wasn't as bad as I pegged him to be.

"Well," said Madeline, "I suggest we all get on with our lives, as Kimberly said. It will be fine. Mr. Ward is taking Angela back to Sunnyside once they've dropped William off. She wants to pick up one or two more items for him. Hopefully, you will stay with us for a while longer, Kimberly."

"I'm not sure. I'll let Desmond know later."

"Even if you are not staying, why don't you come to dinner? It would be nice to have all the family together again."

There was an uncontrollable urge to roll my eyes. What was the queen bee up to? Why was she pushing this happy family thing?

"I've got things to do today," Madeline continued, "so I'll leave you children to get on."

"See you later. I'm going back to bed. I can't remember the last time I was up this early," Leanne said.

"Are you really okay?" Desmond asked me when the two of us were alone.

"Stop asking me that," I hissed. "I'm fine. Thanks to you, I'm late for work."

"But you haven't had breakfast."

"Are you always such a mother hen?"

"First time for everything," he said, grinning. He took my arm. "Come on, at least have a cup of coffee with me."

I gulped the cup of coffee he poured. "Satisfied now?"

"Yes."

"Goodbye."

"Watch out for those cameras at..." His voice trailed off because I was gone.

I left in a hurry. I didn't want him to ask me about my dream and the curiosity was clear in his eyes. And there was no way I was staying another night beneath the Renaults' roof.

As the mansion gates opened, a flurry of light bulbs popped in my face through the windshield and side windows. "Ms. Bennett, when did you know Desmond Renault was your nephew's father... Ms. Bennett, will William..."

I put my foot down on the accelerator and watched as the scrum of people jumped out of my way, then ran behind the car, camera lights still flashing. I looked in my rearview mirror and grinned. *Not today.*

As soon as I reached my office, I called Barbara and relayed everything I discussed with Desmond. She seemed to think that everything he said wasn't out of the ordinary and was to be expected.

"You're overthinking it. He will not bring up anything you don't already know, from what you've told me of previous conversations or the arguments between the two of you. It makes no difference to the judge who wants what. All Sammy will want is a resolution that works for William. So stop worrying and let's fix a time to go over your presentation."

"I can come by later this afternoon or tomorrow."

After my conversation with Barbara, I turned to the next matter on my mind. Justin Thornton. Once again, the call went to voicemail, but I left him a message.

Justin, I know you're avoiding me. I've left several messages, including one at your hotel. Can we meet later? I'll come to your hotel. Call me.

"Ms. Bennett, Desmond is in reception, requesting to see you."

"Bring him in."

A few minutes later, he came striding into my office.

"Hey, I suppose you have something for me to sign."

"I've also brought lunch." He held two Big Belly Burger bags.

My eyes narrowed. "You've taken to this mother hen thing, haven't you?"

"You had a rough night and didn't have any breakfast, so I wanna make sure you eat today."

"While it's nice being your chick, I hope..." I swallowed, closed my eyes, and counted—Three. Two. One. My cheeks were flushed and stung.

There was a huge inane grin on his face; his eyes danced and twinkled. "I like you being my chick very much."

Desmond Renault is flirting with me. "You said you had lunch. Why don't you sit beside the window? I'll get some plates." My heels clicked as I walk back to my office. "So, what do we have for lunch?" I took the chair on the other side of the table and put my phone down.

"You haven't had burgers until you've tasted these. Big Belly is owned by Luke Ward's sister-in-law. You're in for a treat." Desmond removed two burgers from the bag, still in their wrapping, and placed one on each plate.

"And what's in there?" I asked, pointing to the other bag.

"Milkshake."

"I hope its strawberry, for your sake."

"Of course," he said.

"How did you know that was my favorite shake?"

"It's obvious. I'd say there's nothing vanilla about you."

I shot him a look. His face was expressionless. He bit into his burger and chewed with his eyes closed, as if in ecstasy. Then his eyes opened. They pinned me with an intensity that startled me. I swallowed. He was daring me to come back at him.

I let that one pass too. Desmond Renault was backing me into a corner, baiting me. The big cat was pawing the mouse. Well, I would not play.

"Okay, I wanted to ask you something. My mom is having one of her famous fundraising dinners—a black-tie affair in three weeks. Would you be my, um, would you like to be my... um..." he faltered.

"Are you asking me to be your date, Desmond? Don't you have a girlfriend to take?"

"I did until yesterday—well, we didn't really put a label on our relationship."

Desmond Renault was single? Once that hit the papers, all the women in Bayview would show up in his life.

"Oh? Dumped you, did she?"

He looked me in the eye. "Something like that."

"Well, I have a boyfriend and he won't be pleased with me to go on a date with you." Justin and I weren't together. Well, he called me his girlfriend that night, but it caught me off guard.

"It won't be a date, date. It would be more like a family occasion, and I'm sure your boyfriend wouldn't object to that. Who is he anyway? Do I know him?"

At that precise moment, as fate would have it happen, my phone rang and Justin Thornton's face popped on the screen in full view. I picked up the phone and glanced at Desmond. He was staring at me. "Just give me a minute." I turned to Desmond. "Sorry, I have to take this call, then I leave for an appointment right after. See ya at the mansion later, but I won't be staying."

Desmond nodded. "Okay. I enjoyed our lunch. See you later this evening."

I tried to get out of his earshot before saying anything. "Justin, why haven't you returned my calls?"

"I just wanted some space. Can you fucking blame me after the other night? I'm not even in Bayview anymore. I left last night."

"And you didn't tell me? We have to talk, Justin. Nothing is going on between me and Desmond Renault. He was here in my apartment, but that was the second time I met him, because I needed to..."

Justin cut me off. "It's fine. I've thought, and overall, our relationship is not working long-distance, is it?"

I ended the call. A wave of sadness washed over me. Justin and I were friends before we started sleeping together, and apparently that was a huge mistake. I was under the impression it was casual, nothing serious, but it seemed he had a different outlook.

I met Justin on my return to Bayview at a Business Circle event. We had the same business interests and we could help each other. The friendship grew, and we started becoming romantically involved. When an opportunity came up for Justin to broaden his work at STAR Labs, he leased me the top five floors, which he occupied, at a peppercorn rent for my help with certain projects. His tenants occupied the other floors in the building. That gave me the opportunity to move out of my home office and employ Jonas Holt, the technological *savant* and inventor I also met at a Circle event.

There was every expectation of expanding my business and taking more floors in the coming years. I was waiting to sign a contract to provide an implant for servicemen and women with spinal injuries. If it came off, it would make Jonas and I very rich indeed.

They linked all of that to my deal with the FBI. I supposed the golden handcuffs they put on me did benefit me, but all of that would expire in two years. Zachary assured me they would keep their word and there was a signed document in my safe.

23
Kimberly

My hands glided over the back of my neck before I clutched my purse. I sat on the hard bench between Barbara and Barry, who came all the way from Central Bay to support me.

"Kim, chill," said Barbara. "There's no reason to be nervous. What's the worst that can happen?"

"The judge could give Desmond sole custody?"

"We've been over this. You said you trusted Desmond to keep his word, and he's not asking for that."

Barry placed an arm around my shoulders. That was the scene that greeted Desmond when he strode into the building beside his lawyer, who'd been waiting outside for the family. He did a double take at the sight of the guy sitting with his arm around me. His eyes tightened.

He sauntered over and I greeted him with a smile. "Hi. Nervous?"

Desmond nodded.

"Me too."

"Guess it's time to head in. See you later, Kimberly?"

"See you later."

Something wasn't right. The fight had left me. Here I was in court, which is what I wanted, but it was like a big fat anticlimax. A few weeks ago, I was looking forward to formalizing the adoption. Now, I was in a fight with Desmond Renault, who was breaking down every fucking wall I put up.

"Bennett v Renault," the court officer called. "Step this way."

Okay, we can do this. Everything will go smoothly and amicably. Don't freak out, and be precise with your words.

"Good morning, ladies and gentlemen," Gina Samson called the small group of people gathered in the courtroom to attention. "I'm assuming both my petitioners are here."

"Yes, Judge," said our lawyers in unison.

"Alright, Ms. Bennett. I believe you're petitioning for sole custody of your nephew, Mr. Renault's son. Is that correct?"

When put as starkly as that, it was cold and selfish. I glanced at Desmond, finding his eyes locked on me. "Ye-yes, Your Honor, I am."

"I've seen your written petition in lawyer-speak, but I'd like to hear it in your own words. When you're ready."

"Your Honor, for the whole period of my sister's pregnancy, she refused to divulge the name of her baby's father. Cece died in childbirth and my mother raised William until he was about two, when I returned home from Boston where I attended university. My mother and I are the only family William has known since birth. We only discovered who his father was when Mr. Renault turned up in my office exactly six weeks ago, claiming William was his son. This has since been verified by a DNA test and a letter my sister left for William to be opened when he reached the age of eighteen. The reason for my petition for sole custody is spelled out in my sister's letter, and I want to honor her wishes. Mr. Renault would make an excellent father. I have seen evidence of that in the last few weeks, and I know that Desmond loves William. But he is a busy CEO of a major multinational company and travels a lot. His mother and sister are also busy people with jobs. Desmond's, um, lifestyle puts William in the public glare and he is so young."

I hope the judge gets what I can't exactly spell out.

"Sorry to interrupt you, Ms. Bennett, but I see you are also a CEO. Is that correct?"

I nodded.

"So, you and William's father are both busy running companies. What makes him less capable than you?"

My gaze darted to him. When she put it like that, it was ridiculous. She was right. All this time I was so against Desmond when he did nothing but try to prove he wanted to be a father to William. He worked just as much as I did, and actually from the looks of it, I actually worked more. That statement wasn't going to do me any favors.

"Let me rephrase. He travels a lot and all eyes are on him. I believe it would be in William's best interest, for his emotional and psychological well-being, if he were to remain with a fixed point in his life, until he is much older. Before the advent of Mr. Renault, I was to the point of adopting my nephew."

I looked across at Desmond and his eyes were not fixed on me anymore. He'd been watching me the entire time. "I have no wish to deny Desmond access to his son. In fact, we have already agreed he has full unrestricted access to be a father to William. As he should be."

A faint smile crossed his lips.

"Thank you, Your Honor. That's all I want to say."

Fuck, that was hard. I had never been in a courtroom before and it was intense. Barb patted my shoulder as I sat down.

"Just a point of clarification, Ms. Bennett. I don't want to make any assumptions. If you were granted physical custody, I take it you envisage Mr. Renault having legal custody so that he could at least have a say in all the major decisions affecting his son?"

I glanced at Barbara, who gave a quick nod, then I stood back up. "Yes, yes, of course, Your Honor. Desmond is William's father and should have a say."

"And suppose you have a difference of opinion on a particular matter. What then, Ms. Bennett?"

"That could happen in any family. I would hope that Desmond and I could talk it through and come to a decision in William's best interest." I looked over to seek confirmation. Although up to this point, we didn't agree on anything. *Lots of butting heads, though.*

Gina Samson scribbled something on her pad before she continued. "Just a hypothetical, Ms. Bennett. Put yourself in Mr. Renault's shoes. How would you respond to the situation?"

"I'm not sure what you mean, Your Honor," I said, playing for time.

"I think you do."

I shuffled my feet, glanced at Desmond, and then back at the judge. "Well, uh, in Desmond's place, my first desire would be to have my son live with me. It's a natural instinct, but then I'd like to think I could step back and look at where William would be happiest and have the best of everything."

Is she throwing me under the bus? Oh God, Desmond is going to get custody and I will only get to see William at his house. This can't be happening.

24

Desmond

As I took in how magnificent and beautiful Kimberly was, my mind was spinning. She was here fighting on my son's behalf, and I couldn't be mad at her for it. I was glad William had someone in his corner, even when I couldn't be. I wanted them both. Kimberly Bennett and my son. Even though I was used to getting what I want, it might not happen this time. Unless...

"Thank you, Ms. Bennett. You may sit," said the judge.

"Mr. Renault." The judge turned her laser gaze to me. My heart rate elevated as I stood to show respect in the courtroom. "I believe you are petitioning for joint custody with Ms. Bennett. Is that correct?"

"Yes, Judge."

"Very well. The floor is yours. Please proceed."

"Your Honor, my presentation will be very brief, because Ms. Bennett has already set out the gist of our agreement."

Some things changed in the last twenty-four hours. Kimberly didn't know what was going to happen today, and I wanted to keep it that way. There was only one way we would all get what we wanted. She might be pissed at me afterward, but like her, I was someone who liked to have the cake and eat it too.

"As Ms. Bennett said, I found out about my son William six weeks ago. I planned to petition for sole custody of my son, but after several conversations with Ms. Bennett, I agreed if I was awarded sole custody, then I would not demand William's immediate removal from the family who nurtured him from birth. The same powerful arguments made by Ms. Bennett in her presentation about the psychological and emotional well-being of my son persuaded me. I proposed William's transition would take place at a pace that suited him. Once we agreed to that, there would be little point in pursuing sole custody. I trust Ms. Bennett to keep to our agreement, even if she is awarded sole custody. I believe Kimberly is sincere when she says she only wants William's happiness and that between the two of us, he would have the best of everything. Judge, I love my son very much and his safety and well-being are my priority. Ms. Bennett and her mother have been very generous in allowing me unimpeded access to get to know William. I have no desire to get into a tug-of-war over my son. That's all I wish to say, Your Honor."

"Let me see whether I've understood this, Mr. Renault," said the judge. "You and Ms. Bennett already agree that whichever one of you got sole custody, you would behave as if you'd been awarded joint custody."

Kimberly gulped, catching my attention.

"Um, yes, Judge, I suppose you could say that."

"There's no suppose about it, Mr. Renault. You've wasted the court's time."

"That wasn't the intention, Judge. I think we just wanted to have it enshrined in law."

"No, Mr. Renault. Please do not insult my intelligence. William is not some random child up for adoption or fostering.

He is your son and Ms. Bennett's nephew. You're family. It could have been resolved between you. You have both wasted the court's time. Any good lawyer could have drawn up your agreement and it would carry the same weight. I know you know that, as does Ms. Bennett."

"I'm so sorry, Judge. This has been an emotional roller coaster that has been a feature of the last six weeks."

Kimberly exhaled. I was providing cover for her. Her eyes locked with the judge's, who was giving her a penetrating look. "That's why we have lawyers, Mr. Renault, and pay them the earth to advise us. You've either received poor legal advice or ignored the advice given."

"Your Honor, I…"

"Thank you, Mr. Renault," said Gina Samson. "You may sit."

With a certain level of exasperation in her voice, Gina Samson addressed the nine people in the small courtroom. "Before I discuss any potential for resolution with the petitioners, there's further testimony," continued the judge. "Court officer, please, if you will."

The court officer pushed a button on the remote control in his hand. A panel on a section of the courtroom's wooden walls slid back to reveal a screen. He pushed another button, and a room came into view. Angela Bennett was sitting on a sofa with William on her lap. The movie played.

"Hello, William. Do you know who I am?" The voice belonged to Judge Gina Samson, but she was off camera. He shook his head. "Call me Sammy because that's what everyone calls me."

"That's a funny name." William giggled.

Gina Samson smiled at him. "Did Nana Angie tell you why I wanted to see you today?"

"Yes. Because my Kimberly is adopting me, then she'll be my mommy because my mommy died and she's in heaven."

"Yes, that's right, William. And you have a daddy now."

William looked at his nana Angie. Angela nodded her head. "My daddy's name is Desmond, but it's a secret. My Desmond takes me to fish and we play with my robot. Then me and Nana Angie and Kimberly sleep over in my daddy's house and Mr. Ward drives Nana Angie and me to school. Desmond and Kimberly read me stories in a funny voice." William giggled again.

"That sounds like fun. I expect you have fun with Kimberly too."

His eyes lit up. "We go to the mountains to look for bears, that's my favorite. Nana Angie said Kimberly is silly because there are no bears in the mountain. But my Kimberly is the pretend bear."

"Oh wow," said Sammy, "that's exciting. William, sometimes mommies and daddies come to see me because I help them decide if their little boy should live with mommy or daddy. I do that when the mommy and daddy live in two houses like your Kimberly and your Desmond."

William looked at Angela and then back at Gina Samson. "Maurice and Shiloh live with their mommy and daddy," he said. "I like it when we all live in my Desmond's house. I play in the tree house. Can we, Nana Angie? Gramma Madeline said we are family." He buried his face in Angela's chest.

"It's okay, sweetheart," Angela assured him. "Everything will be okay."

"I want to be with my Kimberly and my Desmond. And I want you and Gramma Madeline and Auntie Leanne," William mumbled into her neck.

Angela kissed him and stroked his hair. "It's okay, baby, it's okay." She looked at Gina Samson, who nodded.

The judge stroked the little boy's arm. "Thank you, William. You've done very well. Thank you for coming to see me today."

The court officer switched off the video. There was silence in the room. Ten pairs of eyes, including the court officer, the stenographer, and the judge's clerk, were riveted on Gina Samson.

Following the video, I was almost in tears hearing my son. He wanted nothing more than all of us to live together as one big happy family. Something he never had. Now that he had a daddy, he wanted the rest. The happy parents his friends had.

"Mr. Renault, Ms. Bennett, please approach the bench," said Sammy. Our lawyers stood too.

"Just them two," the judge said.

As Kimberly and I approached the bench, Gina Samson switched off her microphone.

The judge looked at us standing in front of her. There was a softness in Kimberly's eyes every time I looked at her across the courtroom. Kimberly was like a tigress, fiercely protecting her young. But there was something about her I could not put my finger on. The judge folded her arms on the desk and leaned forward. "Mr. Renault, Ms. Bennett, you have both reiterated several times you are prepared to do what would make William happy and be in his best interest. So, I want the two of you to consider the..."

"Before you say anything else, Judge," I said, interrupting Sammy, "I'd like to ask Ms. Bennett to marry me."

What in the hell am I doing? Is this the right time to do this? Kimberly will say no in a heartbeat, but we'd be doing this for William, for his benefit. My feelings for her are all over the place, but they only continue to grow every day as I find out more about her.

Sammy turned to Kimberly. "Ms. Bennett, I believe you've

just received a proposal of marriage..." Gina Samson's voice trailed off. Kimberly looked off-color.

Okay, I know this proposal caught her off guard, but once I explained myself, it would make sense. *I'm done denying the utter fucking chemistry between us and if she accepts the proposal, we will all live under the same roof, and I can show her I am a man worthy of her heart. That is, if she will even give me a chance.*

"Ms. Sutherland, I'm adjourning this hearing for a week. My clerk will be in touch with you. I think your client needs some fresh air and a glass of water."

Barbara took one look at Kimberly and led her away.

"Mr. Renault," the judge turned to me. "Do you know what you're doing?"

"Yes, Your Honor."

"Well, I'd suggest you take a step back and think about this before making any rash decisions. I'll leave it to you, Mr. Renault, to explain what just happened. My clerk will give you a time for next week. I'll wait to hear from him and Ms. Bennett in person before I deliver my judgment, if, in fact, it's necessary."

The judge switched her microphone back on. "Court's adjourned," she announced to the room. Her gavel tapped once and Gina Sarah Samson exited the courtroom.

Everyone stared at me, not knowing what the hell just happened, and honestly, I didn't know either. For once, I let the words spill from my mouth without thinking first.

25
Kimberly

My mother opened the front door as soon as the car pulled into the driveway. "Where's Kimberly?" That was before she spotted me sitting in the back seat with Barry. "What happened in court today? Is it good news? Come inside," she said, holding the door open for us.

"Angela, wait," said Barbara. She and Barry were helping me out of the car.

"What's wrong, Kimberly? What happened? Will someone please tell me what is going on?" Angela demanded. "What happened in court? What did the judge say?"

"There's no decision. We go back in a week," Barbara informed.

"What? Why?"

"Because Desmond asked Kimberly to marry him," Barry said with incredulity in his voice.

Angela's mouth formed a perfect 'O.' "He did what?"

"It's true," Barbara said. "During the hearing in front of the judge."

She looked at me. "Are you alright, baby? Come inside and

tell me what happened." Barbara moved aside as Angela slipped her arm around my waist.

Once inside, I headed straight upstairs to my room, and Angela tried to follow me. "Angela, let me," said Barbara. "I think she's in shock. She hasn't said much since we left court."

Barry and my mother retreated from us and she helped me to my room. My whole body was numb. This wasn't how I pictured it going down. Was this a dream or nightmare?

She plopped me on the bed, and I threw my arm over my face. Everyone wanted to talk about his proposal, but I wasn't ready. Hell, I hadn't even come to terms that it was real yet. We didn't love each other, so what was his deal?

Maybe he did so the judge would favor him and I'd lose William no matter what. Or was this his plan all along? He said he would lay everything out at the court hearing, but he couldn't have planned this that long ago.

I curled on my side with my eyes closed while Barbara took off my shoes and gently eased me out of my coat. "Kim, I know you don't want to talk now, but we'll have to soon. This is just crazy."

For you? Girl, think about what is going through my head right now. She doesn't even know half of it.

"Where is William?" I asked.

"He's still at school. It's only midday. Do you want anything? Something for the headache?"

Barb doesn't need to stay here and monitor me. I was a grown-ass woman. "No, you can take Barry home, but just have my mother bring me some water and a pack of frozen peas."

She gave me an exasperated look and then patted my arm. "Okay, but if you want to talk, call me. No matter what time it is."

That was the one thing I loved about her. She was a kick-ass lawyer, but she was an even better friend. She always told me straight and never fucked around. Guess that was the lawyer side of her.

I curled under the blanket, and Desmond came to the forefront of my mind. The way he looked at me right before he proposed to me in front of everyone in that damn courtroom. I was pretty sure I passed out because it was still blurry from that point to getting home.

Knock. Knock. Knock.

"They left, but Barb said you needed some water and some peas. I'm so sorry for such a weird day. Wanna talk about it?"

"I can't marry Desmond. That's preposterous. What in the hell even made him think about doing that?"

She laughed. "You feel something for him, sweetie. I have known since the first time he came to the house. So much tension. Why are you so against letting someone into your heart?"

Did she forget about Justin? "I just had a boyfriend."

"You mean your casual hookup buddy? I might be older, but I'm not an idiot. There is a big difference between the way you looked at Justin and the way you look at Desmond."

"Mom, I don't want to talk about this anymore. My head is throbbing. Ever since Desmond Renault came into our lives, everything has turned upside down."

"Kimberly, all Desmond has done is claim time with his son. You are overwrought and stressed. Let me call the doctor. You're not looking well. Your face is flushed and your skin is clammy."

"I told you, Mom, I don't need a doctor, I'm fine. I need to sleep."

She patted my legs and then left the room, shutting the door behind her. Finally, some peace and damn quiet.

But sleep eluded me. I replayed the last few minutes of the court hearing but wasn't sure if it was in the right sequence.

Everything was still confused in my mind. My brain was mush.

The words coming out of Desmond's mouth threatened me. They were all jumbled. I unscrambled the words in my head to comprehend.

Staring at him, then at the judge, whose lips were moving, but the words came out in a slow-motion-like distortion. *I... believe... you... have... just... re-ceived... a... pro-posal... Ms.... Bennett.*

The judge's head swiveled round in Desmond's direction. He touched my arm, asking whether I was okay. Then Barb and Barry were on either side of me, holding my arms like some prisoner being escorted to jail. I wanted to laugh because I was somewhere above it all, looking down on myself. The last thing was a loud bang behind me.

I revived outside in the fresh air. The three of us ended up in the nearest Starbucks and Barbara insisted I ate something sweet. I wanted to gag. My stomach was in knots.

I would have to talk to Desmond, but not now. All I could think about was losing William. I was going to lose my baby. I'd been so stupid. The judge saw through my subterfuge and was going to take William away from me. Did Desmond know? Was that why he asked me to marry him?

I could still see Barbara's and Barry's faces. Now I wanted to laugh, but not then. At the time, their faces mirrored how I was feeling. Utter shock and disbelief. I was glad William was with Desmond because I wasn't in a good enough place to be around him.

My headache got worse throughout the night and my nightmares had resumed with a vengeance since that night in the mansion.

26
Desmond

My Renault family was being driven home by Ward. I left Alana Glacey standing bemused on the steps of the court building, staring at my back. All words deserted her.

"What just happened?" Madeline asked. "Why did the judge adjourn the hearing for a week?"

"I asked Kimberly to marry me."

Total silence reigned in the vehicle. Even Ward's eyebrows raised. He glanced sideways. The set of my jaw told Ward I was serious.

"Desmond, what has gotten into you?" said my mother. "You hardly know Kimberly. You can't be in love with someone you met only six weeks ago. Have you lost your mind?"

"Oh, Mom. It's romantic," said Leanne. "Have you not heard of love at first sight? Best decision you've made in a long time, big brother. I like Kimberly, and she'll be good for you. Best of all, William will be living with us."

"Slow down, sis. I didn't ask her properly. I made a statement to the judge."

"I bet she'll say yes. What woman could resist you?" She

chuckled. "Go on, admit it. You've fallen in love with her. I see the way you look at her. Even Mom has noticed."

"She's not like other women. There's something special about her..."

"I just don't want either of you to get hurt, so be careful. Tread lightly since we just got William in our lives." Leanne punched my arm.

The judge adjourned after I proposed so I didn't get to talk to Kimberly. Her lawyer and friend took her away before and were gone before we were out of the courtroom. I didn't know what Kimberly was thinking, but maybe she would say yes.

"Ask her again, properly this time," my sister encouraged.

"I forbid you to do any such thing," said Madeline. "What were you thinking? Marriage is a very serious step. Think about William if it didn't work."

My mother seemed to think this proposal to Kimberly would make things worse for William, and instead, it made things twenty times better. He said himself he wanted to live with all of us together, one big happy family, and I would say that was normal for a kid, and my son deserved that. "Kimberly and I want the best for him."

"I understand, but what you're proposing is not a good basis for marriage. You know nothing about Kimberly Bennett. We'll continue this conversation later."

"The subject is not up for discussion, Mother. You have no say in my love life."

My phone pierced through the tension. I dug through my pocket and pulled it out, seeing her name. "Angela? Is everything okay? Yes, of course. I'll pick him up and bring him home tomorrow. You stay with Kimberly," I said, disconnecting the call.

"Ward, I'm picking William up from school today. Drop me off at the office, then take Mom and Leanne home."

"What is it? What's happened?" my mother asked.

"Kimberly isn't feeling well, so since William is having a playdate at the mansion tomorrow, I'll pick him up from school and he'll stay with us tonight."

Early evening the following day, I brought William home. Angela scooped up her grandson for a hug. "You must be quiet. Kimberly is sleeping. We don't want to wake her."

"Okay," William whispered. "Can I watch TV?"

"Only for a little while. It's your bedtime."

As William ran off, Angela grabbed my arm and propelled me into the kitchen. "You asked Kimberly to marry you in front of the judge? Did you pre-plan this?"

"The judge got real antsy about us wasting the court's time. I didn't know what she was going to say or do. This judge has a reputation for being unpredictable and if there was any chance that Kimberly and I would lose control of the situation... I couldn't let that happen. I jumped in with the first thing that came into my head."

"So, the first thing was getting engaged to my daughter? I suspected that something was going on between the two of you. Is it genuine? Do you truly love her?"

"I have strong feelings for her, Angela. My heart fell for her from the very first day I laid eyes on her. She infuriated me that first evening in her office, yet I found myself inexplicably drawn to her."

"Men have let my daughter down her whole life, so I say this with the most sincerity. Please be the man who doesn't."

Angela and I grew closer since I first met William, and even though her job was to protect her daughter, I loved that she was still giving me advice. Kimberly might need some convincing to say yes, but I hoped she did, because then I could spend the rest of my life showing her she was a woman who deserved to be cherished.

She was in denial about the spark between us, that much I could tell, but like me, Kimberly would do whatever it took to protect William. I wasn't the horrible person she made me out to be in the beginning, and I hoped to God her perception of me in the last six weeks changed.

My hands trembled thinking about the possibility of her rejecting me, which was what I expected. She always defied me at every turn. Not scared to speak her mind.

"Is she okay? Do you think I can see her now?"

"Her nightmares returned, and it's bad. I'll keep William down here." I nodded and squeezed her arm. "Thanks."

Kimberly didn't tell me much about them, and I didn't know how frequently they came, but seeing her so scared the other night, my heart broke.

I knocked on her door. "Kimberly, it's me. Can I come in?"

"Yes. Okay," she mumbled.

"Hi," I said, walking into her bedroom for the first time. She was pale, with dark shadows under her eyes. Just a glimmer of the feisty badass who challenged me at every turn remained. "Angela said you were unwell. Is that the latest cure for a migraine?" I motioned to the bag of frozen peas on her head.

She removed it. "It helps. I don't have a migraine. It's just a bad tension headache meeting too many hours in front of a screen. I don't want to talk right now. I'm furious with you."

"We can talk another time. I just wanted to see how you were."

She looked awful and, of course, that had to do with me dropping the proposal on her.

"Why did you tell the judge you wanted to marry me?"

I hid a smile. There she was. My little firebird, undiminished. I sat on the edge of the bed. "Maybe I can help."

"Help with what?" She jerked away from me.

"Your headache."

She rolled her eyes. "And how do you plan on doing that?"

"I'll show you. May I?" She nodded. "Close your eyes and breathe normally."

I brushed her hair back off her face, placing my thumbs on her cheekbones, close to her ears, and used my fingertips to apply pressure and rub her temples. Using very firm pressure and a tiny circular motion, I edged my fingers along her hairline until they met in the middle of her forehead, then inch by inch I massaged the entire area, including her scalp. Kimberly's breathing kept hitching. I worked on her for a solid fifteen minutes. I smiled when she drifted into sleep. When she opened her eyes, I was no longer massaging her head, but gazing at her with a tenderness that made her blush.

"I'm sorry," she whispered. "I must have drifted off."

"How is your head?"

"Much, much better. Where did you learn to do that? You're good at it."

I took one of her hands in mine and threaded my fingers with hers. My thumb made tiny circles in the space on the back of her hand between her thumb and index finger. "I have many hidden talents. A full body massage would be even better. I'm good at those too."

"I'm sure you are. But I'll pass on that one."

"How about my proposal? Will you pass on that too? Wait..." Still holding her hand, I got on one knee beside her bed. "Kimberly Sandrine Bennett, will you marry me?"

She stared at me for a long while. "Are you serious? Why do you want to marry me? We've only known each other for six weeks."

"I would've thought it obvious. Why does any man ask a woman to marry him?"

She gave an exasperated sigh.

It was unconventional as fuck, but it gave me a chance to show her the man I was. "Yes, I'm serious. We both want William to be happy and have him grow up in a safe and settled environment. We both love him. He loves you very much. And I hope he'll grow to love me too. What better way to hold all of that together than by getting married?" If I didn't know any better, when she started laughing, she was having a breakdown. Her eyes started darting around the room, and it was a little creepy. "Take a deep breath. Don't have a panic attack on me."

"Do you love me, Desmond? Is that what you're saying?"

My brown eyes bored into hers. A small smile played around my mouth. "I have feelings for you. I won't deny that."

I was not ready to tell her she consumed me, that I wanted her, that, yes, I was falling in love with her. That would scare her away, and I couldn't have that.

"Well, I have no such feelings for you."

She might not believe she did, but with all the aimless flirting, she had feelings. We stared at each other for a long time. I bent my face close to hers, and then my lips brushed her ear. "But you do have feelings," I whispered. "I can tell by the way your body responds to me, even right now." I drew back and watched her.

She flushed. "I'll admit I've wanted to fuck your brains out on a couple of occasions, but that's not love or anything close, Desmond. It's just lust."

I grinned. My eyes danced with mirth and my body reacted to her words. "Why, Ms. Bennett, I believe you're talking dirty to me. That's a start, I guess. I'll let you fuck my brains out anytime you want. I'd better go just in case you were thinking of jumping my bones right now."

Kimberly gave me a disgusted look, trying to pull away as the electricity sparked between us. "Where's the ring?"

I chuckled. "Why? Are you saying yes?"

"No. But if a man proposes to a woman, he should come with a ring. I want to see it."

I smirked at her. Thank God I followed my instincts and went to the bank this morning. I removed the blue velvet box from my jeans pocket and opened it.

Kimberly gasped. Inside was the most elegant diamond filigree gold ring with a central stone and two tiny stones encased in delicate carving on each side. "Oh, that's beautiful. I've seen nothing like that."

"It can be adjusted for fit."

"I only wanted to see it. I'm not agreeing to marry you."

"No. You're testing me to see if I'm serious."

She stared at me. I stared right back. "It's Saturday night. Don't you have a woman waiting for you somewhere?"

"I do." I grinned. "Two of them, to be exact." She rolled her eyes. "I'm taking Mom and Leanne out to dinner tonight. It's an unknown event for the three of us to eat out together, especially on a Saturday night. It's one of Leanne's rare weekends off. "I'll see you soon," I said, bending my head to kiss her. It was a very soft and chaste kiss on her lips. "You have less than a week to tell the judge what you want to do."

"Yeah. I got that," she said.

I got up and walked toward the door, but I turned back. "By the way, would you like to go on a date with me before you turn me down?"

"You don't give up, do you?"

Not when I see something I want, my little firebird. "Well?"

"No, I won't go on a date with you. This is not a romantic tryst."

"What is it then? Is that a sign you're at least thinking about my proposal?"

"It's likely that you're the cause of my tension headache. You stress me out," she said.

I didn't want to do that, not to cause her distress, so I would ease back, but I was not giving up. "The judge has given us a week to inform her about our decision," I reminded her. "Although my decision has already been made."

She wafted her hand toward the door. "You should go. You don't want to be late for your family. Say hi to your mom and sister."

"Sleep well. Try and dream about me."

She snorted. "Get the hell out of here."

27
Kimberly

"Have you talked with Desmond yet?" Barbara asked.

"Not in depth, but he proposed. Properly this time. On one knee."

She let out a sharp laugh. "You're joking, right? Desmond Renault? Oh, I'd love to have seen that."

"He even had a ring. It's beautiful."

"So, you said yes, and you're wearing his ring?"

"No... and not yet."

Her head tilted. "I understand this guy has been on your mind since you met him, but you need to think it through. Knowing he is William's dad is one thing, but you really know nothing else about him. It's a risky move, and I don't think you should take it lightly."

"I don't know," I said with hesitation. "There's something about him... I can't help that I'm attracted to him, and I know it's crazy, but sometimes it feels right. Other times, I want to punch him in the face."

I let out a heavy breath, the tension in my chest rising. As the air left my lungs, so did my secrets—secrets that even Barb didn't know, but I couldn't risk it. Desmond could be my key to uncovering the truth, but I'd have to be careful. I knew much more than I let on, but marrying him would be good for William growing up, and more access.

I had to tread carefully. If the FBI were involved, the last thing I needed was for them to trace anything back to me. It presented a dilemma—even though I was known in the underworld as Ghost Fox Goddess, if I created a different persona to outsmart the Feds, no one would know me and I'd get no information. Yet, if I remained as Ghost Fox Goddess, the risk of getting caught became much higher. But I couldn't worry about any of that now.

I let out a deep sigh as the words stumbled from my mouth. "I don't know what to do. Nothing is clear. That's why I'm asking for your help. Put me out of my misery and tell me what I should do. Should I really accept Desmond's proposal?"

"You ignored my advice and now you're in this mess. But that's in the past. Now we have to focus on what's ahead. We know three outcomes, right? You could get sole custody or joint custody or bypass all of that and accept his proposal. I'm not sure which is best for you."

"I don't trust that judge. She doesn't like me. I messed up and should have listened to you."

"I'm pretty sure that Sammy doesn't hate you and is impressed with how protective of William you are. She could suggest a period of reflection—time-limited, so that the three of you spend more time together to see how the dynamics change. Look, I'm making this up. Alana Glacey would have a better idea. This is her territory."

"Well, I'm not talking to Alana Glacey. She'd be on Desmond's side. Wasn't she an ex of his? And you weren't listening in court. Sammy accused me of wanting to steal Desmond's son. That was the first thing she suggested, not overtly, but I heard it. Then she accused us of wasting court time. She was talking to Desmond, but it was directed at me."

"You're just being paranoid," said Barbara.

"I'm thinking about the wild card."

"What are you talking about? What wild... oh God. You mean marrying Desmond Renault?"

"Yep. It would be a marriage of convenience. Inconvenience would be more appropriate."

"You can't. As your friend, that's a dumb idea. You've been reading too many romantic novels. Suppose you meet someone and fall in love?"

When the heck would I have the time to meet anyone and fall in love? I worked sometimes fourteen hours a day, and then any free time was spent with William.

"You're the one reading romantic novels. Do you believe in all that happily ever after crap, like Cinderella? That's never going to happen. Not for me. All men let you down. Justin accused me of having an affair with Desmond. I bet he's dating someone in Central Bay. Then there's that asshole Chad. And my dad and Cece's. At least with Desmond I'd have no expectations and the sex would be good. And he has magical fingers."

Barbara laughed. "So you've gone further than a kiss. You let him get to second base?"

"What? No! That's not what I meant. He gives great head massages."

Something she said pulled me back to the past.

The day I called Barbara asking her to come to the café in the Harvard Bookshop in Boston, which was a strange place to meet. I had simply disappeared with my boyfriend Chad six weeks ago. No one had seen me and my phone was inaccessible.

I looked dreadful, disoriented, with sunken eyes that darted around the room. My skin was pale and my hair dull. Barb took me back to her apartment. To this day, I simply refused to say where I'd been and what had happened.

I told Barb Chad had been arrested for a federal crime plus fraud involving government contractors. I would have to give evidence at his trial. That was all I'd say, and Barbara stopped asking.

When it was over, I went back home to Bayview.

Barbara's voice pulls me back to our conversation. "Kim, you can't do this. It's a recipe for disaster. And what about William in all this?"

"It's all about William. Did you watch that video? He's already so attached to Desmond and wants to be with all of us, his family. Maurice and Shiloh live in a house with both of their parents, and he was comparing himself to them. It broke my heart. If I do this, it's for William's sake. And I'd keep my end of the bargain, if Desmond is prepared to keep his. I know what it's like to be raised by a single parent. I want William to have more. That's what Cece would want for him. He deserves that."

"I think you've just talked yourself into it, Kim. But what is this bargain you want to strike with Desmond? A peculiar kind of marriage."

"What other kind of marriage would you have with someone like Desmond Renault? It's not like we'd live in a house with a white picket fence, a dog, and children."

"We are due in the judge's chambers at ten a.m. on Friday," Barbara said. "You have four more days to think about it. Sammy will give you a specified period to produce a marriage certificate for her records. So don't think you can just say you're accepting Desmond's proposal, and that's it. This is real."

"I don't need to think about it. I'm calling him right now to tell him I'm accepting his proposal. But there'll be rules."

"All I can do is wish you luck with this bizarre plan, kiddo.

I know how stubborn you are when you're set on something. So I'm not even going to talk you out of it."

She got up off the couch, shook her head, and left. My best friend couldn't understand why I would do this, but I knew. I always said my primary concern was William's well-being, and this was what he wanted. Sometimes we sacrificed for our children, no matter what anyone said. He was my son too. He might not call me Mom, but I was the only mother figure he had ever known, and I would be damned if I was reduced to seeing him occasionally.

I can't believe I'm marrying Desmond Renault.

28

Desmond

JOHNNY MORSE SHUFFLED to the mansion, his eyes barely open and his shirt unbuttoned. He gave a dry cough and looked at the enormous building.

"What are you doing here?"

"You and I need to talk. Have you eaten?"

I raised my eyebrows. "What? It's after eleven. Don't you feed yourself at home anymore?"

The smell of stale whiskey and cigarettes followed him, and the darkness in his eyes showed how much sleep he lost. I followed Johnny down the hallway. He was carrying on about the Glaceys splitting up and how Alana went to her dad's. "Johnny, wait!" I called out, breaking into a light jog to catch up with him before he reached the kitchen.

"Hanna, what can a hungry man eat around here?" He rubbed his hands together to create warmth.

Hanna smiled as she motioned for him to take a seat at the kitchen table. "I have some cold ham, potato salad, and some mac and cheese, Mr. Johnny," she said, already dishing up a plate for him. "Or I can make an omelet or scrambled eggs, if you'd prefer. Would you like some coffee?" She held an already-steaming mug and the aroma of freshly brewed coffee filled the kitchen.

Johnny's eyes were wide and wild, with a flame behind them I had never seen before. His hands gestured in the air and he said, his voice a frenzied pitch, "Hanna, you're an angel sent from heaven to take care of a man whose girlfriend doesn't care if he starves. She has no respect for how hard I work. I should marry you, Hanna. We can have a double wedding with my friend here!" I tried to smile at Hanna, who appeared both bewildered and uncomfortable.

"Johnny, what is going on with you? I think he's having a midlife crisis," I said to Hanna. Then to Johnny, I said, "Don't be rude, dude. You know you're older than me."

He shifted his weight on his feet while his gaze darted to the ground. Hanna watched us, her eyes wide with disbelief.

"I'm not the one who had a love child with one woman and proposed to another woman in a courtroom without telling his best friend. They are sisters, dude. You're weird. At least it wasn't a threesome." Johnny laughed.

I made a screwing motion with my index finger pointing to my head, showing that Johnny had a screw loose. My mouth twitched in a half smile, and I let out a shuddering laugh. "It's okay. He's having a nervous breakdown." I was going to strangle Morse. "Johnny, you're rambling a mile a minute. You can barely keep your eyes open and your clothes smell like a brewery. Come with me." I grabbed his arm and pulled him out of the kitchen. In the lounge, I plopped him on the couch. "Stay put," I said, marching back to the kitchen. "I'll grab the food."

I returned to the room with a tray loaded with bacon, eggs, toast, and coffee. Johnny was still sitting on the couch where I left him. I shook my head and poured two cups of coffee. "I know you can't even boil water, but don't you have any food at your house?"

"Never mind about that," Johnny said with his mouth full. "Alana told me you proposed to Kimberly Bennett."

"I did." My voice was heavy with resignation.

"Dude, are you serious? You don't even know her." He squinted at me.

"It's complicated and you wouldn't understand," I told him, running my fingertips along the back of my neck.

"Are you under some kind of spell? Have you even slept with her yet?" he asked, peering at me shrewdly.

"She's not like that, Johnny. And don't fucking talk like that," I replied, a faint flush rising along my cheeks as I clenched my fist.

Johnny's fork clattered against his plate as he dropped it, his eyes wide with shock. "You're going to marry her without tasting her first? Or see how she rides? Bro, that's insane. She could be awful."

"Johnny, please!" I ran a hand through my dark hair and sighed. "She's special, you know? She has this energy, like a phoenix rising from the ashes. Everything about her captivates me—her intelligence, her strength, and her beauty. When she enters a room, it just lights up like the sun. I want her, more than I've ever wanted any other woman in my life."

"Dude. You've got it bad. She's even turned you into a poet. When did all this happen?"

"It's happening, Johnny. She's a wild, defiant badass who never backs down from a challenge. I've known no one like her."

"How does she feel about you?"

I shrugged. "I know she'd like to fuck my brains out."

Johnny laughed. "Okay. That's a start, but not the basis for proposing marriage, my friend. Wait. This is about William, isn't it?"

"Yes, but not all of it. I'm falling in love with her, Johnny. I *am* in love with her."

"But, Des, if she doesn't return your love, then your marriage is doomed. I'm your best friend. And you know I love you, even more than if you were my brother, so listen to me when I say, don't do this, not even for William."

"It's happening!"

Johnny threw his hands in the air. His face was flush, and his mouth hung open. "Alana told me you lost it on Friday when she came home from work." He gestured in the air. "Now I know why. When am I going to meet this Kimberly Bennett? Everyone in Bayview knows who she is after your escapades were plastered all over the papers and TV. But I want to meet her for myself."

I adjusted my collar and cleared my throat. "I'll bring her to the club one night this week."

Johnny nodded, stared at me with a stern look, and replied, "Good. Make sure you do."

"Please keep your mouth shut about our youthful exploits. She already thinks I'm some kind of sex-crazed womanizing rake who regularly indulges in threesomes."

Johnny laughed. "Well, we did. Do you remember what's her name, Bel... Bel something. Belinda, that's it, Belinda and her best..."

I charged forward, fists clenched and nostrils flaring. "Johnny, I'm warning you," I growled. "I'll knock you out."

Johnny stepped closer, eyes defiant and arms crossed in a defensive stance. "Oh, you wouldn't dare. If you lay a finger on me, I'll tell your firebird it wasn't three but four in that bed and we enjoyed every single one of them at the same time!"

Just then, my phone rang. It was Kimberly.

"It's her," I told Johnny. "Get out." As I answered the phone, my stomach dropped. "Hey, are you feeling better today?"

"Yeah," she said. "Can you meet me in my apartment downtown in about an hour? We need to talk."

"I'll be there."

29
Kimberly

The roar of his bike engine sang into the parking lot, and I headed downstairs to bring him to the apartment. His leather jacket flapped in the warm air as he dismounted his Suzuki. He took measured strides toward me, and I stepped back to let him in the doors. I gave my security guard the night off and the office was closed. Before he had the chance to shut the door, I grabbed both sides of his jacket and pulled him close for a kiss. His body tensed for a moment as he hesitated, then he melted into me. His hands traveled up my back, sending shocks of pleasure radiating through my body.

He stooped to meet my gaze, his brown eyes searching mine. "What was that for?" he asked with a low growl.

"Just seeing if it felt the same," I murmured. He cocked an eyebrow, waiting for me to elaborate. I let out a long exhale and responded with a noncommittal shrug of my shoulders, unable to commit to a definite answer.

We waited in silence for the elevator doors to open, anticipation crackling between us. When it dinged, I stepped inside, and he spun me around, pressing the length of his body against me. His hands tangled in my hair, and he claimed my lips with a fervent kiss. His tongue explored and curled around mine with a hunger so intense, my skin flushed as a moan escaped me. Heat surged from my core and made me cling to him as if I'd drown without him. His hand moved against my thigh and the heat of his skin on mine sent shivers down my spine. When he reached the place I wanted to be touched, he paused and looked into my eyes with a desire I'd never seen before. His fingers trembled as if he wanted to keep going, but he held back.

"Not yet," he whispered in my ear, right before the elevator doors opened to my apartment.

I gave him a hard shove and stepped back, panting for breath. He stumbled a few steps, struggling to regain his balance, and I said, "Fine," then walked into my apartment. A smirk played on his lips as he chased me inside.

He breathed heavily, and his eyes were filled with a mixture of arousal and confusion. "Are you sure you don't have feelings for me?" he asked.

I stood tall with my arms crossed and met his gaze. "I asked you here to talk. Not to have a sex romp." His expression fell and he sighed in disappointment. I took his hand and led him to the sofa. I motioned for him to sit before I stepped away.

He looked at me with a deep frown, and the shadows of fatigue beneath his eyes were more pronounced. He removed his jacket and laid it on the arm of the chair, settling back in his seat. I sat opposite him, wringing my hands as I tried to find the words. "I'm going to accept your proposal."

Desmond's face lit with excitement, and a smile tugged at the corners of his mouth. "You are? That's great. What made you decide? It was the massage, wasn't it?"

I stared at him, my jaw set. "I'm doing this for William. It will be a marriage of convenience, not a love match. And I have certain conditions."

He raised his eyebrows and waited.

"We have separate bedrooms, of course. I won't have you womanizing and embarrassing me in public. No more of that."

His eyes hardened and his jaw tensed, but he shook his head in a single nod.

"That means no flirting and no affairs. If I find out you've been with another woman, that will be cause for divorce and I get custody of William."

His face fell. "Not this again. That will never happen because I don't want any other woman. You must change your perception of me. In the last six years, after your sister, I've been with three women. One was an on-off relationship that went on for years, more off than on." His mouth tugged into a sly smile as he looked at me. "What's the separate bedroom thing about? I mean, I hope you're not proposing a marriage devoid of sex."

Heat flushed my cheeks, but I forced myself to stay composed. "No. I'm not. I'd hoped you got that just now."

He chuckled and gave me a nod. "I sort of did. Just wanted to make sure."

"We don't have to share the same bedroom to have sex. It's just that I prefer my own space." *And I don't want you probing into my nightmares.* "I'll also stay here overnight sometimes, but I'll always let you know if I'm doing that."

"What are your other conditions?" I asked. This was only going to work if we could agree on the rules now. This marriage of convenience wouldn't be too bad. Word got around about Desmond's competence in the bedroom, and at least I would get my needs met. Was that awful?

"Same as yours. I don't expect you to see another man.

There'd be no divorce; he'd just disappear. I won't share you. So, you better tell Barry to stay away."

"Barry? What are you talking about? He's just a friend."

"His arm was around you at the court building."

I laughed. "You're such an idiot. Barry is dating another friend of mine, Iris, who is a journalist in Central Bay, where they both live. He came to support me. So, my husband-to-be is the jealous type."

He nodded and cleared his throat, averting his gaze from mine. "I'm assuming we'll live at the mansion."

"We couldn't live anywhere else; otherwise, you'd have to move William's tree house or build him another one."

Desmond chuckled. "Madeline loves It. I think every child in his school has been to the mansion."

"Well, that's because most of the mothers want to get up close and personal with Madeline Renault's rakish son."

He gave me a look. "Kimberly, don't start. You've just agreed to marry Madeline's rakish son, so I guess those sorts of moms will stay away. I assume you'll play the role of dutiful wife and accompany me to business functions and other events."

"To keep the groupies at bay, you mean?" I grinned. "Desmond, I'll play the dutiful wife, except for sharing your bedroom. I also hope we can have our own space at the mansion. I won't always want to have breakfast, lunch, and dinner with your family."

"That's no problem. The whole west wing of the mansion is my domain with its own separate entrance. You can remodel it in any way you want. I rather like how you've done this apartment. The mansion belongs to me, but Mom may live there for the rest of her life if she wants to."

"I'd never suggest or want your mother to move out of her own home. I just want a bit of privacy as a married woman with her own household. Your part of the mansion sounds perfect."

"I have one more question," he said. "I'd like you to tell me about your nightmares. Where are you and who are you talking to?"

There it is. "Desmond, please, I don't want to talk about that now. Let's just finish this conversation."

He stared at me.

"When shall we do the deed?" I asked.

"How about right now?" he suggested, leering at me. "Now is as good a time as any to have your way with me."

"I mean, when should we get married? Is your first waking thought about sex?"

"Yes, with you."

I blushed. He watched me. "Why don't we get a license and get old Sammy to marry us on Friday?"

I giggled. "She didn't like me."

"I was the one she raked over the coals. She was going to hold me in contempt for wasting court time and send me to the dungeons beneath the courtrooms."

I laughed. "I'm so sorry. Thank you for covering for me and taking all the flack."

Desmond's face lit with a warm, genuine smile and he sprang to his feet. He leaned in, pressing his lips to mine. They were soft, yet passionate. He pulled away just enough to look into my eyes, and the seriousness of his gaze sent a chill down my spine. "Kimberly," he said, "I promise I will make you happy and be a wonderful husband to you and father to William."

Great, now my panties are soaking wet.

He sat back down on the couch.

"Doesn't it take at least a week to get a license?" I asked, trying to change the subject.

"I don't know. This is my first marriage." He grinned. "I'll go to the courthouse first thing in the morning. I'll pull a few strings. We need to get it by Friday before we meet with Sammy."

"Perfect." I held my hand out to his.

"What, just a handshake? I'd hoped we'd seal our agreement with at least a kiss."

I got up, walked around the table, and went to give him a peck on the cheek. He grabbed me and pulled me on top of him and held me there. "More than that," he whispered in my ear. "I want you, Kimberly."

"I know, I can see." My eyes fixated on the bulge in his pants, and I licked my lips, knowing that from now on, it was all mine.

"Kim-ber-ly," he begged. "You see what you do to me, what you do every time I'm with you, from the very first time I saw you..."

I loved the power I had over him, but if we were getting married, then maybe our sex life would be hot as fuck. For right now, we had to wait.

"I need to get back to our son. He wanted to come with me."

Our son... It felt so weird to say, yet he was both of ours. We would be raising him together from now on, and truthfully, it would be nice to have someone else to lean on.

"Shall I come with you?"

"I haven't spent any time with William in the last couple of days. Some alone time with him would be good."

He grinned. "Okay. Can I give you the ring now?"

I moved off his body and sat beside him. He took the box out of his pocket and opened it.

"I'd be afraid to wear it in case it gets damaged."

"It won't." He slipped it on my finger.

It was a perfect fit. "I'll have to choose just the right wedding band to go with it, but for now, you should keep it. Too many questions. I'll wear it once we are officially married."

"Okay." He got up and put his jacket on and walked to the elevator. When it opened and he stepped inside, just before it shut, he said, "Mrs. Renault, I could get used to that."

Friday morning glowed as a new day and the start of a new life. A sliver of sunlight crept through the cracks of the wooden shutters, forming delicate patterns on the glass of my bedroom windows. I savored this moment, my last as a single woman.

I was not denying my physical attraction to Desmond Renault. But marriage? I'd taken a wrong turn in insisting on the matter going to court. It was ironic that my action led to my present position. And I wasn't all that keen on living in the mansion.

My hands shook as I finished dressing, and I stared at myself in the mirror, disbelieving. I was getting married—to Desmond Renault, a man I barely knew. I agreed to this to keep William safe. He was the only thing that mattered to me. If I did this, I could protect him and keep him close. I wouldn't let anyone take him away from me. And, for some unfathomable reason, I felt safe with Desmond from the first time I clung to him in his car. He was a rock during a time of turmoil, while being the cause of my distress. I was trusting him to keep us both safe.

I was astute enough to realize there was just a touch of cognitive dissonance between my view of Desmond Renault and my current behavior, but I didn't want to think too deeply about that. Nor would I admit perhaps I wouldn't be marrying him if I didn't find him attractive.

I'd been vulnerable and often exposed after the Chad debacle. I couldn't imagine that at one time marriage had been part of our plan. How was it possible to be so wrong about a person? I'd crafted a tough exterior to keep predators at bay. The world was full of them and they preyed on the weak. I knew a few. But here I was on my wedding day. We got the marriage license, the rings, and Alana Glacey confirmed that Gina Samson would officiate at the wedding. Alana and Barbara would be our witnesses. Apart from our lawyers and Angela, no one else knew our plans. We'd pick William up from school and tell him together.

My mother was happy, but conflicted. In her view, Desmond and I needed to spend more time together, getting to know each other. But the judge rattled me, and I agreed with Desmond that we should keep control of the situation and not let Sammy impose conditions we may not want. Desmond was dependable and brought a solid masculine presence into our lives and William needed that. He needed to be given the chance to be close with his father, especially after losing Cece.

As much as I hated to admit it, Desmond Renault was going to be a wonderful father, and even though this marriage was unconventional, I knew that he would be a good husband.

Mrs. Bennett-Renault...

30
Desmond

IT WAS MY WEDDING DAY, and I was marrying my firebird. A huge smile creased my face. In a few hours, she would be my wife. Madeline might be right; we were too dissimilar to make it work. But if I couldn't trust my heart, then what or who could I trust? She was so different from all the other women. She confounded me, challenged me, made me want to be a better person. To be loved, truly loved by her, would be the best thing to ever happen to me besides finding out about William.

Being his dad made me want to experience the whole thing from the beginning. I would not yet be having that conversation with her. Maybe in a year or two, unless an occasion arose beforehand. I hoped in time she would return my love. Then we could have the 'kids' conversation. I still hadn't been truly upfront about my feelings for her, and right now with her agreeing to a marriage of convenience, there was only so long she could be with me and not figure out the kind of man I was. A man far from what she thought. Sure, I was a womanizer, but what man wasn't in their twenties. Now, that I was older, things had settled down, and I didn't sleep around like that anymore.

Kimberly liked her privacy, and I would give that to her. I knew why she wanted separate bedrooms. She didn't want me prying into the reasons for her nightmares. I could tell by her response to me since that night in the mansion when I'd soothed her. Eventually, she would have to tell me the truth, but I would stay patient until then. The envelope in my safe most likely held the answers, but especially now, I needed to trust her.

There was just one area of my life that needed to be resolved and shut down. And that was going to be a tough conversation between Mark and me. It needed to happen soon.

A little guilt ran through me for not informing my mother and sister about us getting married today. But I knew the whole thing would turn into the type of occasion neither Kimberly nor I wanted. I would deal with my mom and Leanne's disappointment later.

They would be at home waiting. I asked Madeline to prepare a special lunch on the pretext of celebrating the conclusion of the custody battle.

Madeline was more than happy to comply. She ordered some additional champagne and invited Angela to join them, which was perfect. I asked Angela to bring an overnight bag because I planned to take my wife out on our wedding night. It was time for me to get up, shower, get dressed, and go pick her up.

When I arrived at Sunnyside, Kimberly was ready and waiting. She looked gorgeous in a deep-pink dress with matching lipstick, her trademark high ponytail, and black pumps.

"You look fucking hot. Hot damn, am I one lucky motherfucker."

She smiled at me. "Thank you."

"Good morning," said Angela, springing up. "You're looking very handsome today."

"Good morning. Luke will pick you up at around noon," I reminded her.

"Are you ready to go?" I asked Kimberly.

"Wait," Angela said. "It's your wedding day. Look the part." She secured a small white rose to my lapel.

"You told her?" I asked, looking over at her.

Kimberly rolled her eyes. "She beat it out of me... don't be mad."

"I can't believe you two are getting married, and the next time I see you, you'll be my son-in-law."

"We've got to go, Mom. See you later at the mansion," said Kimberly, pulling me out the door.

"Morning, Ward," Kimberly said, sliding into the back of the car through the door I opened.

"Morning, Kimberly," responded Ward, looking at her through his rearview mirror.

"You okay?" I checked.

She smiled and nodded. "Yes."

I slid into the seat next to her and took her hand. Ward caught my eye, and I gave him the barest nod. The car glided away, leaving Angela in the doorway, watching as we disappeared.

When we arrived at the courthouse and were ushered into the judge's chambers, she waited with a smile on her face when we entered with our hands together.

"Good morning, everyone," Gina Samson said.

"Good morning, Judge," four voices said in unison.

The judge beamed at us. "I didn't imagine this time a week ago that we would be here today. Mr. Renault, Ms. Bennett, are you both ready to get married and do you have the marriage license?"

"Yes, Judge," we both said. I removed the document from the inside pocket of my suit and handed it to the judge.

"Good. Let's get this show on the road."

The ceremony went by in just a couple of minutes, and we were out of there as husband and wife.

Madeline Renault's face was a sculpture of incredulity. "You and Kimberly got married without us?" There was a tinge of hurt. "Does Angela know about this?"

Leanne came to my rescue. "Congratulations, Des. That's great news, but you should have told us."

"Please don't blame Desmond," Kimberly said. "It was my idea. I didn't want to wait, and when the judge agreed to marry us, we took the opportunity." *Which is true.*

I squeezed her hand.

"I think Desmond could've said that, then I would've been prepared."

"Mom, that's what we wanted to avoid. Neither of us wanted a fuss."

"Well, I hope we can at least have a party soon. We must celebrate, Des," said Leanne.

"Lea, please, that isn't necessary," I said, my hands rising into the air.

She ignored me and moved toward her new sister-in-law. "Congratulations, Kimberly. I'm happy for you both. Welcome to the family. I'll have to move back home now. You and William are going to be living here."

Kimberly laughed.

"I have a nice celebratory lunch ready. At least Desmond

gave me a warning for that, while omitting the real reason for it. As soon as Angela gets here, we can eat."

My mother touched my face, squeezing my cheeks like I was only a child. "Let me arrange a small gathering in honor of the event. It's not every day my son gets married. We must make an announcement in the papers. I'll speak to Eric."

Kimberly and I looked at each other. "No, Mother. Please don't do that. We want to keep this low-key. People will find out in time. We don't want to make a grand announcement to the world."

"Fine," Madeline said. "Whenever you call me mother, I know you're serious. But I hope you'll let me have a few close friends for dinner tonight to mark the occasion. Is there anyone you'd like me to invite, Kimberly?"

"Just Barbara Sutherland and my business partner, Jonas Holt," she said.

Madeline looked at me. "It's okay, Desmond. I'll keep it small, only about a dozen people."

"If you must, but no more than that, Mom, and please include Luke and Lorna."

"It'll be fine, Desmond. Just a few close friends to share in your happiness."

It wasn't but four hours later that everyone was gathered in the Renault Mansion and my mother insisted on making a speech during lunch.

"Angela, Leanne, Hanna, please join me in a toast to Desmond and Kimberly," she began.

"To my dear son, I know how much you wished your father was here with us today. But I want you to know how proud he'd be of you, especially the way you've stepped into the role of CEO of the company and now you are a married man with a wife and a lovely little boy, his grandson. Damien would have been delighted that you married someone who enhances the Renault name."

I dare not look at Kimberly. All I could do was squeeze her hand beneath the table.

Madeline continued. "And to my new daughter-in-law, Kimberly, welcome to the family. This is your home now, my dear. The only thing I ask is that you and Desmond give me a lot more grandchildren."

Everyone laughed, including Kimberly, although she looked as if she'd sucked on a lemon. *This will not be so easy.*

"I wish you and Desmond every happiness. To Desmond and Kimberly, Mr. and Mrs. Renault," Madeline said.

"To Desmond and Kimberly," echoed Angela, Leanne, and Hanna.

"Kiss her!" trilled Leanne. "I know you didn't do it in the courtroom, or it was just a peck. The bride and groom have to kiss on their wedding day. It's part of the ritual and we all have to see you do it."

Kimberly glanced sideways at me, and I couldn't hide the uptick of my lips. I reached for her hand beneath the table. I liked the sound of Mr. and Mrs. Renault. Why did I know she would want to be known by her own name? I smiled and leaned in. We gave each other a chaste kiss on the mouth.

"Oh, come on, Des, you call that a kiss? You can do better than that!" Leanne admonished.

I smiled and gave Kimberly another kiss on her cheek. The three older women laughed, and Leanne snorted.

Kimberly smiled at everyone. I'm sure she couldn't wait for it to be over.

"I have a wedding gift for you. Come, I'll show you." I took Kimberly's hand and led her out of the dining room into the mansion's rather large sitting room, from which we could view another aspect of the grounds. Everyone else followed. They wanted to see too.

In the middle of the room stood a high gloss dark red wood grand piano. Kimberly gasped. "Oh, Desmond. Oh my God. It's a Steinway Grand. They cost the earth. Concert pianists use these!"

"Only the best for my wife," I told her. "You have one at Sunnyside and one in your apartment. You need one here. You can move it into the west wing."

"Oh, Kimberly, you play," said Leanne, grinning at her sister-in-law. "We can hold concerts here. Is there anything you can't do?"

"I can assure you, I'm not anywhere near concert level, not by any stretch of the imagination. Thank you, it's beautiful." She reached to kiss me. And my arms enfolded her.

The room emptied as Madeline, Angela, and Hanna gave the us two lovebirds some alone time. But not Leanne. She stood watching us. "Erhmm..." She cleared her throat. "Are you two going on a honeymoon?"

We ignored her, and without raising my head, I shooed her away.

"I didn't get you anything," Kimberly said.

"I have everything I want."

Kimberly had little time to explore the piano before we had to pick up our son. I loved it. It just rolled right off the tongue. She might not love me now, but over time, as she realized she pegged wrong, she would come around. I knew it.

I stared at my watch, not wanting to stop her, but we couldn't be late. "Sweetie, we have to go get William, but you can play later for as long as you'd like."

She played much better than I could.

Ward drove us to get William, and we were both nervous about how this would go.

"Hello, Daddy," William greeted me as Kimberly helped him into the back seat of the Trailblazer. "I didn't know you were coming to get me."

"That's because we have a surprise for you, buddy."

Ward smiled as he drove us away.

Seated between the two of us, the small boy looked from one to the other. "What is it?"

"I had to see the judge about adopting you," Kimberly said. "She said I can be your mommy now."

"Yay!" He maneuvered himself in his seat belt and hugged her tight around the waist. "Can we live with Daddy, so I can play with my friends in the tree house all the time?"

"Yes," I replied.

The little boy's eyes shone. "Can Nana Angie come too?" he asked.

We looked at each other. Kimberly rolled her eyes at me. This was a conversation we'd started with Angela. I'd feel better if she came to live in the mansion. There was more than enough room for her to have her own self-contained space. But she would have none of it. All she'd say was, 'I have my own plans.'

"Nana Angie will stay with us sometimes, buddy," I said. Perhaps William would be the one to persuade Angela. "Why don't we talk to Nana Angie about it later?"

"Okay," William said and then launched into a graphic description of his day at school.

Me and my new wife looked at each other again over William's head. We rehearsed what to tell him about being married. But none of that happened. We leave it for another occasion. For now, the little boy was cheerful because he had a mommy and daddy living in the same house like Maurice and Shiloh.

We made his dream come true.

"But tonight we are going out together and you're staying at the mansion. Okay?"

He nodded.

After dropping him off at the mansion with Angela and my mother, we ended up ensconced in a secluded corner of the restaurant, talking about the day. We were at ease with each other, but the surrounding energy thrummed with sexual tension.

I couldn't take my eyes off my bride all night. Her locks tumbled over her bare shoulders and down her exposed back in soft curls. This gorgeous woman was my wife now. She was going to meet Johnny.

"Are you ready to go, Mrs. Renault?" I said with a grin and waited for her comeback.

Kimberly raised her glass before finishing the last of her champagne. "Here's to a long and happy marriage, Mr. Renault, as long as you remember my name is Bennett. Not Renault."

He chuckled. "Not even Bennett-Renault?"

"Nope."

"What about our children?"

She gaped at me. "*Our* children?"

"Poor William, you're not going to let him grow up in that vast mansion all by himself, are you?"

"Desmond, are you being serious? I'm making that a condition of this marriage right now. No children."

"I think we should seek mediation on it."

"From whom? Not your mother."

"No. From William."

"That's not fair. He's bound to say yes to a baby brother or sister. Who will breastfeed and get up at one every morning? *You* will have to take care of it in every sense."

"Okay. Deal."

"Fine." Kimberly smiled. "We can go now."

31
Kimberly

"So, this is where you located your glitzy club, on the edge of the Bush, amidst dereliction. I'm surprised."

He shrugged. "Best location for a club. Nobody to disturb. It was an abandoned Renault Tech factory and was a good idea to renovate and restore it to new glory. The idea was to encourage new development in the area. It's also given Leanne an outlet to shine. She's fantastic at it. She and Johnny are a great team."

As we approached, we could see the long line of people waiting to get in. We recognized a few Bayview luminaries who could walk right in along a red carpeted path in a roped off area.

"I see you have two unique types of clienteles."

"Yep. the Bush caters for all types. Members sit in a VIP area and drink the best, most expensive champagne all night long and pay a small fortune for the privilege. Then there are those who just want to come and have a good time, have a few beers and let off steam on the dance floor."

It was a successful business model. I didn't have time for

clubbing. Especially now. My life revolved around William. The car stopped close to the red-carpet entrance to the club. Within seconds Ward was opening my door and Desmond was right beside me.

"We won't stay long," he said. "I just want to introduce Kimberly to Johnny and maybe have a drink."

Ward nodded. "Just text me when you're ready to leave."

He took my hand. "I suppose we'll be the talk of the town by tomorrow."

"You'll get used to it, Mrs. Renault, then you won't notice." He grinned. "We still have news of our marriage to come out."

I groaned. "Yeah. I forgot about that and don't think I didn't notice the Mrs. Renault. What did I say less than half an hour ago?"

He laughed. "My apologies, Mrs. Bennett."

"Good evening, Mr. Renault," said a dressed doorman, the gatekeeper for the VIP entrance. He bowed to us as someone ushered us inside. Two burly bouncers oversaw the entrance for those with less deep pockets.

Inside, I scanned the surroundings. There were hundreds of tiny muted spotlights embedded in the high ceiling. Half-naked women danced, raised above the ground as the music boomed. The strobe-lit dance floor throbbed with gyrating bodies. The place was packed to the rafters. It was a Friday night, the start of the weekend, and everyone was having fun.

I directed my attention to a waving Leanne fighting her way through the crowds, heading in our direction. "Why didn't you tell me you were coming tonight?" she shouted. "Are you staying?"

"For a little while," he shouted back.

"Okay. Make your way upstairs. I'll get some drinks sent up. Johnny is around somewhere. I'll ask Dan to find him. By the way, I have said nothing to Johnny about your nuptials. I'd leave that pleasure to you," Leanne said, trying to make her way back through. "It's very busy tonight, so I can't stop," she yelled over her shoulder, wanting to be heard above the cacophony.

The pounding rhythm pulsed through our bodies, drawing me to the dance floor, but he was leading me to where another gatekeeper guarded the upper level. As soon as his eyes alighted on me, he released a red cord-rope to let us through. "Enjoy your evening, sir."

"Hey, Hal, you're still here," Desmond greeted him. "Good to see you." With a hand on the small of my back, he guided me to a table overlooking the dance floor. It was quieter there.

We settled in our seats, when a man appeared with a tray of vodka shots, a bottle of wine, and some glasses. "Des, my man." He grinned. "You came." He put the tray on the table.

"And this must be the delectable Kimberly. My God, Des, you're right. She's stunning, even more gorgeous in person. No wonder she's knocked you into a cocked hat." He took my hand and brought it to his lips. "I'm Johnny Morse, your faithful servant and illustrious wingman to this guy whom you appear to have transfixed. You've turned my buddy into a..."

"You've said enough Morse," he interrupted.

I giggled. "Do continue. What have I turned your friend into?"

"Please call me Johnny. We'll have to meet without him." Johnny jerked a thumb in his direction. "I'll tell you everything."

I laughed again. "Good. I'm going to hold you to that."

"If you're done with the BS, Johnny, may I introduce you to my wife?"

The look on Johnny's face was priceless. That shut him up, which was what Desmond intended. Johnny stared at me, then at the ring on my finger, then back at Desmond. "Your wife? But you said, what the hell... You're married?"

He laughed. "Didn't Alana tell you? She was one of our witnesses today."

"No, she didn't." Johnny took one shot and gulped it back. "Probably because I left before she got home, and anyway, she's so secretive about anything to do with you."

Desmond's facial expression changed. He was looking over Johnny's shoulder at the person approaching us. Marsha, whom I only know from living here, was with an unfamiliar man in tow.

"Hello, Desmond, Johnny," Marsha said. She looked at me. "Hi. You must be Kimberly. I recognize you from your photographs in the papers. I'm Marsha Hannigan."

I gave a slight nod. "Hi."

Marsha turned to Desmond. "Can we have a word in private?"

"Will you excuse me for a moment? I won't be long." He planted a soft kiss on my lips after standing up. My guess was he did that to comfort me. He remembered my rule—no sharing. Desmond only took a couple of steps away from me.

"So, you're with her now? That didn't take you long, did it?"

"Marsha, who I'm with is not your concern. Our relationship is over. I tried to talk to you, but you bundled me out of your apartment."

"Because I didn't want to break down in front of you, Desmond. You hurt me. I love you."

He looked over at me talking to Johnny, but I wasn't actually paying attention to a word he was saying, because my man was over there talking to his ex-girlfriend. Was I already getting jealous?

"Don't look at her. I'm talking to you. At least have the courtesy to look at me when I'm talking to you."

Fuck. Why tonight of all nights?

"Marsha, please, don't make a scene. There's nothing more to say. I told you about William and what I needed to do. I've moved on; you should too."

"So, have you fallen for your son's aunt? Is that it? Why could you not be honest with me?"

"Sorry for interrupting. Marsha, would you mind? I need my husband," I said, resting my hand on his arm, revealing my ring.

Marsha gasped and the bright-red color suffused her face as her eyes fell on my ring. She gaped at us. "Excuse me."

We watched as an embarrassed Marsha walked back to her companion and dragged him away. The two of them went down the stairs and disappeared into the crowd.

He took my hand. "Thank you. That was awkward. Are you ready to go home?"

"Not yet, we've only just arrived," I said. "Come dance with me."

"I don't care how fast the music is, we're doing a slow dance."

"My sentiments exactly," I whispered in his ear.

When we passed by the table where Johnny was sitting, Desmond tapped his shoulder. "I'm going to dance with my wife, then I'm taking her home."

"Okay, buddy," was all Johnny could say.

He took me in his arms, and I slipped my arms beneath his jacket and around his waist. He stared into my eyes. "I'm sorry you had to do that, but thank you for rescuing me."

"We agreed that one of my roles is to keep the groupies at bay. We can add ex-girlfriends too." I grinned.

He bent and placed a quick kiss on my lips. His arms tightened around me as we swayed to the fast dance music. I moved my arms and wrapped them around his neck, pulling him closer. His hand moved to my butt and pushed my lower body into his. My lips parted and eyes closed.

"Come on," he said, his lips close to my ear, "we're leaving. We're spending the night in your apartment, where I plan on making you scream all night."

The touching began in the back of the car. Desmond's hand meandered beneath my skirt and he stroked my inner thigh. My lips parted as my breathing started to hitch. His finger moved my panties aside so he could tease me. I opened my legs to give him better access.

"The club is doing great Ward, don't you think?" Desmond said as he inserted that finger into my hot, wet, and already throbbing pussy.

My eyes flew open. Was he holding a conversation with Ward while finger fucking me? But it was hot. Like doing it in public. I turned my head to look at him. He was watching me with a grin on his face. He knew exactly what he was doing.

"Leanne and Johnny have it banging. I must take Lorna one night," said Ward.

"I've been encouraging them to think about opening a second club," Desmond said.

"Leanne was telling me about that tonight," Ward said. "Was it your first visit, Kimberly?"

Desmond chose that moment to pump his finger. I faked a cough to cover the moan that escaped my lips. I was aware of Desmond's enjoyment of my predicament and wanted to glare at him, but honestly, I was enjoying the sinfulness of what we were doing. One day I'd make him pay for taking unfair advantage, though.

"Uh, yes, Ward, it was my first visit. An amazing place and a great business model by the look of things."

My juices flowed over Desmond's fingers just as the Bennett Tech building came into view. Desmond withdrew his finger and arranged my skirt seconds before the car pulled up outside. He opened the door and stepped out, turning to help me. I was a little unsteady on my feet and he slipped an arm around my waist.

"Good night, Ward," Desmond said.

The touching and kissing continued in the elevator. My dress was off and flung onto the couch. Fuck! My back hit the door as he pressed hard against me. He shrugged off his jacket and flung it toward my dress. I rocked my hips against his already hardened bulge, making him gasp. *"Kim-ber-ly,"* he breathed, as I pressed open-mouthed kisses against his neck.

He lifted my arms above my head and held my wrists in place with one hand. My dark-pink nipples spoke to him as he traced a figure eight around my breasts. He tweaked each and watched me. I made a strangled noise in my throat.

Desmond bent his head and licked my nipples, then grazed each one with his teeth. I moaned and my body jerked forward. I struggled to free my hands. He raised his head and shook it.

"Desmond, please," I moaned, "Fuck me. Now."

"I'm going to, my adorable firebird, but not yet."

He was going to take his sweet time with me. My lips parted and his tongue licked them.

His tongue probed and explored. I sucked it. His hand cupped my pussy, the dampness of my underwear. "You're so wet. When did that happen?" he whispered.

I squirmed and thrummed against him.

Desmond slipped his hand inside my panties and stroked before plunging a finger inside. I moaned and my body jerked forward. He removed his finger and used it to press on my bottom lip, then he inserted it into my mouth. I sucked on it, tasting myself. My pupils were wide and dilated as I stared at him.

Slowly, he removed his finger from my mouth and kissed

me hard. His finger and thumb rolled and squeezed a taut nipple. I moaned, and my body bucked and jerked. He gave the same treatment to the other breast. *Fuck!*

"Desmond, please," I moaned, pinned in place while he took complete control of my body and commanded it according to his wishes. He was playing my body like an instrument.

"What do you need, baby? Tell me."

"Please, Desmond, please," I whimpered.

Without warning, he ripped off my flimsy lace underwear and plunged two fingers inside of me and pumped. In and out. He watched as my mouth opened in a silent cry. I ground down on his hand, seeking more friction. Desmond inserted another finger, curling them deep inside, seeking my sweet spot. His thumb rubbed my throbbing clit. I whimpered and my body undulated in time with the rhythm of his fingers. My orgasm ripped through me, leaving me gasping.

Desmond released my wrists and slipped his arm around my waist and held me while he pumped me through to recovery. "Wow," I whispered. Desmond grinned and kissed my clammy forehead.

I placed soft kisses on his exposed chest while I undid his belt, unzipped his pants, and pushed them and his boxers over his ass. I gripped his straining erection and squeezed. "I need you inside me right now!"

He grinned. "Yes, ma'am," he said before hoisting me off the floor. I wrapped my legs around him. His body shifted, and I gasped as he plunged his cock in all the way, filling me. He stilled, giving me time to adjust to him. I whimpered.

"Fuck." The expletive fell unbidden from his lips. "You're so tight. You okay?"

"Yes. Please, Desmond!"

He chuckled and sucked a nipple, wrapping his tongue around it. Desmond withdrew his cock, pulling back until the tip was once again pulsating against my clit, then he slammed hard inside, pushing me against the door. Stunned by the sensation, I screamed his name. The breath caught in my throat.

He nipped my bottom lip with his teeth. "This is going to be quick and dirty," he breathed in my ear. My head fell onto his shoulder, and I held on to him for dear life as he started pounding into me, gathering speed as he pushed me to the limit. He was not gentle, but my loud moans and cries betrayed me, revealing the intense pleasure my husband was capable of.

Desmond squeezed his eyes tight to maintain momentum and control. His breath stuttered. "Kimberly, come with me," he rasped into my ear. Before the words left his mouth, my walls tightened around him. I was ready. He pumped into me hard. Once, twice, three times. I screamed out his name just as his release exploded inside me.

We clung to each other, breathing hard, until our orgasmic high receded and we returned to the present. His legs shook from his exertions and the electrical storm engulfed us both.

"Holy fuck, firebird. I'm never gonna get enough of you." He kissed my forehead, then with one arm around my waist and a hand clasping my thigh, he moved me into the bedroom. He let me rest for a while, but he wasn't done with me yet. That was just the prelude to the night.

32

Desmond

THE SPACE next to me was cold. She must have left me some time ago. A momentary panic set in. There was no noise from the bathroom. I got out of bed and searched for my boxers, slipping them on and then going to the bathroom. Putting on the larger of the two white bathrobes hanging behind the bathroom door, I wandered back into her bedroom. It was quite plain for a woman's room—no girly fluff. The walls were a plain cream color, but there were vibrant prints of paintings depicting Parisian scenes—a couple sitting outside a bright café, lovers walking in the rain with a red umbrella beside a river—probably the Seine. I recognized Monet's impressionist view of Notre Dame and The Eiffel Tower.

I knew I was being nosy, but I couldn't help myself when I opened a nightstand drawer of hers. My eyes widened. *So, my firebird was a wild one.* I'd never minded a little light bondage, and I'd make use of that vibrator today. I got a sense of Kimberly some time ago, and especially after last night. Sex with her was just out of this world, and I couldn't get enough of her. I'd fallen asleep beneath her.

This was going to be a fun marriage, if bizarre. My wife was a mystery. I was looking forward to uncovering the whole of Kimberly Bennett. I went out into her living area, but she wasn't there either. After picking up our clothes, I draped them over the back of a chair. Where the heck was Kimberly Sandrine Bennett-Renault? I smiled at the memory of her response to my teasing. Did she run out on me already?

I found her in another bedroom. Her back was to me, her hair splayed out over the pillow. I could tell by her breathing she was still asleep. Why on earth did she leave me and come in here? I removed my robe and eased myself into the bed and spooned her. My cock jumped to life. She shifted and wiggled her bottom into the curve of my body. I put an arm over her waist and listened to her breathing.

She turned and faced me, her eyes still closed. "Good morning."

"What are you doing in here?" I asked. "I woke up to find you'd left me."

"I told you, we sleep in separate rooms."

"Why? Tell me why. I don't think it's going to work."

"Desmond, that's our agreement. You can't bail out now."

"Is this about your nightmares?"

She looked at me. "Yes. Will you leave it alone now?"

I kissed her. "Okay. I won't pry."

She sighed with relief. "Thank you. What are we doing today?"

"Not a lot. You. Are. Not. Leaving. The. Bed. Today." I kissed her between each word.

She giggled. "You're insatiable."

"Mm-hmmm," I hummed, as my lips sucked the soft skin just below her earlobes. Her breath hitched as I slipped a finger inside. She hooked her leg over my hip and ran her fingers over my taut, well-defined abs, then along my side. I put another finger inside her and watched her as I pumped in and out. She looked into my eyes. "You're so sexy," I breathed. "I can't get enough of you." I took a breast into my mouth and sucked her nipple at the same rhythmic pace as my fingers moved. Then I raised my head and bit her shoulder. She was more than aroused as she stroked my cock, rubbing her thumb over my tip.

I removed my fingers and moved her leg off my body and laid it back on the bed, shifting my position to crouching between her thighs. I raised her legs up, bending them at the knees so her pussy was opened to me. As I fingered her, I kissed the inside of her thighs. She rocked her hips upward and moaned, grabbing my hair and directing my mouth to where she needed attention.

I could fucking live here!

My head went down. She cried out as I thrust my tongue into her, then moved to her clit and sucked on it. "Oh yes, baby, don't stop. That feels so good!"

My hands cupped both of her butt cheeks and raised her as I devoured her. She moaned and pushed her hips up. She wanted more. I used my strength to hold her still as I continued to eat her out until she talked gibberish. *That's my firebird.*

I was controlled, intent, and purposeful at driving her wild when my mouth moved back to her swollen clit. She could not stop the scream as her orgasm exploded, leaving her gasping for air. I stayed where I was, using my tongue and lips to soothe her.

I raised my head, kissing along her thighs. She giggled as my scruff tickled her. We lay together, holding each other.

After a while, I moved. "Shower, then breakfast."

"Breakfast? Are we going out? There's nothing here for breakfast."

"It's all taken care of. There should be a hamper downstairs with your security man. I'll pick it up once we've showered."

She grinned at me. "You planned this out, didn't you?"

"Yep. Since you rejected a honeymoon, I arranged a twenty-four-hour mini-moon."

She laughed and palmed my face. "Are you for real, Desmond Renault? Who knows about this?"

"Our mothers and Ward. Oh, and Hanna, who prepared all the food." I smiled, picked her up, and carried her into the shower.

There had to be shower sex. I could not keep my hands off her; she went out of her way to entice me. This little firebird was all mine.

33

Kimberly

HANNA SENT enough food for the week. Our breakfast table groaned with smoked salmon, cream cheese, Spanish omelet, bagels, muffins, his favorite damson and ginger jelly, fresh fruit, and juice. He even made us coffee.

"What do you think about Angela moving into the mansion? I don't feel right about her living in Sunnyside by herself," Desmond said. "And William will miss her."

"Good luck with that. She's looking forward to a break. She has plans to spend time in Vegas where she grew up and going on a Mediterranean cruise."

"She can do all that and still live at the mansion."

"The more you badger her, the more she'll dig her heels in, so just leave it for a while."

His phone rang. It was Leanne.

"Aren't you going to answer that?"

"Nope. If it was an emergency, Madeline, Angela, or Ward would call."

I tapped the answer button and put the phone on speaker. "Hi, Leanne, what's up?"

"Hey, Kimberly. Why are you answering? Where's Des?"

"I'm here, Leanne. What do you want?"

"Where are you? Mom won't tell me. Are you two having a dirty weekend somewhere?"

"Yes, we are. The dirtiest weekend you can imagine. That's what newlyweds do."

"Eww, please spare me the details."

"Well, if you don't want to know, don't ask. You're interrupting us. What do you want?"

"To tell you that TMZ announced you and Kimberly are married. Someone took a photograph of the two of you in the club last night with your hand on her ass and it's on the front page of a tabloid this morning."

"I don't care. Since the entire world knows now, thanks to TMZ, I can touch my wife's butt if I want."

"But, Des, the article that goes with it isn't very nice. It says... wait, I'll read it to you."

"No, don't. I don't want to hear it."

"I do," I said. "What does it say?"

"No. I'll let you read it yourself. I'll save it for you, but it says something like, there must be something special about the Bennett women. Desmond Renault is on to his second one. That's horrible."

I snickered. "Well, they're not wrong. Cece was a McCormick, but we both have Bennett blood."

Desmond glared at me. "Thank you, Leanne. Goodbye." He ended the call.

"It's not a problem for me. I don't have the time or the capacity to worry about stupid tabloid stuff."

"It's okay if it's about me. I've had years to get used to it, but I hate it when you are dragged into it."

I got up and kissed him. "Don't let it spoil our mini-moon. I have an idea."

"What?"

"Follow me and you'll find out," I said, and he started chasing after me.

In the early evening we were together on one of my deep comfy couches, my head on his lap, sipping the champagne he asked Hanna to include in the hamper.

"I think our peculiar marriage has gotten off to a good start. Leanne is right; it's the best decision I've made in my life. I think we should have a mini-moon once a month."

"Your wish is my command, Renault, except that you're a Bennett."

"What are you thinking about?" I asked.

"You, us, and how much I want this to work."

"You think too much," I said as I got off the couch. I threw a cushion on the floor and knelt in front of him. I undid the tie. He was stark naked underneath. We had not dressed all day. I grinned and nudged his legs apart and settled between them.

Desmond didn't take his eyes off me as I ran my hands over his abs, kissed his chest, and continued down his thighs. He hardened as I brushed my fingers over his cock. I bent my head and licked him from the base to the swollen tip. My hand stroked his balls. I took my time before taking him into my mouth.

Desmond sighed with pleasure, closed his eyes, and surrendered to my touch. He groaned as my tongue swirled around his tip and I took him in deeper. I massaged his balls and my hand clasped him in a fisted hold and moved up and down his swollen cock.

It's nice to see him succumb to me.

I felt his hand hold my head and his fingers tightened in my hair. "Oh yes, baby," he moaned. He arched his back, struggling not to thrust into my mouth, but he couldn't stop himself. I was driving him out of his mind. His fingers tugged my hair to keep himself anchored. The sounds that came out of his mouth mingled with the erotic slurping, sucking noises of my mouth on his cock. He rolled his head from side to side, his whole body twitching, and he struggled to get air.

"Kimberly..." he groaned. "I'm... I'm..."

I sucked deeper and hollowed my cheeks. Desmond shouted out as his release filled my mouth. I swallowed and stroked him through an earth-shaking orgasm that rattled his very soul. His head was resting back against the couch, his chest heaved. He laughed, a reaction to the adrenaline that coursed through his veins.

He raised his head and looked at me, his hair tousled. He looked undone. It made me grin. This was payback.

"You'll be the death of me," he said at last. "That was one hell of a way to end our mini-moon."

"Anytime, Mr. Renault." I enjoyed making him lose control after I discovered that my husband's lovemaking verged on the tantric. My orgasms lasted longer and were shattering and powerful.

I loved how he'd been with me the first time after the club, not gentle, but it was fantastic. I never experienced such pleasure. But later, in bed, he'd been soft. He loved, honored, and respected me. He used lovemaking to worship me as if I was the most precious thing in the world. Shit, I couldn't remember a time when I'd been so giving of myself during sex.

I was still refusing to acknowledge I was falling in love with Desmond Renault.

He pulled me into his arms and kissed me. "Thank you. That was just awesome, but I need a nap. I'm shattered. You've worn me out today."

I stood, took his hand, and led him into the bedroom. Pushing him on the bed, I got in beside him and pulled the duvet over us. We slept, both exhausted and satisfied.

The next day, after returning to the mansion, I awoke to Desmond talking in the other room.

"What's going on between you and Kimberly?" Leanne whispered.

"What do you mean?"

"Well, it looks good on the surface. She's mostly here and around a lot with William, but you're not really together, together, are you? I assume you're having sex, but why do you have separate rooms?"

"I'll thank you for keeping your nose out of my marriage and keep your running commentary to yourself."

"But, Des, I don't understand. If you and Kimberly are..."

"Let it go, Leanne," he interrupted. "Kimberly and I are fine. We'll work things out."

"You'll work things out? What does that mean? Not exactly what newlyweds should do; only couples with issues need to work things out."

"I said let it go, Leanne. I have to go," he said.

No one considered us to be anything other than a couple in love besides her. He was a different person when I was around. I shouldn't be eavesdropping, but then again, they shouldn't be having this conversation so close to our bedroom.

Only Desmond and I knew we occupied separate bedrooms, but I guess the jig was up and his sister found out our secret. The thing that worked for us was sex. But I'd leave him after making love. Or if he went to my room, I insisted he returned to his own bed.

We were adventurous in our lovemaking, trying out different things, including some light bondage when he was willing to indulge my fantasies.

But as far as I was concerned, I wasn't quite willing to move fully into the mansion. Our part of the mansion was being renovated according to my specifications, including the installation of a kitchen separate to Hanna's domain. Not that I was going to use it much, but it made the mansion feel more of a home and less of a house share with my mother-in-law. Meanwhile, I spent at least one night per week in my Bay apartment and an occasional night with Angela.

The intimacy we captured during our twenty-four-hour mini-moon evaporated except for when we were in bed. I had sex with him, fantastic sex, but when he was put on the spot, as Leanne just did, it most likely made him wonder about my commitment to him.

Desmond asked me to fully move into the mansion, but I wasn't ready for that. My heart was getting closer and closer to him, but I needed to keep some distance. This was supposed to be a marriage of convenience, and the second I made it real, my heart could be broken. He was working hard to earn my trust and prove he wasn't a womanizer even before we got married.

Our first opportunity to step into the public eye as husband and wife came with our appearance at Madeline's annual fundraising dinner for the Renault Technologies Foundation.

Madeline asked me to be a board member of the foundation and suggested what was an excellent idea. I should say a few words at the event, introducing myself to the assembled group, the movers and shakers of Bayview, as a member of the board, but also as part of the Renault family. I was reluctant, but Desmond persuaded me it would be good exposure for Bennett Technologies and would give me some business contacts.

On the night of the fundraiser, he was sitting on the edge of the bathtub, watching me soak in sweet-smelling bubbles. He reached out and took the sponge and washed my chest and shoulders, paying particular attention to my breasts.

Unable to resist, he leaned over and ran his tongue over each pink nipple poking through the bubbles. My body jumped in the water, splashing him. I palmed his face and kissed him. Our tongues explored each other, and his hand disappeared into the warm water to stroke my stomach and upper thighs. We both moaned as the longing for more took hold. His hand wandered lower to cup me. I placed my hand over his.

He moved back and frowned at me. I shook my head at him. He reached for a towel, stood, and held it open for me. I stood, and he wrapped it around me, lifted me out of the bath, and hoisted me over his shoulder in a fireman's lift. I giggled.

He laid me on my bed and leaned over me with his arms on either side of my body. I stared at him, my eyes filled with lust. He parted my legs and inserted two fingers inside, then leaned down to take a nipple into his mouth. I threaded my fingers through his hair. "You know we're going to be late and your mother won't be impressed," I said with a soft smile.

"I don't care. I want to make love to my wife." He kissed my neck and continued over my shoulders and down my arm. His lips moved back to my breasts.

"Desmond Renault, you need to get dressed and let me do the same or your mother will come looking for us and will find me on top of her son, fucking his brains out."

He laughed. "You're so literal. Okay, I'm going for now."

34

Desmond

THE BREATH CAUGHT in my throat as a vision of loveliness—my wife—came into view. Kimberly wore a simply cut red couture dress, the uppermost part of which consisted of a sheer skin-colored material. It covered her chest, creating both a demure and voluptuous look. The outfit, partly chosen by an excited Leanne, hugged her slender body and showed it off to perfection. *Did she have on any underwear?* Oh God, I hope she didn't so I could have some fun with her under the table tonight.

Her hair was swept to one side, held in place by something apparently invisible that allowed her blond curls to cascade over one shoulder. The only jewelry she wore were the earrings that matched the diamond pendant necklace, a gift I presented to her earlier. My eyes were glued to her as I watched her walk down the stairs.

"You are positively glowing," I said, "and you look absolutely stunning. I'm not sure I'll be able to stop myself from ravishing you in a dark corner somewhere."

"Thank you. My husband is looking particularly dashing

too. I'll have to make sure I stay close to you tonight," she said. "I hope your mother hasn't invited any of your exes who are looking to drag you off into a dark corner because they'll feel my stiletto heel."

"You're lethal, Mrs. Renault," I teased. "Come on, Mom and Angela have left. Ward is waiting."

Our limousine pulled to the beginning of the red carpet a few minutes after Angela and Madeline. The waiting paparazzi surrounded our car.

Kimberly looked anxiously at me. I took her hand and gave it a little squeeze. "It's okay," I said, "I've got you."

Ward opened the car door, and I stepped out first, to a babble of voices shouting my name. I reached a hand out to Kimberly. As soon as she stepped out, more than a dozen cameras flashed in her face. Expecting a scrum, Ward brought in extra security to flank us. They elbowed out of the way anyone who got too close. Disembodied voices shouted out intrusive and impolite questions.

What's it like being a member of the Renault family, Ms. Bennett?

Did you not have a girlfriend until very recently, Mr. Renault?

Did you know him when he was with your sister, Ms. Bennett? Is it true that William is really your son?

Why such a quick marriage? Are you pregnant, Kimberly?

Is this a marriage of convenience, Mr. Renault? A woman's voice pierced through the jangle of voices.

My arms slipped around Kimberly's waist and pulled her close. I kissed her temple. And that was the photograph which would dominate the following day's papers and various magazines over the coming weeks, with articles about how Bayview's most eligible bachelor was no longer available.

We hurried into the hotel and joined Madeline in the

receiving line to welcome the guests. When everyone was finally seated for dinner, Kimberly and I found ourselves at a table with other board members, plus Johnny and Alana as well as Gordon and Angela. Leanne remained at the mansion, with Hanna, to be on hand for William.

Much too soon, Madeline was on stage, making introductory remarks, including presenting the newest board member of the foundation and her new daughter-in-law, whom she invited to say a few words. I knew how nervous she was. That was Kimberly's cue to step on stage. I made sure she was aware of the discreetly placed photographic lenses zooming in on her. She already rehearsed what she would say. It was going to be very brief.

"Ladies and gentlemen," she began... "Good evening. I look forward to getting to know most of you. As you know, The Renault Foundation is about engaging with and investing in our local communities by bringing together the skills and resources to help and support the most disadvantaged. My husband and I, as CEOs of our respective companies, are committed to the development and growth of the community in which we live and work."

She smiled at me to keep herself focused.

"I encourage you to regard the community in which you trade or do business as crucial to your success. Apart from the moral reasons for doing this, our bottom line is also dependent on the health and sustainability of our wider community. Thank you and have a pleasant evening."

There was silence in the room. I was the first on my feet and then followed by others, as applause broke out, directed at the attractive blonde, my beautiful, intelligent wife.

Madeline Renault beamed at her. My mother was right in her assessment. Kimberly was an asset who enhanced the Renault brand. My heart swelled with pride at my firebird. She was everything and more I could want in a life partner. I watched as people swarmed around her, wanting to meet the attractive and younger Mrs. Renault.

When the band started to play, someone asked her to dance, then a second partner stepped in. I looked at my watch and timed the guy. She must be loving all the attention and seeing me in at the corner of the dance floor with my eyes focused on every man that dared to touch her. I was given exactly three minutes before I claimed my wife. It was my turn to rescue her from her groupies. If only I could recapture our mini-moon time and extend it into our everyday life, everything would be perfect.

Later that night, in her room, I leaned back against the door and watched her. "Kimberly," I said softly, "come here."

She came to me. I reached behind her to pull the zipper, letting her dress fall to the floor. "I've been wanting to do that all night long, then bend you over the dining table."

She looked at me with smudged eyes and a soft smile, as she kicked her dress aside. She stood before me naked with just her earrings and silver sandal shoes on.

I stared at her as her hands moved beneath my jacket and pushed it off my shoulders. Fuck, she was going to be the death of me. Every moment of the day I was thinking about what I would get to do next with her. She undid my bow tie, leaving it hanging around my neck, and then she moved down to my belt and zipper. I kicked off my shoes and lifted one knee, then the other to remove my socks, all while keeping my eyes locked on hers.

She pulled my pants and boxer briefs to my ankles to free my erection, and I unbuttoned my dress shirt. She placed open-mouthed kisses across my chest while stroking my rock-hard cock.

I grabbed her ass and pulled her into my body. My hands

roamed all over and a finger found its way into her. She was already wet for me. Our tongues delicately explored each other.

I picked her up, walked to the bed, and laid her on it while I removed my shirt. She was going to be screaming my fucking name tonight. I settled my body between her legs and took hold of my cock and moved it up and down against her until I was coated with her juices.

I cradled her with one arm as I guided myself inside and pushed in slowly. She moaned, holding me close, and then wrapped her legs around my waist. With long, pulsing thrusts, I lost myself in her in the way I loved to do. Kimberly moaned beneath me and called my name.

Desmond... fuck... oh God... please...

The noises she made always excited me. I looked at her as her hips gently rolled beneath mine, our bodies meshed in a slow and sensual dance. It wasn't long before her first orgasm pulsed between us.

———

Today was the day I was going to put an end to my work with Mark, but I had to do it undisturbed. After four long years, I'd had enough of the whole sordid business. Kimberly and William were my life now. They could be endangered. More than that, I no longer wanted to participate in this long-running saga. Even if that meant I'd never get justice, then so be it.

My phone rang before I could make the call. I looked at the screen and shook my head. I really didn't want to deal with the subject of my pending call to Mark right now. But I took the call.

"Svetlana," I said.

"Desmond, *darling*, I've missed you. I haven't seen you for much too long. You're being so mean to me."

"Life has moved on, Svetlana."

"For whom? For you? You're married now. I'm married too, but I told you, it makes no difference to us. I love you. Does your new wife please you as I can? Are you in love with her? Your marriage happened pretty quickly. Is she the mother of your child? That's what the gossip says."

I closed my eyes at the nauseousness while remaining silent.

"Desmond? Are you still there? What is it? You haven't been to Moscow for an entire year. I long to see you. *I miss you, baby.*"

I sighed. "Our relationship is over, Svetlana. We had this conversation a year ago, and we're both married now."

"My being married is of no consequence. Is that why Gerard comes to Moscow, not you? You've been absent from my bed since taking up with that little whore you kept. What was her name, the policewoman? Are you still seeing her?"

I wished I didn't agree to start this. It was fun at the beginning, when I'd taken up with her, not knowing who she was. That was five years ago, after my father died. It was only after Madeline dispatched Svetlana that the FBI made contact, informing me of the plot against my father and his murder, after Damien refused to allow the Bratva to use Renault Tech as a money laundering outlet. The greatest shock was the discovery that my best friend's father, Michael Morse, was the Russian mafia's number one contact in Bayview. He enlisted the Shade's help to bring about the demise of Damien Renault.

At this point, I brought Luke Ward in on everything and we'd ramped up the security at the mansion and around my family. It was part of my motivation for wishing to safeguard William, Kimberly, and her mom, but I was not able to share that information with my wife. The less she knew, the better.

35
Desmond

Sleeping with the enemy was part of the game, but she was part of the pack that killed my father. Instead of getting out, I plunged in deeper. I agreed to work with security agencies to help expose the secretive network in Bayview linked to the Bratva. I visited Moscow to see Svetlana to get further information on the plotters, especially Michael's whereabouts, and also to identify who replaced Michael in Bayview. It became apparent to me I was being targeted as Michael's replacement and Svetlana was being used to reel me in, as my father was before me. Svetlana would drop snippets of information but never enough to get to the mother lode the security agencies were seeking. But now I wanted out; I had for over a year now.

I forced myself to focus on what Svetlana was saying.

"If you cannot come to me, then I'll have to come to you. I need you, Desmond. When I've made my travel plans, I'll let you know."

"What travel plans?"

"Why are you being so slow today, Desmond? You haven't been listening. I've just told you. If you won't come to me, then

I'll have to come to you. It's been too long. I need you inside me."

I breathed. All my senses screamed in disgust. Right now, I'd prefer to slit my wrist than be with her. I didn't want to see her, not even for a casual drink. But the voice in my head pushed that all away. At last, here was light at the end of the tunnel. We could end once this and for all.

"Svetlana, that might be a good idea, but we'd have to meet outside of Bayview."

"Why? Because of your wife? I'd like to meet her, as one of your business contacts, of course. Or is it that bitch Madeline? She hates me for no reason and forced us apart."

I closed my eyes. *No, Svetlana. She had a bloody good reason, and I didn't know. She never said a word.* I'd taken Svetlana's abuse of my mother all this time, and now there was a way to shut her up once and for all.

To this day, I was ashamed of the fact that unbeknownst to me, I took up with my father's former mistress soon after his death and my mother didn't say a word. I was ashamed after I found out that Madeline was repatriating Svetlana Gorev.

"Desmond? Are you still there?"

"Yes, I'm still here. And you need to stop badmouthing my mother. I've told you before."

"It's her fault that I'm languishing over here when I'd prefer to be with you. I know you still have feelings for me and I long for you every day. When I've arranged my travel dates, I'll let you know."

"Goodbye, Svetlana."

"Goodbye, my sweet one. I'll see you soon."

I left my desk and walked to the window. My hands were jammed into my pockets, my shoulders hunched. I stared out at the Bay, where something dark and alien was lurking, waiting to get a stranglehold on it. *Over my dead body*. Which it might well be. That same dark force which operated stealthily, unseen, and underground had taken my father away from my family. I would have justice.

I pulled out my phone and called Mark.

"Hey, buddy. I was going to call you sometime this week. We need to meet. Things are stirring. The buzz in the undergrowth says the Pakhan is planning a visit, but he is sending an emissary out first, and we don't know who it is. We need you to pump your girlfriend for more information."

"Mark, you need to stop calling her my girlfriend or I swear to God…"

"Okay, okay. Don't get huffy. We need you to make a trip soon, like within the week."

"That's why I'm calling you. I just talked to her, and she's coming here."

"What? They're sending Svetlana? Are you sure?"

"That's what she said. She'll give me a date when it's arranged. Why? Isn't that what you wanted?"

Mark hesitated. "We do. It's fantastic. We've got her. See, I knew you were worth your weight in gold."

I lifted an eyebrow. "No, Mark, that's not it. You used and manipulated me when I was at my most vulnerable. It's been four years. Four fucking years, and very little has changed. I caused pain to my mother by doing what you wanted, but I won't destroy my marriage. Do you understand? I will not do it."

"Desmond, you were fucking the Gorev bitch before I came along. You had free will, my friend. You could have said no. Yes, it's been four years, but we have a shitload of valuable intel thanks to you. The end is in sight, Desmond. You can't stop now."

I sighed. I wasn't a hypocrite. Mark was right; I could have said no. But the opportunity to avenge my father's death, to make those responsible pay, was too good to pass up. To this day, except for Luke, nobody knew about my work with the FBI. Not even Johnny knew about Michael's role in the death of his father, and I'd never tell him.

Damien had been more present for Johnny, who only knew that his dad had vanished. If he was grieving, then he never showed me any sign of that.

"You wanted to avenge your father's death," Mark said, "and sometimes we have to do unsavory, unethical, dirty, and underhanded things, Desmond. That's the nature of the beast. Someone has to keep our country safe and pollution free."

I fucking hate this guy.

"As soon as we have our hands on her and know who their connections are in Bayview, we can close the operation and you'll be free. You will get a Presidential Medal of Freedom for your sterling work on top of our Balkan friend, in defense of our country." Mark sniggered.

I snorted. "You're disgusting. I'm hanging up now. I will let you know as soon as I hear from our Balkan friend, as you call her."

"Wait. I need to brief you in person about what to say to Svetlana. She's been ordered here on Bratva business, but she's a pawn and dispensable. That's why they're sending her. You're the prize they want. She'll put a lot of pressure on you to use Renault Tech. Appear to go along with it. We need vital intel, and I don't care what you have to do to get it. This is the opportunity we've been waiting for. Don't screw up, even if you have to screw her to get it."

His voice was annoying as fuck, and I couldn't take any more of his shit. After I hung up, I dialed Ward.

"Desmond?"

"We need to talk."

"Okay. What time shall I pick you up?" Ward asked.

"Late. Pick me up from the office at about nine p.m. Let's drive out of the Bay and have a drink or two at some anonymous bar."

"I'll be waiting."

I texted Kimberly to tell her I'd be working late and to kiss William for me. I let her know Ward and I were having a drink afterward and not to wait up.

It was close to midnight when I got back to the mansion. After too many vodka shots, I was in a foul mood. It made matters worse when I heard the message left by Mark. He was coming to Renault Tech after close of business the following day to brief me, and suggested eight p.m. when the office would be empty.

The mansion was quiet. Everyone would be in bed as I expected. I wanted to hold my firebird in my arms tonight, to bury myself deep inside her and forget, to let go of the dark thoughts that plagued me ever since Svetlana's phone call. But I promised. I wouldn't disturb her, and it was best if I went nowhere near her tonight. For once, I was glad for the separate bedrooms.

I took off my jacket and tie, flung them on the central table, undid my top button, and walked to the living room. It had been a long, tiresome day, but I wasn't ready to go to sleep just yet. The music hit my ears. She was playing. I opened the door very quietly and walked in.

She was sitting at the Steinway in leggings and a baggy t-shirt, her hair tumbled around her shoulders. *My firebird*. I was irreversibly in love with her. Kimberly filled my thoughts. I'd die for her. I watched her and listened to her play. She was unaware of my presence.

Kimberly kept on playing, then stopped and turned to gaze at me.

"It's late," I said. "What are you still doing awake?"

"I couldn't sleep, so I waited for you. You look terrible. What's wrong? Are you okay?"

I stared at her for a long time. "Play something for me," I said. "What were you playing just now? It's familiar."

"Beethoven's *Sonata Claro de Luna* or Moonlight Sonata."

I went over and stood beside her and watched as her fingers moved over the keys, and she got lost in the maestro's haunting strains, powerful and deep in its yearning for something unattainable. There was a lengthy silence once her hands stilled on the last chord. Neither spoke. She turned and looked at me. "What is it, Desmond? Did something happen today? You're tense and on edge. Is that why you went out for a drink with Ward?"

I remained silent.

"Talk to me, please. What's going on? I'm your wife. If there's a problem, we should be able or willing to share with the other."

I stroked her hair. "I just need you. Play some more."

I got a chair and sat beside her. She stared at me, then played 'William's Lullaby' as she called it. I closed my eyes and let the gentle strings soothe me.

When she finished, she stood and took my hand. "If you won't talk to me, let's go to bed."

"You go. I'm okay. I just need to unwind for a little while."

"It's late. Come on, let's go. You can unwind in my bed. I might even let you stay." She grinned.

"I don't think that would be a good idea tonight," I said. For one, I didn't want her to push me, not tonight. And secondly, given the mood I was in, I didn't want to touch her.

She stared at me, perplexed, then sat on my lap. "In that

case, I'm not going anywhere. I'm staying here with you." She put her arms around me, and my arms went around her waist. I laid my head on her chest and listened to her heartbeat. Kimberly rested her head on top of mine before she lifted my head and kissed me. I returned her kiss and my body stirred. I moved my lips away from hers. "You should go to bed."

"I want you. Since you won't come to bed, you better make love to me right here."

"That's not a good idea right now."

She smiled. "I want you to fuck me, Desmond. Now! I won't ask you again."

I chuckled. "You're so bossy."

She pulled me up. Her hands went to my belt and my zipper. In a short time, my pants and boxers were around my ankles. She gripped my already stiffened cock and smiled. Within seconds, Kimberly's leggings were off, and she reached over and closed the piano. *God, she's so fucking sexy.* She placed both hands on top and pushed her ass out.

"I won't ask again, Desmond. Fuck your wife... hard and fast or slow and sensual... whatever you need to get you out of this funk..."

I pulled her panties down to her feet and slapped her ass; she jumped at the unexpectedness of it. "You're such a little temptress," I whispered in her ear. I kissed the reddened spot on her ass, soothed it with my tongue, and pushed two fingers into her slick passage from behind. My other hand reached beneath her t-shirt to massage her bare breast. I closed my eyes, enjoying the feel of her. She moaned and ground on my hand.

My thumb rubbed around her clit, making her hips jerk upward. My fingers brushed a spot inside of her that made her cry out. I removed my fingers and grabbed her hips as I pushed myself inside her. Her body was like a temple and I would worship it for the rest of my life.

I groaned and moved, thrusting into her hard, my hands gripping her hips to keep her still. My pelvis smacking into her ass made raunchy noises that spurred me on and added to the heat in the room.

"Let me hear you," I growled as she tried to muffle the noises spilling from her mouth. I fucked her hard and fast. Just what I needed, and she knew. I pounded into her until she was speaking in tongues. "Come for me baby, now!" I growled. My fingers rubbed her clit. I was ready and exploded inside her as her own orgasm rumbled through us both.

I bent down, resting my head on her back, my cock twitching inside her. "Are you okay?" I asked. "I didn't hurt you, did I?"

"No, that was fucking amazing."

I helped her straighten up. Anyone could have walked in on us, and that was even more thrilling. I dressed her and fixed my own clothes before heading upstairs.

"Stay with me tonight," I said as we reached my room.

She nodded.

36
Kimberly

AFTER PUTTING WILLIAM TO BED, I drank a glass of wine with my new mother-in-law, Madeline Renault. She wanted to know if there were any points of collaboration between Renault Tech and Bennett Technologies. I wasn't in the mood to talk much. Though I found Madeline to be quite pleasant, which was not at all her typical demeanor. All I could think of was my husband, Desmond. I wanted to be with him, figuring out what was going on that was making him angry and so I told Madeline I needed to go back to the office for a while.

"You work late, then?" she asked, sipping her own glass of wine. It came across more like a dig than a compliment. We both knew that if Desmond was going back to the office, she wouldn't hesitate to pat him on the back, but women didn't get the same treatment even from other women, I supposed.

I nodded. "It's the only way to get things done these days." I decided to go see Desmond, despite it being late. After all, he was my husband now, and I had needs that weren't fulfilled yet today. He was slacking. So, after changing into some lingerie under a short black dress, I threw on a heavier coat and couldn't wait until he caught sight of me. Maybe he would take me right there on his desk and say fuck it to whatever was keeping him at the office this late.

"Well, I won't keep you any longer," Madeline said, rising from her chair. She gave me a hug and a peck on the cheek. "Be safe. And enjoy your evening."

Living with Madeline was one thing, but a peck on the cheek was almost taking it too far. She never quite appeared a maternal figure, and now I was second-guessing myself. Maybe she wasn't as bad. "Thanks, you too."

I made my way out of the house. The night air was cool, and the stars twinkled in the sky. I took a deep breath, got into my car, and took off toward the Renault office building. The streets were empty compared to dinner hours, and my heart was pounding.

When I arrived, Ward was sitting outside the building in the Trailblazer. I drove my car into the small executive parking lot. If this was another boys' night out, I was going too.

I took the elevator to the executive floor and headed to Desmond's office. When I arrived, he was sitting at his desk, eyes closed and head in his hands. I watched him in silence, blinking back tears. He looked so peaceful and content in that moment, and I wanted to be in that moment forever. I wanted to be with him, holding him and feeling his warmth, until someone else was pacing in his office. So, he was working?

I opened the door, not wanting to interrupt, but at least let him know I was here, so I didn't look like a creep. He opened his eyes and smiled at the sight of me. The strain in his eyes proved he was not having a good day, and the man was waving his hands around before I went in, almost like he was scolding my husband.

"What are you doing here?" Desmond said, standing at his desk.

When the man turned around, I gasped. My eyes widened and my face froze in a stricken expression. I howled like a wounded animal.

Before either of them could move toward me, I was gone.

I ran to the elevator to get away, but changed my mind. Desmond was bound to come after me. I removed my heels and flew down the stairs, then stopped short. I'd never make it to reception before Desmond, and I couldn't chance the elevator. So I headed for the ladies' restroom two floors from the executive floor and locked myself in a stall. My body doubled over. The perspiration was streaming off me and my heart was thumping. I was going to pass out. What was my husband doing with someone I'd hoped I'd never seen again in my life?

The only person I could call was Barb. I tried to calm myself long enough to dial her number without dropping my phone. I didn't want to draw attention to the bathroom and since no one else was in the office, any noise would be a distraction.

"Hey, what's up?" she answered in a cheerful voice, having a great night at home that I was about to ruin.

"Something bad has happened. I'm okay, but I need you to pick me up." I try to keep my voice as unwavering as possible, because I didn't want her to call the police, but I couldn't tell her any more until I was out of this fucking building.

"Where are you?"

"Come to the back of the Renault office building. I'll meet you there. Whatever you do, don't stop in the front. Ward is parked there and he must not see you. I'll meet you at the entrance at the back of the building. How long will you be?"

The shuffling on the other end told me she was rushing around trying to get dressed. "At this time of night... about twenty minutes. I'll text you when I get there."

The wait for Barb was excruciating and felt like ten years.

Everything startled me, thinking that man was going to find me. Why was he here with Desmond? How did they know each other? Was this all a setup?

When Barb's text came through, I took the elevator down to reception and took the last flight of stairs to the parking garage.

"Mrs. Renault..." Bert, the security guard, tried to get my attention, but I was gone.

37

Desmond

UNABLE TO FIND KIMBERLY, I took the elevator back to the executive floor and strode into the ladies' room. I pushed the door of every cubicle. She was not in there. Frustrated, I went back to my office. "Do you want to tell me what just happened?" I said to the man waiting in my office.

"Desmond, I don't know... I..."

"Cut the crap, Mark. Kimberly recognized you. Did you see the look on her face? She was terrified. How does she know you, Mark, and why do you scare the shit out of my wife?"

Mark sighed. "Yes, I know Kimberly Bennett. She works for the FBI."

"My wife is an FBI agent. Is that your answer? I'm going to ask you again. How do you know my wife?"

"That's not what I meant. She's not an agent. She is a contractor for the security services. The app on your phone that you use make secure calls to me was produced by her company."

I stared at the man. "Okay, but that does not explain her

reaction to you. What is going on, Mark? And none of your bullshit."

"Have you read that report I sent you, Desmond? Most of it is in there. She got in trouble with her boyfriend in Boston and we had to question her."

"You questioned her about something that happened with her boyfriend? You need to be more specific."

"For God's sake, man, read the damn report," said Mark, exasperated at being interrogated.

"I'm sure the report won't tell me why my wife ran as if all the bats of hell were after her when she saw you."

Mark ran a hand over his face. "We interrogated her."

"By we, you mean you."

"Yes, I was there."

"You tortured her," I said in a flat, even tone. The strong urge to grab the man by the throat and squeeze the life out of him grew.

"No. Of course not. Don't be so melodramatic."

"What's your definition of torture, Mark? You scared a young woman witless and left her having horrendous nightmares. Did you know that? She has terrible nightmares. What did you do to her? I swear to God if you don't tell me what you did to Kimberly, I'll throw you through the damn window."

"You know it's a crime to lay a hand on a federal officer, right?"

"I don't give a damn. Tell me what happened to Kimberly."

"Okay, okay. She had information we needed. It was a matter of national security. She might have experienced a bit of sleep deprivation, that's all."

"And how long did that go on for?" My voice was calm, and it scared the hell out of him.

"Six weeks."

"Six weeks? What are you, a sadistic monster?"

"I told you, we don't torture peop—"

"Stop talking," I shouted, striding to my office door and opening it. "Get out! I need to find my wife. You and I will talk after I've found her."

"We haven't finished our conversation. Gorev could arrive any day and we have to get this right."

"I don't give a damn about Svetlana Gorev. She's your problem and you need to leave before I forget you're a federal agent." My tone was cold and unemotional.

Mark grabbed his jacket from the back of his chair and scuttled past me. I stared at the agent's back as the man walked away. My eyes were glacial. All I could see was Kimberly's beautiful face, stricken in terror. I didn't want to think about what she might have endured. I had no doubt that he used psychological torture to get what he wanted. It broke my heart to think about my firebird in Mark's clutches, even for an hour. I now knew what her nightmares were about and who she was talking to.

My office phone rang. "Yes, Albert?"

"Your wife left through the parking lot, sir," he answered.

"Thanks. By the way, Albert, my visitor is on his way down. Once he's left, please remove the film from the security camera. I'll pick it up on my way out."

Ever vigilant since Damien's murder, I trusted no one, and Mark least of all. I might require evidence of Mark entering and leaving Renault Tech at some stage. I called Kimberly and for the third time, the call went to voicemail. The next call was to the mansion. Hanna told me Kimberly went to her office about an hour ago. The next call was to Ward.

"I've lost Kimberly. She was here and left. Now she's not answering my calls. There are two more places she might be. I think she's avoiding me."

"I saw her drive into the parking lot and she hasn't left, Desmond. She must be in the building somewhere."

"No. Security saw her going to the parking lot just a minute ago. I'll meet you there. Look for her car."

We found her car, but there was no sign of Kimberly. I ran my hand through my hair. I was losing my mind. "Let's go to Sunnyside. Either she's there or Angela will know where she is."

We squealed into the driveway, and I jumped out of the car, worried for my wife's safety. Angela met me at the door. "I'm confused, Desmond, what's going on? Did the two of you have a fight?"

"No. Nothing like that. She came by my office and the person with me upset her. Where is she? What did she say? I need to talk to her."

"Who was it? Did this person do something to her?"

"It was somebody she knew in Boston. I don't think the relationship ended well, but that's all I know. Angela, I must see Kimberly. Please tell me where she is. Is she with Barbara?"

"Yes, she is, but she doesn't want to see you. She sounded like something, I don't know. Scared?"

My heart was breaking. If Mark caused her nightmares, as I suspected, and then she found him with me... "I need Barbara's number, Angela. If Kimberly won't talk to me, I need to talk to Barbara."

"Yes, okay. I'm worried. Was the person with you Chad Norton? Do you know him?"

"No, Angela. It was someone I've known for years. He works for the government."

"I think I should come back to the mansion tonight. I don't know what's happening to my baby girl, and I want to be around for William."

"Yes, of course. My mom will take care of him, but there

can never be too many grandmas. You know, you need to move in with us. The mansion has plenty of room."

"I want to stay in my own home. But I'll spend time with my grandson as often as I can. If you and Kimberly met and fell in love in the normal way and got married, I'm sure you wouldn't want your mother-in-law cramping your style."

"Yes, I would. I want you to come and live with us in the mansion, and I won't stop trying to persuade you. And I've told you, your daughter is the love of my life. I fell in love with her the first night I met her."

"Yes, you have, and I'm glad to hear that. You must tell her."

"We were doing so well, but today has been an enormous setback. Come on, let's go home. I mean, your other home," I said with a grin.

I was relieved to hear that Kimberly was safe.

As soon as I got home, I called Barbara.

"She's not okay. I've seen her like this once before, in Boston. I think she needs you, but she keeps saying she can't trust you. What happened in your office today?"

"She saw someone from her past who hurt her, but I didn't know. When he told me he knew Kimberly Bennett, I thought nothing of it. Barb, I need to speak to her, see her."

"I don't know. I think you'd only make it worse if you tried to speak to her. Look, it's late. Why don't you leave it until the morning? I'll call you when I know how she is. Try to get some sleep."

I couldn't sleep; instead, I tossed and turned. Images of Kimberly with Mark drifted past my mind's eye. The broken sobs and her begging to be left alone from that first night in the mansion. I got up and went downstairs to get myself a large whiskey. When I returned, I was surprised to see I missed a call from Barbara.

"What's wrong?"

"It's Kimberly. You need to get here as soon as you can."

"On my way," I said. "Text me your address."

When I arrived at the door of Barbara's apartment, I texted her. The door was opened almost immediately. Barbara put a finger to her lips and ushered me into the kitchen, the room nearest to the apartment door.

"She's only just gone back to sleep again, but I got scared. She had a terrible dream. When I went to her, she lashed out at me. I told her I was calling you and she cried. She kept talking about you and someone called Voldemort. I can't get any sense out of her. What's going? Who's Voldemort, apart from that character in *Harry Potter*?"

I shrugged. I'd neither read *Harry Potter* nor seen the movies. "Someone was in my office tonight. He's a federal agent and Kimberly knew him from before. She was terrified of him."

"That makes sense," said Barbara. "This is how she was before and during Chad's trial. She had terrible nightmares then."

"So, who is this Voldemort character?" I asked.

"He was a dark sorcerer who killed Harry Potter's parents and wanted to kill him."

"Barbara," Kimberly's voice called. "Is Desmond here? I told you I didn't want to see him."

"Wait here. Let me talk to her."

She left me in the kitchen and went into the living room where Kimberly was now sitting up on the couch, wrapped in a blanket.

"He's here, isn't he?" Kimberly said. "I told you I didn't

want to see or talk to him. I don't trust him. No, in fact, get him. I want some answers."

I could hear the conversation from here, so I strolled into the room.

"Stay there. Don't come any closer," Kimberly said.

"Okay," I said and stood still. I unfolded my arms. "May I sit?"

Barbara moved to pass me a chair from the dining table.

"What was Voldemort doing in your office? Are you spying on me?" asked Kimberly.

"Shall I leave you two to talk?" asked Barbara.

"No. I want you to stay, Barb," said Kimberly.

"His name is Mark," I answered, "and I know he hurt you. I'm so sorry, Kimberly. I'm not spying on you. I knew Mark for several years before I met you."

"Is that his name? I prefer Voldemort. How do you know him? Is he your friend?"

I hesitated and looked at Barbara.

"Look, Kim, why don't I leave you and Desmond to talk in private?"

"No. I don't want to be left alone with him. If you won't stay, then he has to leave."

Her words made my heart ache. My firebird feared me. She put me in the same bracket as Mark. "I'd never hurt you. Mark is not my friend. I have been working with him. When I found out what he had done to you, I wanted to kill him."

"What did he tell you?"

"He said he interrogated you for six weeks."

Kimberly laughed hysterically and then sobbed.

"Make her some sweet tea, lots of sugar. I have some red berry tea bags in a jar beside the stove. The sugar is there too. Hurry," said Barbara, who went and sat beside Kimberly and put her arms around her friend.

"Let it out. You've carried it for too long," Barbara told her.

Kimberly nodded, lifting her tear-stained face to look at Barbara. They sat in silence until I returned with three cups on a tray. "I think we all need something hot and sweet," he said.

We all sat in the room in silence. Two of them waited on the third. Neither of us wanted to push her.

Kimberly's eyes were red, her face blotchy. Terror filled her eyes and he was scared because not even her best friend knew the whole story. She had been keeping this to herself for years.

"Before I tell you about Voldemort, I want to know why you are working with him. And I want the truth, the whole truth."

I hesitated. My natural inclination was to hold back to protect her from the sordidness of it all, from the truth about Michael and Svetlana, from the truth about myself, my preparedness to fall in with Mark and sleep with Svetlana after I knew of her role in my father's death. *Fuck.* What kind of person was I? I slept with my dead father's mistress, whom I now despised. I couldn't share that with her, and especially in Barbara's presence. I was too ashamed.

I was filled with self-disgust, but I took one look at Kimberly's face and knew I risked losing her if I was not as open with her as possible. But there were certain things I couldn't tell her.

"I need to know what that hateful man was doing in your office." Kimberly's voice was tremulous now.

"Mark contacted me a year after my father died," I began. "The FBI had knowledge of a conspiracy to kill him, which originated with the Russian mafia."

"You know about that?" Kimberly said with incredulity.

My brow wrinkled. I stared at her. "What do you know about it? Did the FBI tell you? Mark said you worked for them."

Barbara stared at her friend. "Kim? Is that true? You work for the FBI?"

"It's a business arrangement. I'll get to that in a minute. I know about you and the FBI, because when you stopped me from adopting William, I got a report on you, searching for something I could use against you. The authorities had surveillance on you because you were involved in some sort of criminal activity."

"You thought that and still married me? How did you get this information? Why am I asking? I should know Mark can't be trusted. He sent me a report on you, too."

Kimberly's eyes widened. "When?"

"I expect it would have been around the same time as you were investigating me and for the same purpose."

Kimberly laughed. "So, we spied on each other, and didn't trust each other. Remind me why we got married again?"

"Because I asked you to marry me, and you said yes, even if I were a criminal, because we both wanted custody of William. A marriage of convenience is the easiest way to solve a problem."

"Yes," said Barbara. "One week you were sworn enemies, the next week husband and wife. I just don't get the two of you and this weird marriage."

We both ignored her.

"But that's not the reason I married you, Kimberly. I asked you to marry me because I love you; I fell in love with you." *There. I'd said it. She needed to know.* "It took just six weeks for me to fall head over heels in love with you. In fact, it took less than a day. I wanted you in my life the moment I saw you. The custody hearing just provided a shortcut. I love you and I would never, ever knowingly do anything to hurt you. And I don't want to lose you. I can't lose you."

Kimberly stared at me. Her eyes filled and she shook her

head. "You don't love me; you only think you do. I'm unlovable and I have proof of that. You're only saying it for fear that I'll leave you and take William. Tell me about Svetlana. When was the last time you were in Russia with her?"

I got up from my chair and paced the floor. *Jesus Christ. She knows about that too?*

"And what about Michael Morse," Kimberly continued. "Was he part of the conspiracy too? Is that why he disappeared from Bayview?"

I stopped pacing and stared hard at my wife. My eyes narrowed. "You're well informed," I said. "Perhaps even better than I am. What else do you know? Did you get that information from Mark?"

"No. I want nothing to do with that man, and I want you to stop working with him. You can't trust him. He's a monster."

All I could think about was killing that man with my bare hands, but then I would go to prison and William would grow up without a father.

"He held me in indefinite detention without trial, like some sort of terrorist. He interrogated me for six entire weeks. I'd be woken at some ungodly hour every night and taken to a room where he and a sidekick, some callow youth probably learning the trade, waited for me. I never knew their names, so I christened the evil one Voldemort, a perfect fit for who he is."

She shuddered. It was becoming too much for her, and she recoiled.

"He is indeed an evil man," I said.

"They interrogated me for hours. It happened day after day after day until I lost my mind. Voldemort enjoyed his power over me. He threatened me with thirty years to life for conspiracy to defraud the government and hacking confidential information to sell to foreign interests. It was all a lie."

I couldn't believe she was involved in something like this.

Or that she was even on the FBI's list. Although, with her tech knowledge, it kind of made sense.

"Yes, Chad used the code I created to hack into government computers and erase data on student loans. It was an act of liberation. But then he stole money from government contractors because he could access their financial information, again using the super-virus I produced. They had proof that the hack originated from his personal computer where he lived, not from mine. He even admitted it."

So, he was the one who did that.

38

Kimberly

"My detention had nothing to do with selling information endangering national security. Voldemort made that up. Do you know what he wanted? He wanted information on my father, a cybercriminal known as The Calculator, wanted by the FBI. He sold government secrets he acquired to the highest bidder. I didn't even know that until Voldemort told me. He wanted me to tell him my dad's whereabouts because he believed I either knew where he was or how to contact him. I didn't. I do not know where my father is and have had no contact with him since he left when I was eight years old."

When my eyes locked on his, his mouth was open and he rubbed his forehead. Now my husband knew what he was getting into with me. I came with baggage, a lot of it, and my nightmares would probably never go away. After all this time, the thing that was haunting me was out in the open. I expected them to throw me out of their lives after that, but they didn't.

"So, your wife is the daughter of a wanted criminal, and her former boyfriend is in jail. I'm sure that information is in your file on me. Why didn't you give it to the judge? She would have given you sole custody of William." I cried softly, holding my elbows tightly at my sides.

Barbara and Desmond looked at each other. I was helpless. Barb, who was sitting on the couch next to me, touched my arm. "It's okay, continue. You need to tell all of it."

My dry mouth was soothed by the warm tea, and then my chest tightened. I never wanted anyone to know about my time with Mark. In fact, I did everything I could to erase those six weeks from my memory, but nothing worked. "They kept me in a cell in some FBI *out of the way* place. They took my clothes and gave me their standard kit. Other than when someone brought my meals, I saw no one, and nobody spoke to me for an entire week. They only let me out to have a shower every few days. Then, for the next four weeks, they would wake me up every night for interrogation. Voldemort played bad cop. He did all the threatening and banging on the table."

Desmond's fists clenched, but I tried not to watch. The more I spoke, the madder he got, and I didn't want him to do anything stupid. We had William to think about now.

"He would yell in my face, his saliva spotting my skin. I feel sick just thinking about it." Barbara passed the trash can as I started to gag. I shook my head. "It's okay," I told her with tears rolling down my cheeks. "I want to talk about this. By the fifth week, I was a total wreck. Every day, I begged his henchmen not to take me, but they did. Can you imagine what that was like, week after week for six whole weeks? Can you? It was a dehumanizing experience."

Barbara's eyes didn't leave me but once to look away so I couldn't see the tears shed.

"The following week they told me I was going home, and they put me in a proper room with a bed and a bathroom. The people who brought my food talked to me and I never laid eyes on Voldemort again until today. In return for my freedom, I had to give evidence against Chad and agree to work for them for five years as a private contractor. They pay me, but not the true value of what I do for them. They monitor my movements online and told me they would put me in jail if I was ever found engaging in specific activities online."

I glanced at Desmond, not ready to divulge my cyber-Goth identity. The Master Hacker, Ghost Fox Goddess who traversed the dark web, could get any information required and obliterate my enemies. My husband didn't need to know that, not yet, if ever.

"They gave me a minder, an older retired FBI guy," I continued. "I know him as Zachary Warner, if that's even his real name. I had to see him once a week until Chad's trial, and I have to keep in contact with him once a month until the five years is up. Zachary is kind and fatherlike, but I'm sure that's just a façade. He got me the report on you, but I don't trust any of them. Now I find my husband working with them. How do you think I felt, Desmond, when I saw that man in your office?"

He came to me then and sat on the floor beside me, but didn't touch me, although I wanted him to gather me in his arms and tell me no one would ever hurt her again.

"Kimberly, I'm so sorry. I didn't know any of this."

"What did the report say about me? I'm betting Voldemort told you nothing about what he did to me."

"I don't know what the report said. It's in my safe in the mansion. I haven't read it. That first night you had a nightmare, I wanted to read it then, but I waited until you wanted to tell me yourself. I'm sorry that it had to be like this, that you had to go through the trauma of seeing Mark again."

"I don't want you to work with him. I understand you want revenge or justice for your dad, but can't you work with someone else?"

Desmond shrugged. "Whatever happens, you'll never have

to see Mark, or Voldemort, again. Whether I work with him, I have to see this through. After many years, it's almost over. Svetlana Gorev is coming here soon, and we've been trying to get her here so they can arrest her as part of the conspiracy."

"Svetlana Gorev is coming here? Are you going to see her?"

"That's the plan," he said.

I stared at him. Did my husband still have a sexual relationship with that woman? I wouldn't put up with that. There was more I needed to say and to know about Svetlana and Morse and about whether Madeline knew how her husband had died. We had more to talk about, but not now. My eyes were burning and every muscle in my body ached with a vengeance.

"Can I hold you? I need to hold you. I love you so much," Desmond said.

I nodded because his warm embrace was just what I required.

Barbara made her way out of the room, leaving us together. It had been a dramatic and shocking night for me. Such revelations. One thing I was certain of, I'm in love with my husband.

Desmond sat on the couch beside me. I shared my blanket with him. His arms went around me, and my head rested on his chest. He closed his eyes and we were both asleep within minutes.

We woke the next morning.

"Hi," he said. "Good morning. How are you feeling?"

"Much better," I said. "We still have to talk. There are some things I want to know."

"Okay. I've made coffee. Do you want some?"

I wrinkled my nose. "No, not yet. We don't have to talk now either. You should get back to the mansion."

"I don't want to leave you. Why don't you come home with me? I don't think you should go into the office today, and you should talk to Angela. She's worried about you."

"I know. I'll call her later, but I need to go to work. My car is in the Renault Tech parking lot and I don't want to ask Barb, she needs to get to work."

"Tell you what," he said. "I'll ask Luke to pick you up and take you to your car. How about we have lunch and you can ask me whatever you want to know?"

"No. Let's talk tonight. Can you pick William up from school with me? Let's spend some time with him and have dinner at home. We can talk then."

He nodded. "I'll make that happen." He bent to kiss my cheek. "I better go. Tell Barbara I said goodbye. I'll see you later," he said, walking away.

At the door, he turned. "Kimberly, I love you."

I stared at him. That was difficult for me. I'm not lovable, so whether he loves me, I couldn't open myself up to let him truly love me. My heart wouldn't allow it after being shredded so many times. Men didn't stay. All they did was break my heart.

Later that night, once we put William to bed, the two of us sat at the dining table eating the meal Hanna prepared. Madeline was out with Gerard, and Leanne left for the club. Apart from William and Hanna, we were alone in the mansion.

We talked about William and his upcoming school performance, and Madeline's interest in collaboration between our companies. We both avoided the subject of Mark.

"Come on," I said when the meal was over, "let's clean up and then take the rest of the wine into the living room."

"Okay, but only if you play something for me."

Desmond relaxed on the couch while I played a medley of theme tunes from various movies. When I finished, I got up and went to sit beside him. He took my hand. "That was wonderful, thank you. We should do this more often."

I stared at him. "Do Madeline and Leanne know Michael murdered Damien?"

He stiffened and his brown eyes bored into me, as if searching my very soul. He withdrew his hand from mine and got up and walked to the floor-to-ceiling windows that looked out over the mansion grounds to the summerhouse where he first kissed me. His jaws were working. He remained silent. Of all the questions I could ask, this was one he hadn't bargained for. I went and stood beside him. "Desmond, tell them. They deserve to know."

"No, my mother and sister went through enough heartbreak at the loss of Dad to last them a lifetime. It was an entire year after his death before I knew the truth. I'm not putting them through that again."

"But, Desmond, I... wouldn't you..."

"Kimberly, that's enough. I have some work to do," he said, cutting across my words. "I'll be in the study for a couple of hours. Good night. I'll see you in the morning."

I was left staring at his retreating back. *Uh-oh, that is obviously a taboo subject.*

I hadn't seen this Desmond before, brusque and uncommunicative. Not since that night in my office building, when he'd walked away after telling me I would hear from his lawyer. Then he'd been cold and angry. This was something else. I knew him as an attentive and passionate lover. This person was almost scary. He disengaged from me.

A lot had happened since that night when he'd strode into my life, asserting that my nephew was his son. This man whom I'd disparaged as a man-whore a few months ago was now my husband, and the weirdest thing of all was I was falling in love with him. In a short time, he became my husband, my lover, and my rock. Yet I was not ready to give him my heart.

The only knowledge of what happened to his father came from Zachary's report, and I'd been wrong about Desmond not knowing of his father's murder. I would leave him in his own space and whatever was going on in his head.

I went back to my piano and played until I was tired enough to sleep. I went to my own room and prepared for bed, then I crawled between the sheets.

When Desmond walked into his room, if he was startled to find me in his bed, he didn't show it. Without saying a word, he went into the bathroom. He came out, got into bed, and lay on his back beside me. I sat up and turned to him, palming his face. His brown eyes stared at me. "I'm sorry," I whispered before laying my head on his chest.

He put an arm around me and closed his eyes.

I couldn't imagine a life without him in it anymore.

39
Kimberly

"Are you serious? You want me there?" I asked, shaking my head and pulling at my clothing as my stomach quivered.

"Yes."

"Why? I don't want to meet Svetlana." She peered at him through her lenses. "Oh, you want me to be the buffer?"

"Kimberly, please," he pleaded. "It's not that. Well, it is sort of, but it's more that I want to avoid any ugliness in the tabloids. We should meet outside of Bayview, but on the off chance someone photographs us together, it would look worse. If you are there, it stops the gossip."

"Okay, but will she talk in front of me?"

"No, she won't. You'd arrive with me and perhaps stay for a drink, but only if you want to. Then you and Luke can wait in a nearby bar, and I'll call you when we're done. I'll try to keep it to under an hour."

"Okay. That works for me. So, tell me what's going on with Gorev, what's the plan?"

Desmond surprised me by asking for my attendance. Especially with everything involved. We were sharing a pint of mint chocolate chip ice cream, sitting side by side on the couch in my penthouse before he had to leave to meet with Svetlana in her hotel bar.

"Come on, Desmond, no holding back. You need to tell me what's going on. Unless you don't trust me."

"I trust you. But the less you know and are involved in all this, the safer you are and the better I'll feel."

"I'm not in any danger here. You are. Besides, if anyone's in a threatening situation, the more they know, the less vulnerable they are. I'm not some whey-faced Victorian damsel." I stared at him. The set of his jaw was telling me that this was going to be like pulling teeth. "Tell you what," I said, "why don't I ask you a question to begin with?"

He looked at me through narrowed eyes. He agreed. "Okay."

"If she's not here to fuck you, what does Svetlana want?"

He chuckled. "I can always depend on you to punch me right in the solar plexus. The Russian mob has been wanting to hook Renault Tech into money laundering. It began with my dad. When he threatened to expose them, and Michael in particular, well, you know the rest."

This was dangerous. My husband was going into dangerous territory and my stomach clenched, thinking the worst. What if something happened? The Russian mob didn't play games and what if they found out that Desmond was working with the FBI?

"So now they're coming after me. They see me as Michael's replacement. If I agree, the Pakhan will pay me a visit to put his seal of approval on it all and that's what the FBI wants. We need to know more about him, his name and what he looks like. No one knows his name or who he is. Secondly, there are the small fries who run minor operations in the Bay, but they are so well camouflaged, the FBI could not get a handle on them. We think Svetlana will contact them while she is here. They'll track her and will identify and eliminate the foot soldiers."

"Is this Voldemort's plan?" I asked.

"His name is Mark. It might help you work through that horrible experience if you made him a real person, not some looming menacing shadow that has power over you. He doesn't."

Not happening. "No. I won't make him a real person. He knew my name; I wasn't allowed to know his. I'll stick to the name I gave him. I'm a real person, but he didn't treat me like one. The name suits him. He abuses his power and is evil. He should not be allowed to interact with human beings. I don't know why you want to work with him. To me, he will always be Voldemort."

And one day I'm going to take him out.

I wished he could take the pain and distress of that experience from me. It emotionally exhausted me from having to dredge up and relive that experience with Mark I'd kept locked away all these years.

"Let's not talk about that man," I said. "This isn't about him; it's about you. This whole thing doesn't hang together; it's too easy. How do you know this Pakhan person will visit you and when? While Svetlana is here? I don't think Voldemort is telling you everything."

"I'm certain that I don't know everything, but they need to know who he is. Up to now, he's been faceless. All they know from assets in Russia is that he will be coming here once Svetlana has confirmed I'm on board."

"I don't like it. Something's off. You said they plan to arrest Svetlana, but that's stupid, unless they arrest the Pakhan as well. I'm not minimizing your importance or Renault Tech's, but if this guy's identity is so hush-hush, what makes you so important that he will come out in the open to meet you on foreign soil? That makes no sense."

He grinned. "My wife is quite the little forensic analyst, I see. They've been grooming me for the last five years. I've had to do a few things to give them confidence in my trustworthiness, but it's all been monitored and managed by the FBI, who provided the funds. I just played a part. Plus, Renault Tech has subsidiaries all over the world and that's an enormous advantage for them. They can spread their tentacles with little effort."

"Does Gerard and your mother know about this?"

"No, of course not. We had to keep the circle as tight as possible. That's why FBI funds were used whenever the Bratva wanted me to pay my dues. I'll tell them once it's over."

What would he have told me if I hadn't walked in on that man in his office?

"The flaw in the plan is still the arrest of Svetlana," I said. "That will not happen. It would blow the whole thing wide open. Surely you see that. Voldemort is playing games. He has no intention of arresting Svetlana, I'm telling you. He's devious. He'll use any means necessary to get what he wants and doesn't care about the collateral damage."

"The plot is thicker than that. It surprised us that she was the one being sent to the advanced party. That means she is expendable. She is the price the mob will pay to get me. They already know that our government suspects her of being involved in a conspiracy with Michael to kill my father. That ground has been laid over the last few years. They suspect they will pick her up if she ever returns to this country. That information has been fed to them, too."

I shook my head. The alarm bells rang. It was something Desmond said earlier which made little sense, and I couldn't for the life of me remember what it was. But it made everything implausible, on top of which Voldemort was not to be trusted and I couldn't make Desmond take that on board.

"So, will Voldemort be listening to it all? He should because they have my tech."

"Is it a two-way earpiece that looks like a thumbnail?"

"Yup. Did they give you one?"

He nodded and showed me the tiny nondescript item, which indeed looked like a thumbnail but was a powerful two-way transmitter to fit into his ear.

"Are you in?" he asked.

"Yes, okay, but I don't think I should have a drink. I'll stay for five or ten minutes, then leave."

"Fine," he said. "Time to go."

Desmond's left hand landed on the small of my back as we stepped out of the revolving doors into the lobby of the InterContinental Barclay Hotel, the newest and most expensive appendage to Bayview. He glanced toward the bar shaped like a donut ring and spotted Svetlana. Desmond propelled me forward. "Hello, Svetlana," he said as we approached her. She got off the barstool and waited to greet him.

"Desmond, darling." She kissed him on both cheeks. "It's so nice to see you after such a long time." Svetlana focused her entire attention on him while ignoring me at his side.

Desmond turned. "Kimberly, this is Svetlana Gorev, Svetlana my wife, Kimberly Bennett."

"Oh my dear," Svetlana gushed in my direction. "I'm so sorry. I thought you were Desmond's assistant. Please excuse my rudeness. It's so nice to meet you. I've read a lot about you in the tabloids. Congratulations on your marriage."

"Thank you, Ms. Gorev," I said. "I don't believe I know anything about you, except that you were Damien Renault's assistant at one time. I'm told those tabloids carried more photographs of me than words about me." There was a flush that subsumed Svetlana's face.

"Are you going to stay for a drink, honey?" Desmond asked me, knowing full well that was not the plan.

"I need to go, actually. I have a meeting in half an hour. It was so nice to meet you. I hope we'll meet again sometime."

"I hope you'll call me Svetlana because I'm sure we're going to become friends. I've known Desmond for such a long time. I'd hate to lose our friendship."

The woman looked at me with an icy stare. *So Svetabitch, that's how you want to play it? Well, I'll fix you.*

I turned to Desmond and whispered in his ear, "If you let Gorev lay a grimy paw on you, I'll pickle your you-know-what."

He chuckled. "I love you too, my sweet," he said. "Call you when I'm finished here. Won't be long."

"Miss you already," I said, giving him a wink.

40

Desmond

I couldn't contain my laughter. She was outrageous. She walked away with that provocative sway to her hips. We were looking forward to our weekend. For the entire two days, I was going to impose a no underwear rule. I was looking forward to fucking her into oblivion.

"My, my, Desmond Renault," said Svetlana. "Do my eyes deceive me? You're in love with her, aren't you?"

"Yes. I love Kimberly very much. And you were being rude with that little stunt you just pulled. You know she is the CEO of her own company."

"So, are the rumors true? She is the mother of your illegitimate son and the sister story is just a smoke screen, pardon the pun." Svetlana's laughter rang out around them.

"All you need to know is that we're the parents of a beautiful little boy. Now, let's get down to business."

Svetlana stared at me. "Now that you're married, Desmond, this whole thing is looking less secure to my people."

"Oh? Why is that?" I asked.

"Can your wife be trusted? We've done our research on

her. She has a double master's from Yale. Her former boyfriend is in prison for trying to cheat the government. The FBI is looking for her father, a cybercriminal. Did you know that? Did she tell you that? Who knows what you might divulge to her in the throes of passion or because of this delusion you call love?"

"Yes, Svetlana, I know all of that. What difference does it make? I would imagine that her proximity to criminality is something you would appreciate."

She laughed. "Touché."

"Now, can we get down to business?"

"Only if you have dinner with me. We can have room service and spend an hour before you need to get back to the little wifey."

I looked at her and let out a deep sigh, wondering why once upon a time I'd found her attractive. I could now see the cruelty around the set of her mouth and the coldness in her eyes she couldn't disguise. Repulsion rose in me. "I can leave now. I have half an hour before I need to meet Kimberly for dinner. So, are we doing this or not?"

"Okay, okay. I don't know what's got into you. You've changed," she said. "In a minute, I'm going to show you a photograph of the Pakhan so that you'll recognize him when he shows up. Burn the image into your brain. You'll have twenty seconds to do that before it disintegrates. Okay?"

I nodded, watching Svetlana tap a code into her phone, placing it on the bar in front of me. Sure enough, an image of an average-looking middle-aged guy appeared. There was nothing noteworthy about the man, except cruel eyes and rather thin lips. I would recognize him again. I looked at the image until, as Svetlana said, it broke and disintegrated on the screen.

"What's his name?" I asked.

"You don't need to know that. He'll introduce himself as the Pakhan. That's all you need to know."

"Okay. When will he be here?"

"I'll let you know."

"I won't be around this weekend."

"It's not a problem. He doesn't intend to meet with you until next week. I hoped we'd spend a little time together." She held up a hand to stop me from responding. "But I can see that won't be happening. I'll contact you and let you know when and where to meet the Pakhan. He will discuss the next steps with you and will want a last gesture of good faith."

"What will that be?" I asked.

"He'll tell you when you meet."

"Fine," I said. "Is there anything else?"

"No, that's it. You better go home to your wife. I'll find my entertainment," she said, staring at some guy on the other side of the bar who had been giving her the eye.

I followed her gaze to the man who seemed to fixate on Svetlana. "Have a good night. I'll wait to hear from you."

"Bye," she said without another glance in my direction.

"Did you get all of that?" I asked the listener as I stepped out of the hotel.

"Yes. You need to get to the police precinct, where an artist is waiting to get an impression of the Pakhan from you. Well done. Call me when you hear from her so we can position various tails along the different routes you might take from your office."

"I could be at the mansion."

"That's fine. We are geared for this. It's what we've worked toward for years. Just keep playing your role. By the way, you must give me some tips on how to attract them. And I'm sure your wife knew her whisper was a bellow in my ear."

I grinned. *That's the least that you deserve.* "Good night, Mark," I said.

I called Ward. "Coming over to you. Is Kimberly there?"

"No. She went back to the mansion. She wants you to bring her some mint chocolate chip ice cream."

I frowned. "Okay, but we need to go to the police precinct first."

When I got home, Kimberly was waiting by the door in sweatpants and one of my hoodies. "What took you so long?"

"Why, have you missed me?"

"No, I need ice cream," she said, taking the bag from my hand.

I smiled and shook my head, put my briefcase down, removed my jacket and tie, and followed her to the kitchen.

"What's going on with you? You ate a whole pint of that stuff earlier."

"That's not true. You had some."

"Two or three spoonfuls. You had the rest."

"Well, I like ice cream, and mint choc is my favorite."

"I'm starving," I said, looking into the fridge. "Have you eaten?"

"Yup, that's why I left Ward and came home. So how did you get on with Lady Svetlana? A little hard-faced; I wouldn't have pegged her as your type."

"Kimberly," I said in a warning drawl, "we're not going there."

"Okay, okay. So, what happened?"

"Well, Mark was happy, so I guess it went okay." We sat around the island together while I ate some cold chicken and salad and drank a beer. She attacked another pint of ice cream. I told her about my conversation with Svetlana.

"So, you'll be meeting this guy in a few days."

"Sometime next week."

"That reminds me, where did you say we're going tomorrow?"

"I didn't, Miss Sneaky. It's a surprise. Just lie back and enjoy it," I told her with a smirk.

She got up and put the rest of her ice cream in the freezer. "I'd prefer if you could lie back and enjoy it," she whispered in my ear, before making her way out of the kitchen.

"Kimberly, wait, where are you going?"

"To bed, Desmond, where do you think?"

Twenty minutes later, I entered my bedroom expecting to find her in my bed again. And she was. She had taken to sleeping in my bed the whole night, ever since her encounter with Mark. I wasn't complaining. I took off my shoes and yanked off my socks. The rest of my clothes came off on the way to the bathroom.

I was totally naked when I slipped into bed beside her, having washed off my time with Svetlana and the time in the police precinct trying to reconstruct the image of the hitherto faceless Pakhan, whom I would meet soon.

I needed her. She alone could erase my past and unwanted present. She reconstructed me anew, and I wanted that. I wanted her. She wasn't sleeping and was naked, too. "What kept you?"

I returned her smile and ran my hand all over her body, exploring every curve. I licked and sucked her nipples while my fingers tested her level of readiness because I couldn't wait. Satisfied with my explorations, I lifted my body up and over hers, entering her, and immediately thrust fully, watching her the whole time. Her eyes widened and her breathing hitched. I closed my eyes and continued to thrust. I groaned with the pleasure that her body gave. When her arms wrapped around me, I looked at her and pulled one of her legs up high over my waist. My cock touched that secret spot, making her gasp. She moaned as my deep rhythmic thrusts awakened her erotic wantonness. She undulated her hips in a slow sensuous movement, which slowed down my pace. "Yes, baby," she whispered. "Just like that."

I forgot who I was and lost myself in that sensual, timeless rhythm. And she was right there with me. My head fell on her shoulder, and her hand stroked my hair. "Don't stop, baby. This feels so good," she whispered.

Her lips fumbled over my ear and temple, searching. I lifted my head and pressed my lips to hers. My tongue immediately explored her mouth, then I sucked on her tongue and bottom lip.

The universe opened to enfold me and the warm, fragrant woman moving sinuously beneath me. In my mind, my physical body dematerialized as my essence merged with hers. I didn't want this to end, and it wouldn't for now as we kept climbing the stairway, going deeper and deeper into sweet ecstasy.

"*Kimberly*," I drawled her name in a husky whisper as her first orgasm rumbled through us. She was in for several more before the night was done.

41

Desmond

Kimberly marveled at the scene, taking in the breathtaking panoramic view of the ocean from the window of the luxurious Post Ranch Inn room. She gasped in delight, taking in the sun's beauty dipping into the horizon, the waves crashing against the cliff, and the seagulls soaring in the sky. The sun was setting, leaving behind oranges, pinks, and purples.

"This is wonderful. I can feel the tension falling off my shoulders already."

"This is your weekend, baby. We are going to do everything and anything you want. We can shop, walk along the beach, and watch movies. The hotel has two heated dipping pools, great yoga and workout facilities, and a gourmet restaurant. I've booked two massage sessions already."

She laughed. "Are you getting a massage, too?"

"Of course. Us boys need pampering. Isn't that the new man thing to do?" I laughed.

She came to me and put her arms around my neck. "Thank you. You'll make a great husband someday."

"I'm already married."

"Oh well, she made a splendid choice."

She attached her mouth to mine, and I cup her ass with both my hands, pulling her body closer to mine.

"We should eat," I mumbled against her lips. "Why don't I feed you, then we come back here and finish this after we have built our energy up."

She grinned. "Deal."

The day went by in a blur once we left, strolling hand in hand along the beach after filling our bellies, stopping at the souvenir shops to buy gifts for William, and then heading to our massage appointment. The smell of jasmine and lavender permeated the air, and the sounds of tinkling wind chimes and soothing music filled the room. Then it was time for FaceTime with William. Later, we went to a seafood restaurant and had an exquisite, candlelit dinner. When we returned to the hotel room, I lay on the bed, fully clothed, and watched as she moved around the room, unpacking her things. Now and then, her eyes would meet mine, and the warmth radiated between us.

She walked to the bed and asked me to unzip her dress. Kimberly moved back, keeping herself in my direct line of sight, and slowly slipped the short dress down her body to reveal black lace panties and a matching half-cup bra which accentuated her breasts.

Her hand moved to unclasp her bra and pushed each strap over her shoulder, while holding an arm across her breast to keep the cups in place. My face settled into a huge grin. I gave her a sweet smile and lowered the cups to reveal her firm round breasts with the dark-pink nipples already swollen with her own arousal. She began to caress herself.

I let out a low growl and in one smooth move, I was on my feet, reaching her in two steps. My fingers reached for her nipples and pinched them while I stared into her eyes. She moaned and her body swayed toward me. Her hands reached for my Henley, and I helped her to remove it. My lips fell on hers, forcing them apart. Our tongues vied for ascendency as she pushed me backward toward the bed.

The backs of my knees hit the edge, and I went down like a sack of potatoes, pulling her on top of me. Her hands cupped my face as we stared at each other.

"You're so beautiful," I whispered.

She kissed me then and my hands caressed her back and squeezed her ass, pushing her on my hardening cock. She ground on me. We both moaned with the sensation we gave each other. She moved off my body and undid my zipper. I lifted my ass off the bed to help her remove my pants. She pushed her hand down my boxers and I gasped as she gripped my cock.

Soon I was naked. I groaned as she stroked my length and her tongue flicked over my tip. When I tried to sit up and grab her, she pushed me back and straddled me. Her hot wetness slipped on my cock, and I hissed when I was fully sheathed inside of her. My hands reached for both her breasts. They were just a little rounder to me and very enticing.

A long while later, when all desire was thoroughly sated, we lay in each other's arms on the cusp of sleep. In the softest of whispers, I heard, *I love you, Desmond.*

My eyes flew open, and I waited, forcing my body to remain totally still. She was still as well, her breathing easy and rhythmic. I smiled and closed my eyes again.

The primal scream pierced through the final veil that separated the dream-sleep world and the awake world. It came again, and I sat upright in bed.

"Kimberly."

She was sitting beside me, her arms wrapped around herself, staring straight ahead. "No, don't touch my baby. Please don't take him. Desmond, Desmond, stop him. He's taking my baby."

She was still asleep, so I pulled her into my arms. Her body was rigid. "Kimberly, wake up. Wake up, honey. I've got you. Nobody is going to take your baby. He's safe." I assumed she was talking about William.

Now awake, she moved back and stared at me. "Oh Desmond, I dreamed that Voldemort had William and was taking him for interrogation to punish me for not telling him where my father was."

"Kimberly, I'm so sorry you met him at all. Come here." I pulled her back into my arms and rocked her back and forth until she was calm.

"I woke up earlier and was watching you, but I must have fallen asleep again." She stroked my face. "I'm worried about you meeting this Pakhan."

We looked into each other's eyes.

"I'll be fine. I'm not in any danger. The FBI will keep a close eye."

I was startled when she leaped off the bed and dashed into the bathroom. I jumped up and went after her. We were completely naked. She was throwing up in the toilet. Why was she so sick? The look on my face was one of alarm.

When she finished puking, she sat on the floor, looking exhausted. I wiped her mouth and her face.

"Tell me what you're feeling..." My eyes widened. "Did you throw up yesterday while I was packing? I thought I heard you."

She nodded.

"When did you last have a period?" I asked.

She stared at me. "No," she said. "No, no, no, no. I can't be. I just can't be." She got up and left the bathroom to find her phone.

42

Kimberly

I WAS as regular as clockwork. My periods came every twenty-eighth day and every time it did, I inserted a red dancing lady emoji in my Google calendar. I'd done that since the time the FBI had held me and I didn't have a period. I'd gone straight to a pharmacy as my first act on release and was overjoyed when the result came up negative. The last thing I wanted was Chad's child. My doctor told me that stress often impacted the menstrual cycle. I needed to heed that as a warning and take care of myself.

The red dancer lady last appeared seven weeks ago. I didn't read the obvious signs. But then, how would I know? Cece concealed her pregnancy for as long as she could, and then only spoke of her cravings, but it didn't register.

He came behind me until his arms were around my waist. "Tell me."

"I'm pregnant, but I can't be."

"Madeline said I should persuade you to go to the doctor because she'd found you sleeping on the toilet, and your ice cream eating splurge has been a little excessive. It also explains your tiredness, plus you've gone off coffee, haven't you?"

I nodded. I couldn't exist without caffeine, but the smell made me nauseous. He moved to stand in front of me and lifted my chin with his finger. "Are you okay?"

"No. I'm not. I can't be pregnant. I shouldn't be pregnant. I must be the joker in the pack that got handed the short straw. IUDs are supposed to have over ninety-nine percent success rate."

"What do you want to do?" he asked. "I suggest we have breakfast and talk about it."

"No. We need to find a pharmacy, so I can do a proper test because I don't believe it."

"Okay," he said.

We found a pharmacy where I purchased three First Response home testing kits. Back at the hotel, Desmond sat on the couch and watched as I paced with my phone, counting the minutes. I ignored him once I'd used the kit.

He waited while I went back into the bathroom and emerged again with the three sticks in my hand. I came and stood in front of him, staring at him.

"What's the consensus?" He pulled me onto his lap and took the sticks from me. He lifted my chin with a forefinger. "Tell me what you're thinking, Kimberly."

"Do you want this child, Desmond?"

"You know I do. I want our child with every breath in my body. I love you."

I nodded.

"Does that mean it's okay with you, too?"

"Yes, but I'm scared."

"Oh, honey, there's nothing to be scared about. It will be fine. Do you want to go home today?"

"No," I said, "we need to talk."

I was sitting with my tablet on the small terrace outside our bedroom with its sea view, waiting for him to join me. I giggled at the memory of his rendition of Foreigner's "I Want to Know What Love Is" while he was in the shower earlier. My shoulders shook with silent laughter; he never sang in front of me before.

When a bare-footed Desmond in jeans and t-shirt padded out to join me, I shaded my eyes from the morning sun and gazed at him. He looked gorgeous, as always. Our relationship had taken a turn after my truth poured out about Voldemort. It was something I had been keeping inside for so long, but I trusted Desmond with that information. My heart was full and Desmond had truly shown me the man he was.

"What?" he asked.

"Come," I said, beckoning him to my level.

He bent over, and I gave him the tenderest of kisses. "There," I said, "do you know now?"

"I have no idea what you're talking about, but I'd like another one of those," he said, leaning in.

My mind went blank as I kissed him again. "I love you."

He pulled back and stared at me and I stared into his infinite brown eyes and knew without any doubt that I loved him. "So, do you know now what love is?" I asked.

"Oh, you've made me so happy. You said it last night in your sleep, and I didn't dare hope. Is that what you were referring to earlier? That you love me?"

"It was more to do with your singing about wanting to know what love is. I loved being serenaded by my husband, but our baby was cringing." I laughed. "You'll have to take some singing lessons."

"It's one of the few songs I know the words to. I was practicing singing her lullabies," Desmond said.

"Her?"

"Yes, we're having a daughter, duh."

"I want a boy."

"We already have a boy."

"I like boys."

"I know it's a girl."

"Well, we'll know soon enough."

"What are you looking up?" he asked, eyeing my tablet.

"All things pregnancy and babies. I've ordered a couple of books. But more about that later. I want to talk to you."

"I'm listening," he said, "but I want to be close to you, so move a bit."

He slipped his arms around my waist as he pulled me back against the lounger. "You're the first person outside my family whom I've loved, and it scares me. When my dad left, I was devastated. It left an enormous empty space in my heart and in my life. I loved Chad, but now I'm not so sure, and if I did, it died a pretty quick death. I think I was looking for validation that I was enough. But I wasn't. He only wanted to use me." I took a deep breath because it was time for me to talk to my husband about things. "I can't help but be vulnerable about this child we're going to have. Trust is a huge issue for me."

"You need to turn around and look at me," he said.

I changed position so that I now faced him with my thighs resting over his. He cupped my face and kissed me. "Have I given you a reason not to trust me?"

"It's not that, although I didn't trust you at the beginning. It's about secrets and lies; they can hurt our children. I knew nothing of my dad's criminal persona until Voldemort told me. When I asked Angela, she said she didn't have any proof, only suspicions. But if she hinted at that possibility, it would have been less devastating to find out from the FBI. It left me even more vulnerable to their manipulations."

"This is about what you questioned last week, isn't it? I can't talk to you about that because I don't know how to, because I cannot even talk about it to myself. Why do you think Angela kept her suspicions from you?"

"She said it was because I loved my dad so much and he'd left. It would have destroyed me to then tell me she suspected he was a criminal."

"And do you think she was right?"

"I don't, Desmond. You've known about your mom and Michael for years. Face the truth and tell your mom and sister how their husband and father died. All I know is it feels better to know the truth."

He shook his head. "I get that, but Angela had no actual proof, just suspicions. You got to know about the allegations about my mom and Michael the same way I did. The information came through Mark. He said my mother had an affair with Michael and he was certain she knew how my father died. I don't believe it, and I'm never going to ask her that."

Holy shit!

"I cannot and will not do that. Mark is manipulative and I don't trust him. He would have to provide irrefutable evidence before I'd even think about doing something which would destroy my family."

"But there are ways we could find out."

"How?"

"I don't know, maybe ask him to give you proof," I suggested.

"That was the first thing I did. He says its sensitive information related to national security and I don't believe that for one second. The question is, why would he say that?"

"You can't have peace of mind about this. Find out the truth."

He stared at me. "I'm not sure I want to know, even if I knew how to find out."

"You can't mean that. Lies and secrets are destructive; they can hurt our children."

"You're the best part of me. It feels as if I've loved you forever. I'll never hurt you or our children, Kimberly, and I won't let anyone else hurt you, either."

"You can't promise me that."

He palmed my face. "Let's not spoil our weekend. I'll ask Mark again, and even demand that he provide proof of his assertions, okay?"

"I think it may be lunchtime," he said.

"Mmmm," I hummed. "In a minute."

I pushed a hand beneath his t-shirt and caressed his back and nuzzled his neck. My other hand unzipped his jeans, and I stroked him through his boxers.

He groaned and then whispered, "You're so bad."

I swung one leg over the side of the lounger, stood, and took his hand. "Come with me."

43

Desmond

Kimberly and I were being driven back to the mansion by Ward after our weekend away when I received a text from Svetlana.

Meeting in Moscow on Friday.

I called her. "Svetlana? What the hell? What's going on?"

"I said I'd let you know when and where. My message is obvious."

"You said he'd be arriving here."

"Did I? I don't think so. He has no reason to come there. You must go to him. You'll receive further instructions when you arrive." The phone clicked in my ear.

"What is it?" Kimberly asked.

I ignored her and tapped the only unlisted number on my contacts list. They answered immediately. "Ah, Desmond, I was expecting to hear from you."

"What's going on, Mark? I've just spoken to Svetlana. I've got to be in Moscow at the end of the week." The sharp intake of breath from Kimberly was audible, causing me to glance at her.

"Good," said Mark. "Their plans have changed."

"Good? Is that what you said? This isn't a good thing. You were supposed to arrest Svetlana. Where is she?"

"She's about to board a plane back to Moscow."

"What?" I shouted at the phone. "You let her go?"

"We had to. Can't you see? The most important thing is that you meet with the Pakhan. We must know who he is. If we didn't let Gorev go, that may not happen."

I brushed my hand over my face. "I'm on my way back to the mansion. You and I will talk later."

"Desmond, wait..."

I ended the call and met Ward's eyes in the mirror as he nodded. If this was going to go ahead, then I had to get Lorna Michaels on board. There was no time to waste.

"What just happened?" asked Kimberly. "Svetlana wasn't arrested, was she?" The 'I told you so' inflection in her voice was loud and clear.

"Desmond, are you hearing me?" Kimberly stomped into the bedroom after me. "You *can not* follow that woman to Moscow," she said, giving sharp definition to her directive. "The Pakhan would never show his face here."

I put our bags down and closed the door I left opened. I took her hand and led her to our bed, then sat and pulled her onto my lap. "Shhhh," I said, trying to quiet her. "You worry too much. This is the endgame and I have to see it through. It'll be fine."

"No, you don't. It was supposed to be the endgame when the mob boss came here. Now you have to go there. It's a trap."

"What can they do? They need me. Anyway, Ward is traveling with me, and we'll take every precaution. I promise."

She jumped off my lap. "You are the most stubborn person I've ever met. When will this stop? What will you be required to do next, before this ends? Voldemort is controlling you, and it's time you said no."

I stood, took her in my arms, and held her close so her head tucked beneath my chin. "Please, you're pregnant, Calm down," I whispered.

"What does that have to do with anything?"

"I don't want you getting upset and making your blood pressure rise. Our little poppy seed is at her most vulnerable right now. We need to tell our respective parents so they can take care of you while I'm away."

"Well, don't go on this ridiculous wild goose chase and I won't get upset. And I don't want to tell anyone about the pregnancy. Your mother hen response is enough to deal with for the moment."

The agitation in her body was clear. "Come," I said. "Dance with me." I moved around the bedroom, swaying.

Almost against her will, she allowed me to hold her close and moved with me. She slipped her arms around my waist and laid her head against my chest.

"A poppy seed? Where does that come from?" she asked.

"I've been doing some reading too. It's the size of our baby in your womb at this stage."

She giggled. "I'm impressed. Such a little thing to wreak such havoc, throwing all my hormones into disarray. We need you. You shouldn't be going anywhere."

"It's only for a few days. I'll be back before you even know I've gone."

A mischievous look planted a smile on her face.

"Desmond."

"Hmmm?"

"If you are going to Moscow, I want to track you."

"Okay," I said. "How will you do that?"

"Through your clothes. I don't like invasive trackers. It will go on everything you wear, as I've done with William, and through your cell phone."

"You track William through his clothes?"

"Yep. Since the time you appeared on the scene. It's ironed on to the existing labels on the clothes. You'd literally need X-ray vision or a machine to detect it. Where things like socks don't have a label, then it goes directly onto the material but will look like a label. I will also link your phone to mine so I'll know where you are, or at least where your phone is, at all times, unless you turn it off or it's been destroyed. Do you stay at a particular place when in Russia?"

"Yes. At the InterContinental in the Bay Centre. Why do you need to track my phone if someone already tagged my clothes?"

"It's a failsafe. The program that tracks you through your clothes is different to the one I'll use for your phone. In case they separate you from it, I need to know that, and it will tell me the last place you were. The only way I'll lose you is if they stripped you naked. The more clothes you have on, the stronger the signal."

"How will that work? Unless you're in the Bay with an electronic map."

"Simple. I'll download the planning grid for Moscow. If I can't find you, I'll extend the parameters until I do."

My eyes widened. I would not ask how she'd get the planning grid of a foreign city. She was getting a little paranoid about the situation, but I would not say that either. Anything that made her more comfortable about his trip was fine by me.

"What is it about you I don't know, Bennett? Hmm? I quite like it though, that my wife is a mysterious woman, and a remarkable one too."

"I'll always find you. Don't think you can ever get away from me. Besides, who's going to satisfy my needs?"

I chuckled and kissed the top of her head. "I'll never want to get away from you, and I am always willing to take care of your needs. Fancy a quickie before I go to the office?" I winked at her.

"No. I'm still mad at you and I need to make a prenatal appointment. So go to the office; I know you're itching to do that. I'll be fine."

"Okay," I said. "I need to go in because I'll have to leave again in a few days, but I'll take care of my horny woman later." I grinned, giving her a quick peck on the lips.

There was a lot to put in place, including talking to Mark again and planning with Ward and Special Ops because I didn't trust Mark. I'd noted Kimberly's concern, but I couldn't back away now. I had to see this through. I hated leaving her, but I'd only be away a couple of days, three at the most. Then I'd be able to focus on my family.

44
Kimberly

As I turned to walk away from William's bedroom, my husband's presence was behind me like a weight on my shoulders. He watched me all afternoon and I could sense his hunger radiating off him. I tugged on his arm, and when he looked at me, the tinge of desire in his eyes mirrored my own. He could no longer resist me, and he took my hand and led me into our room, my heart pounding with anticipation.

I took a step forward and pressed Desmond's body against the door. His arms embraced me and he paused, waiting for me to take the next step. I tugged his head closer to mine and kissed his earlobe. "I've been expecting this moment all afternoon," I whispered.

He grasped my hair, its chestnut waves cascading down my back as his fingers entangled in its flow. His tongue traced my lips before they opened and welcomed his hungry invasion. I sucked him in deeper, tasting his essence as his arousal pressed against me through his pants. His firm hand crept up my skirt, grazing my thighs as his fingers explored my skin, leaving a trail of fire wherever they touched.

"Desmond." My voice was quiet and pleading. "Touch me."

Without hesitation, his hands were on me, yanking my panties off my hips. He ran his fingertips along my swollen clit before pushing two fingers inside. I gasped and writhed against his touch, shivers awakening at my core, but every moan that escaped my lips urged him deeper and further into my pleasure.

"Kimberly," he moaned against my mouth, "you're so wet already, baby."

I ground my hips against his as his fingers moved within me, and I moved my knee, inviting his fingers to go deeper. His passionate kisses blazed a trail down my neck, making me gasp, and my body shuddered in climax, my legs giving way to the intensity.

"Oh my God," Desmond groaned as I collapsed against him, drained of my energy. "You are insatiable."

With one arm wrapped around me, he picked me up and placed me on the bed. Taking my glasses from my face, he looked into my eyes and slowly undressed me. I watched as he peeled away each item of clothing, until I lay there, exposed. With aching desire, he removed his own clothing and lay beside me, his muscular body radiating a delicious heat. As his hands explored my body, he caressed every inch. I felt his eyes pierce me. He pressed his lips against my skin. He explored the depths of my femininity with his fingertips. I moaned in pleasure as his lips encircled my nipple, and his tongue and teeth sent shock waves of pleasure through me. His expert touch drove me wild as it teased my clit. An electric tension built between us.

"Oh, please," I whispered. "Let me feel you inside me."

He moved me into position, leaning his lower body toward me and lifting my legs over his hips. With one hand, he guided himself inside me and I gasped with pleasure as he filled me. His hand caressed my breast as the other held my backside against him, allowing him to move in the most tantalizing way. As he teased me with gentle thrusts, I ran my hands through his hair. I purred with pleasure. His hands, now on my hips and ass, held me close as he made love to me, exploring and pleasing me in a slow, sensual rhythm. The peak was coming.

My body moved with his as he thrust into me with deep, urgent strokes. Each powerful surge sent an undulating wave of pleasure through me. I cried out his name as I felt my orgasm crest. His movements intensified, pushing me over the edge, until he, too, was caught in the throes of pleasure. He held me, burying his face into my neck as his last passionate thrusts stilled inside me. We lay in utter bliss, my legs still entwined around him, basking in our high.

Some time passed before Desmond stirred, awakening from his slumber. My head was propped up by my arm as I smiled at him, my hand taking pleasure in his cock beneath the sheets. "Looks like someone can't get enough of me. Now who's insatiable?" he uttered with a cheeky smirk.

Desmond was powerless against my siren's call, and a mischievous grin graced my face. "Keep fucking me this good and I'll never get enough."

He pulled me on top of him, kissing me while his cock twitched. I wriggled away from his grip and straddled him, pushing him inside me once more.

"God, woman, I swear you're going to kill me before this child is born. How many times have we had sex today? Six times?"

Okay, I had never heard of a man complain about too much sex. Something about the orgasm gave me such a high, way more than before I was expecting. Hell, I was horny all the time, from the time I woke until my mind shut off and I fell asleep. "Enjoy it while you can. Sometimes a woman's libido changes after pregnancy."

"Oh yeah? From where I am right now, I think you'll buck the trend."

"Then you'll die a glorious death," I said as I began a slow and sensuous rise and fall rhythm, all the while smiling at him.

He chuckled and watched my breasts dance before his eyes. "I can think of no better way to go," he said as he held on to my hips and thrust up, hastening my meltdown into my third orgasm for the night.

In time, we made our way to the shower and then downstairs to scavenge for food.

It didn't take long before we parted ways and I went into my makeshift home office, putting the second phase of my plan into action. First, I asked my assistant to book me on the nonstop flight from JFK to Moscow on Friday, the day after Desmond was leaving, and to book me into the Radisson for three nights in the name of Megan Bennett.

The other thing I wanted was a wig to hide my blond hair, just in case it was needed when I arrived in Moscow. The tracking of Desmond had a third prong that I didn't share with him.

I arranged to have dinner at the mansion with Angela and Madeline the next day. By then Desmond would have left. How would I explain my decision to go to Moscow? I would play it by ear and hoped something would come to mind in the moment.

I secreted myself away in my apartment to program a specific 'find me' algorithm for the chip to be inserted into Desmond's phone and linked to my phone and tablet.

I set up an exponential search algorithm with a twin-track programming sequence, which I would leave to run until I found what I was looking for, a name and a profile. Then I disguised my cyber identity and got down to some serious hacking for the first time in a long while. This search required a foray into the dark web. In the unlikely event, because of my superior skills, anyone tracking my cyber persona spotted me, then I would deal with the consequences. My priority was to protect my husband and the father of my children. I had every intention of removing Voldemort's hold on him in more ways than one. It would also satisfy my seething need for revenge. No, atonement. That's what it would be. Mark needed to atone for crimes against humanity.

The next morning, it was still very early. We woke and reached for the other, as if even in a state of unconscious we knew our impending separation meant we needed time to say goodbye. I trembled as I clung to him.

"Kimberly, honey, it's okay." His voice was low and somnolent as he became awake.

"No, it isn't. I don't want you to go." I still couldn't understand how, in a relatively short time, Desmond became a deeply ingrained part of me. If I lost him, I would lose myself, lose my reason for being. My body glued to his as I sought his lips.

He pressed his lips to mine to comfort and to reassure. This was the first time we would be apart since that night I discovered Mark in his office. He stroked my hair. "I love you so much and I hate leaving you, but it's just for a few days, honey. There's nothing to worry about."

I tried to push away the sense of foreboding. "Please stay close to Ward."

"I promise. I will call you every day," he said.

He ran his hands all over my body and I touched him, too. The ever present heat that ignited whenever our bodies touched leaped urgently into life. He made love to me with a reverence bordering on the worship of divinity. I was his only love, his goddess.

"Kimberly." He whispered my name when my inner muscles clamped around him. Lost in mutual pleasure, we forgot time as the soaring sensation reached its peak and consumed us.

In time, he rolled off me, taking my body with him. We lay, bodies glued together once again, but in silent repose. He waited until he thought I was asleep before gently easing himself away and out of bed.

He took a shower and left me an envelope on his pillow, telling me of his love for me. It was the last thing he did before exiting our room.

45

Kimberly

I LEFT the office early to return to the mansion for the special dinner for the two most important women in my life, but I had no inkling what reason to give them for my travel plans the next day. There were other, more important things on my mind vying for attention. I hoped something plausible would emerge.

"Dear," said Madeline, "this is such a wonderful idea. We should do it more often, don't you think, Angela? But next time have Leanne come too."

I nodded, looking at the two women. What was about to come out of my mouth? I'd be following Desmond to Moscow. "I planned our dinner for a reason."

"Oh, baby girl, what is it?" asked Angela, her eyes twinkling. "Is it the good news that we've been waiting for?"

I snatched at the cover Angela just provided. That was not my plan, but I would go with it. They would be so excited with the baby news, it would push all else to the sidelines. "Yes, I'm pregnant, but that's not what I..."

Angela Bennett squealed and rushed around the table to give me an all-encompassing hug.

"Congratulations," said Madeline. "I'm delighted. A little brother or sister for William. We must put an announcement in the papers, dear. Would you like me to arrange that?"

"No. Madeline, please, don't do that. It's much too early. Desmond and I want to keep the news to the family for now. We're not even telling close friends."

"Alright, dear, I understand," said Madeline.

"There's another reason I wanted to have you both here tonight. I'll be traveling to Moscow to join Desmond. This is a spur-of-the-moment decision. I want to surprise him," I said, bracing myself for a barrage of questions.

"Oh," said Madeline, a little surprised. "Is everything okay?"

I smiled. I could read my mother-in-law's mind. "It's okay. I know about Svetlana Gorev. It's not about her. I just miss Desmond and feel needy."

Angela smiled. "We remember, don't we?"

"Mom, please. You're embarrassing me," I said, glad that my mother provided the perfect cover, even a cringe-worthy one. I read about hormonal changes in the first and second trimester and admitted I was starting sex more often. My sex drive jumped up at inappropriate times. I grinned at the thought of marching into Desmond's office in the middle of the day and locking the door while I had my way with him. When we come back from Russia, I might do that.

"I've explained to William that I'm going to get his daddy and will drop him off at school on my way to the airport. I feel guilty that both of us are away again for a second weekend, but we should be back by Monday or Tuesday."

"You never have to worry about William," said Madeline. "Between Angela, Leanne, Dan, and Hanna, he doesn't have a spare moment, and I hope Angela will keep me company this weekend."

"You go be with your husband," said Angela. "Don't worry about anything."

I heaved a sigh of relief. That had been easier than I'd expected. All I needed to do now was pack. My assistant had a driver ready to drive me to the airport. I packed a few days' worth of clothes into the carry-on bag and headed downstairs and out the door, handing my bag to the driver and getting into the back seat.

Sitting in the departure lounge, waiting to board my flight to Moscow, I logged the precise time that I lost the signal to Desmond's phone. My body froze and fear gripped my senses. *Don't panic. You were expecting this. Now breathe.*

I closed my eyes and inhaled several times, forcing my heart to stop behaving like a runaway train. There was nothing I could do from here, and there was a nine-hour flight ahead before I'd be able to trace Desmond. Part of me wished I insisted on traveling with him, but that would've been a counterproductive thing to do. Nine hours was a long time to be out of touch with my husband.

Sitting on the aircraft, I began the nine-hour long mantra: *please keep Desmond safe. I can't lose him now.*

I checked into my hotel and in the relative safety of my room, I pulled out my tablet. The downloaded grid gave me Desmond's exact location, somewhere north of where I was right now. The signal was weaker than it should be, which meant that he was undressed. I took a quick shower, dressed, and put on my wig. The long dark-brown hair formed a curtain which hid most of my face. It was a long time since I saw that old self.

I made my way to Desmond's hotel.

At the InterContinental Hotel, the concierge confirmed

what I already knew. Desmond was not in his room. I called Ward.

"Hey, everything okay?"

"I'm at your hotel. Where are you?"

"What are you talking about? Where are you?"

"I just told you. I'm at the InterContinental. Where are you?"

"You're here? Okay, don't say another word. I'm coming to get you."

Luke walked into the hotel.

"Do you know where my husband is?"

He turned his head in the voice's direction. It was amazing how a long brunette wig could disguise a woman sitting in an armchair on the other side of the room facing the revolving doors.

"Are you staying here?" Luke asked.

"No."

He looked around. "Good. Let's go to your hotel. I'll wait for you outside while you pay for your drink."

"Then what?" she asked.

"I'm taking you to a safe house."

Something was going on and Luke would not give me the details. After all, my husband was the one who paid him.

"Is that where Desmond is? So, he's safe?"

"Kimberly, I'll explain everything once you're at the safe house. Until then, let's maintain silence," he said, leading me to the waiting car parked a little distance from the hotel.

At the Special Ops safe house, it rendered me speechless to discover that his wife was a secret service agent.

"Hello, Kimberly, I'm glad to meet you. Luke has spoken of you."

"Oh," I said, peering from one to the other. "Ward has said

little about you, but then he wouldn't, given who you really are."

Lorna Michaels grinned. "Would you mind telling us what you're doing here?"

I ignored the question. "I know where my husband is, Lorna, and I want to know why he hasn't been rescued. It's been over twelve hours since he's disappeared."

Lorna and Luke looked at each other and then at me. "You know where Desmond is?"

I nodded.

"How?" he asked. "How could you know that?"

I took out my tablet and showed them the stable but blinking red dot. "This is where he is. Where is this safe house in relation to where Desmond is being held prisoner?"

Lorna looked at Luke and back to me. "I have a hundred and one questions right now, but I will not ask any of them. All I'll say is you're showing us a location about fifteen minutes' drive from where we are, but Desmond is on the other side of the city at least twenty-five miles away."

"What evidence do you have that he's where you say he is? Have you seen him there? He's not where you think he is. How do I know that? Because the implant you placed somewhere inside his body has been found and removed, which is what I would do. Right now, my husband is half-naked somewhere close to here, and we need to find him. Now."

They both stared at me, speechless. Lorna recovered first. She picked up her phone and tapped on an icon. "How many people are in the building under surveillance right now?" she said.

"There were four last night, but there are only two there now. One is moving around, but the other is stationary," said a voice at the other end.

"I need eyes on those two people. Identify Desmond

Renault and confirm that he is one of the two people in the building," said Lorna.

"What? Now?" asked the voice.

"Yes, now," Lorna countered.

"But boss," said the voice on the other end, "that's not a good idea. We'd be exposed. We should wait until it's dark."

"I don't care what you have to do; just get back to me with confirmation as soon as possible," she said with exasperation.

Her people were right. They wouldn't put themselves or the operation at risk. It would be several hours before anyone could get eyes on my husband.

She turned to me. "Show me again where you think Desmond is located."

"I need to talk with our friend," Lorna addressed me. "I think we need a second lookout position. We can't afford to take any chances."

Luke nodded and Lorna pushed another contact on her phone.

46

Desmond

On the drive I tried to memorize landmarks, but it was dark and I was only familiar with the inner part of the city. I soon gave up once we were beyond that. We were heading south, and it had been about a half an hour's drive already.

Within another ten minutes, the vehicle slowed and came to a stop. The driver got out and opened the door for me. I stepped out of the car and glanced around. As far as I could see, I arrived at a desolate landscape. It was dark and sparsely spaced streetlights illuminated the road. The handful of two-story houses on the road looked dark and foreboding.

"Follow me, Mr. Renault," said the driver, who began walking toward the house nearest to the parked car, but set back from the road. I knew that Lorna's people would be on my trail and could pinpoint my whereabouts even if they did not yet have eyes on me.

The driver knocked on the door and allowed me to enter the house first. My eyes blinked as they tried to adjust to the gloom. The sharp pain at the back of my head started as I descended into darkness.

There was a metallic taste in my mouth. I was thirsty and had a pounding headache. Abruptly, I remembered being hit at the back of the head, and I was sure they had drugged me. I tried to open my eyes, only to stare into blackness. I moved my body, becoming aware then of the slight pain in my left shoulder. They'd found the tracker and removed it? I was sitting in a chair with my hands tied behind my back with a hood on my head.

"Mr. Renault." It was an English sounding voice without a trace of the guttural cadence.

I closed my eyes again and licked my parched lips. They dragged the hood off my head and I squinted into the bright light which beamed onto my face, leaving the rest of the room in near darkness, almost as opaque as it was behind the hood.

"Mr. Renault, can you hear me? Can I get you anything?"

"Water," I croaked, now a little more accustomed to the gloom of my surroundings. I could just make out the shape of a person sitting in a chair some distance away from me.

Someone who'd been standing behind me stepped to my side and held a bottle of water to my lips. I sucked at the bottle until they removed it, but I wanted more.

"Slowly now, Mr. Renault," said the voice across the room. "You can have as much water as you need, but drink slowly." They placed the bottle back to my lips, and I drank again until they removed it once more.

"Who are you? I'm supposed to meet with the Pakhan. I didn't expect to be assaulted."

"Yes, I'm sorry about that. A necessary precaution."

"Are you the Pakhan?"

"We're not that stupid, Mr. Renault, as you people believe. You must realize by now we know you're being tracked via your phone, but also through that tracker we found in your shoulder.

So amateur. I expected the FBI's technology to have evolved way beyond that."

My heart sunk. They knew. Kimberly was right. This was just a trap. "What happens now?"

The interrogator held up a hand and removed his vibrating phone from his pocket.

"What is it?" he asked in clipped tones. The interrogator's eyes widened as he listened to some very unexpected news. He looked at me. "Okay, I'll take care of that and will let you know when we're on the move again."

The interrogator signaled to the third person in the room. "Take off his clothes, remove his watch and shoes, and bring them to me," he said. "Leave his underwear and socks on, then find me a hammer and a sharp knife."

The man standing behind me untied my hands, then stepped in front to remove my jacket and shirt. They retied my hands before the man removed my belt, unzipped my pants, and tugged them. I watched as he took a key and unlocked the metal rings around my ankles, attached to a short chain bolted onto the floor.

The whole thing took place in complete silence until they shackled me once again. Undressed, a sense of vulnerability invaded me. I did a quick scan of the room. I was in a basement with no way out except through the one door.

The interrogator's eyes observed me. "No surveillance can penetrate this basement. So, they have placed your implant in a decoy, so there will be no unexpected callers."

The interrogator took the hammer from his henchman and smashed my watch to smithereens. He used the knife to dismantle the pair of shoes, but found nothing. The man searched through every inch of my clothing.

He stripped off the waistband of the pants and ripped the jacket to shreds, removing the lining. Nothing. He found nothing. The shredded garment was thrown to the floor, satisfied that the second tracker, in the watch, had been obliterated.

"Take these things and burn them," he instructed his man.

I was perplexed. What the hell was going on? Why didn't they strip me before since they knew I was being tracked? The interrogator had only taken action after that phone call. Who was on the other end?

Only Kimberly and I knew about the second tier tracking device on my clothes. I'd not even told Ward. Hopefully she was still receiving me from the label in my socks and underwear, if indeed she didn't lose the signal already. Thank God for my wife.

"You and I are going to have a little talk," said the interrogator. "May I call you Desmond? Mr. Renault is so formal, since you and I are family."

My mouth gaped. I squinted my eyes again, trying to zoom in on the features of my interrogator. "You and I are related? I don't think so. How?"

"All in good time. First, you must be honest with me."

"Honest about what?"

"About why you're here."

"I told you, I'm here to meet with..."

"Yes, yes," the interrogator interrupted me. "Please stop repeating yourself. I'm the Pakhan's emissary and he's not happy that you're trying to double-cross him. We know about your relationship with the FBI and your little subterfuges over the years. So, I'm asking you again. Why exactly are you here?"

"If you are the Pakhan's emissary, then you would know that someone invited me here and by whom," I shot back.

"That's true. I know all about you and Svetlana Gorev. She told you to come here to meet the Pakhan, but none of that tells me why you're really here. I want to know, Desmond. What were your real objectives in coming here? If you don't cooperate, things will go badly for the Renault family, including for your wife and son, William."

"Leave my family out of this. This is about me and Renault Technologies, not them. If you try to hurt my family, I will kill you."

"I don't want to hurt your family, Desmond. I told you, they're my family too. I'm a reasonable man. Something from you is what I want. Once I have it, all will be well."

"Who are you, and what do you want?" I snarled.

"It's very simple. One billion dollars is what I want. I have some debts."

I closed my eyes and sat still. The silence hung in the room for long minutes before the interrogator spoke again.

"I shall leave you to contemplate in peace and will be back later. There is no need for you to respond to my request. I'm sure your mother will pay a ransom for her precious son and will keep paying until we have destroyed Renault Technologies. That is the price to pay for your father's treachery, and for yours."

Fuck! This was a trap!

"Do not harbor any thoughts of being rescued because you are no longer where the FBI thinks you are," continued the interrogator. "Once we've made a short movie, we'll be on the move again. And by the way, you must become a better judge of character."

They placed the hood over my head again, and then I heard footsteps receding before the door closed. I shivered in the cold basement and wondered what fate awaited me. What had I done? Stupid fool. Kimberly was right. I was now a husband and father. Those three people were my priority now. I was so anxious to rid myself of the whole mess, I'd lost perspective.

47
Kimberly

FRUSTRATION OVERCAME ME. Ward persuaded me it was not a good idea for us to leave the apartment now in search of Desmond. They were planning in place. But I had put Desmond at risk with twentieth century technology. I could not believe they were still using body implants. That was so old school and the first thing that would be checked, especially if Desmond was not completely trusted by his captors.

When Luke and Lorna tried to pry into how I knew where Desmond was and how I'd been able to access a grid for Moscow, all I said was that I ran a hi-tech company and Special Ops might wish to consult Bennett-Tech to bring their antiquated equipment up to date. Ward grinned and gave Lorna an 'I told you so look.'

I liked Ward, especially since Desmond trusted him, but he was out of his depth, and I suspected that the 'friend' Lorna referred to earlier was none other than my arch enemy, Voldemort, and there was no way I trusted him. I already dealt with him in my own inimitable way. Plus, I'd hacked his phone, but nothing suspicious came up.

I watched Ward and Lorna observing me when they thought I wasn't looking. "Okay, you two," I said. "I'm here to surprise Desmond. Since we didn't have a proper honeymoon, I hoped we could spend a few days here. I also know about Desmond's work with the FBI and was worried because I don't trust Voldemort or Mark, as he's known to you."

Ward choked. "I don't trust him either, but Desmond has to work with him. How did you track him?"

"Desmond agreed to it because he knew I was worried about this trip, especially when the FBI failed to arrest Svetlana. Implants are too obvious, though. It's the first thing anyone up to no good would check for."

My trackers were in every item of clothing Desmond packed, but I would not divulge that information. It was just an instinct, and I went with it. There was something I needed to check first. "Is Mark here with you? Does he know what's happened to Desmond?"

"Yes, the FBI's sister agency is here on the ground, but Mark is managing the operation," Ward informed. "Lorna is moonlighting and is not assigned to this, but a couple of her men are now in the vicinity where Desmond is being held. Everyone's monitoring Bratva activities."

"I suppose he knows I'm here and tracking Desmond?"

Ward nodded. "We had to tell him; otherwise, we wouldn't be able to persuade him to set up another stakeout at your location."

"Yes, I know." I sighed. "Will Mark be going with you to get Desmond?"

"Yes, we have a plan. Hopefully, we can extract him without incident."

"Then what?" I asked.

"We'll come back here and get the first flight out of Russia.

It means your additional stay here is not in the cards, Kimberly."

It never was.

"That works for me," I said. "I'm going with you to get Desmond. You're not leaving me here, especially if Mark will be there, too." There was no way I was going to rely on Voldemort to keep Desmond safe.

"Mark is calling the shots. It's better if you wait for us here. Desmond would never forgive me if anything happened to you."

"No, that's not happening. He is not here, and I'm calling the shots. Either you take me with you or I'll hitch a lift from someone and follow my tracker. What's it to be? It's up to you."

Ward looked at the defiant set of my face. They would not win this one. He looked at Lorna and shrugged his shoulders.

"Okay," said Lorna, unsmiling. "It looks like we have no choice. I'm still waiting for the guys at the original stakeout to confirm whether Desmond is there. Are you hungry? Why don't you have something to eat and have a little nap? We have a few hours yet before we leave."

I narrowed my eyes. If they thought they could get me to sleep and then leave without me, they had another thing coming. "Yes, I didn't notice how hungry I am. I'd like some coffee too if you have any."

"Coffee and sandwiches coming up," said Lorna.

"Thanks," I said with a slight grimace. I hoped it was only in the mornings that the smell of coffee made me want to gag. Whatever happened, I had to get a cupful down my throat. It would help me stay awake.

Once they'd gone, I leaped up, opened my bag, and removed a small red pouch which contained some innocuous-looking items that looked like stud earrings, lapel pins, earplugs, and paperclips. I smiled at how creative Jonas was. I removed a tiny microphone, an ear stud lookalike, and attached it to the best concealed edge I could find, which was beneath the table in the room. If they insisted I took a rest, then I could listen in on them. There was no way they were going to leave me behind.

Next, I checked the signal on my tablet. My heart plummeted. There was now no color to the signal, just a slow, intermittent pulse at the spot where the red dot had been. It meant that Desmond was now down to his underwear or even just his socks, or even to some place that deadened my signal.

I rushed out of the room to find Ward and Lorna. "Hello," I called, "Ward, where are you? I have something to show you." Ward appeared through a door, followed by Lorna.

"Look at this," I shouted. "The signal was loud and clear when I got here. Now it's almost nonexistent. See." I shoved my tablet under their noses. "Can you see how different the signal is from when I first showed you? Apart from you, Mark is the only other person who knows Desmond has a secondary tracker."

Ward nodded. He looked at his wife. "If she's right, Lorna, we have no way of knowing whether Mark is staking out the place where Kimberly thinks Desmond is being kept. I believe her. As the person responsible for Desmond's security, I need to check this out now. There's no time to lose."

"Are you sure it's not just your battery dying?" Lorna asked.

I gave Lorna a withering look. "I may look blond, but it's hair dye. My batteries are not dying. I have a double master's from Yale. We have to make a move now before they move my husband again."

"You two eat. I need to think," said Lorna.

"What are you going to do?"

"Give me a few minutes, Luke. Go. Let me think about this."

Lorna paced back and forth, and I watched her from the other room. Did she believe Mark wasn't who he said he was, and if I was right, all of our lives were at risk?

She said fuck and then picked up her phone. I could hear everything from the other room.

"You've put yourself at risk without telling me, Lorna. And before you say anything, I know your motivation was to protect your husband and, by extension, Desmond Renault, but this is not a matter someone has directly charged our agency with. That is unfortunate, and I'm not impressed. You and I need to have a talk once you're back here. I have to make a call and will get back to you in about fifteen minutes. Do nothing until you hear from me."

"Thanks, Amanda, I'll wait," said Lorna.

Lorna continued her pacing back and forth until her phone rang again. She listened, this time without it being on speaker.

"Yes, Amanda," she said. "I understand."

Lorna rejoined us. We both looked at her. "Plans have changed," she said. "Luke, you better show Kimberly how to use a Glock. She's coming with us."

Luke and I stared dumbfounded at Lorna Michaels.

Ward stared hard at his wife after she'd instructed him to show me how to use a Glock.

"What's happened, Lorna? Who were you talking to on the phone? Amanda?"

"Yes. I explained our situation, and she's none too pleased about it. I'll probably be hung, drawn, and quartered when we get home." Lorna grimaced. "It took a while because I was waiting for her to get back to me. It turns out Mark is in Russia on vacation and is not part of any operation here."

"I knew it," I exclaimed. "Nothing has felt right about this whole thing from the time Desmond told me about it. Whoever is holding him probably knows that we know where he is. There's no time to lose. We must go now."

"She's right, Lorna. There's no time to show Kimberly how to use a gun," said Ward.

"Fine," said Lorna, "but you'll stay in the vehicle while we go in. No arguments."

"Fine," I said. "I hate guns."

"There's just one minor problem," said Ward. "You and I cannot rescue Desmond by ourselves. That's too dangerous. We don't know how many people are in that building. Let's move your men from the original location. They have the infrared sensor and we need that."

"No. It will take at least an hour to get from where they are to where Kimberly says Desmond is being held. Plus, we need to cover all our bases, just in case. The powers that be have instructed our embassy to send back up, so it's not just the two of us, Luke. By the time we get there, they will arrive too."

"I can help with that heat seeking thing," I said, "but we have to get to the building first. I have a gadget you can attach to the outside wall. It will transmit images back to my tablet."

Lorna Michaels looked at me. "Of course you do," she said. Ward shook his head and grinned. I came prepared.

48

Desmond

What time was it? They took my watch, so I had no concept of time. It must be close to twenty-four hours since I'd left the hotel. I hoped Kimberly was in contact with Ward and they were on my trail by now. Every nerve in my body was on alert for any sign of a rescue attempt. There might be a way I could get my hands free, but my feet were another matter.

I was shivering, hungry, and perplexed. The interrogator was not the Pakhan. For the first time since my arrival, I thought about Svetlana. I expected to be met and briefed by her. What was she up to? And what the hell did the man mean that we were family? I racked my brain but could not come up with anything rational. All I knew was that whoever this person was, I was not related to him. Kimberly and Angela had not referred to other family members. I knew Cecily's dad was deceased.

Kimberly's father!

A lightning bolt out of the blue hit me in the solar plexus. It couldn't be. Kimberly described him as a cybercriminal. Could he be working with the Bratva? He knew a lot about my business with the FBI. I couldn't restrain my runaway thoughts. I chased after them and ended up at Mark. Once I homed in on him, things began to both make sense and become confusing.

The door opened, and the interrogator was back. He was carrying an old-fashioned camera with a flashlight. Behind him came his henchman, wheeling a small table with a computer screen on a short pedestal.

"Now, Desmond," my captor said, "I hope hunger and a little time in this rather cold basement has focused your mind and you're ready to cooperate. I've brought you some clothes and am going to untie your hands so you can put on the sweatshirt."

Yes, please come fucking closer so I can rip your head off.

"Once we've done a short video to send to your mother, my man will unshackle your feet so you can put on some pants. Please try nothing or he'll shoot you. I don't want that to happen because I hate violence. Secondly, it would be an inconvenience."

I nodded. "Tell me who you are."

"All in good time," said the captor, handing me the sweatshirt. "You and I will be together until they pay your ransom. I've been rather lonely these past years. I look forward to having some company. Can you play chess? I'm fed up with playing against the computer."

When I had done what I was told, the captor handed me a newspaper. It was *The Times*, a British newspaper with yesterday's date. *That's clever. I was taken to Russia but would be holding a British newspaper, which means I could be almost anywhere in the world.*

I looked at my captor, who was staring at me with cold eyes, devoid of expression. "I see you've noticed my little subterfuge," I said. "An English newspaper will suggest that you could be anywhere."

I studied the man. He was tall, over six feet, I'd say, with iron-gray hair. His well-educated background was obvious, and he lacked thuggish demeanor, but something quietly predatory was present. I tried to discern anything which resembled Kimberly in the man's features. There was nothing I could see.

The captor moved a few steps back and positioned the camera. "Now hold the newspaper beneath your chin and smile, although I suppose you're not inclined to smile," the man said.

I held the newspaper as instructed and stared into the camera. A loud cracking sound came from the door being kicked off its hinges. Everything happened in a split second. My entire body was on alert mode since I regained consciousness and found myself bound, hooded, and in pain. I knew Ward would find me with Kimberly's help.

My eyes swiveled toward the door as it burst open. I dived to the ground, shouting, "Gun to your right!" I glimpsed Ward and Lorna, whom I recognized even beneath their ski masks, as I moved as far away from my chair as possible and curled my body into a tight ball, shielding my head with my arms. The gunshot exploded into the wall nearest to where I'd been sitting just a few moments before. A grunt of pain followed it. It was only then that I looked up to see Ward had the man pinned face down on the floor.

Two more men came charging into the room, followed by... *Kimberly?* Her name fell from my lips. I couldn't believe my eyes. My heart thumped in my chest as I stared at her. She moved toward me in a slow motion. Then things sped up. She was kneeling beside me, showering me with kisses and asking if I was okay. I could only stare at her.

"Desmond!" she screamed my name. "Talk to me. Say something. Are you hurt? Did they hurt you?"

"No. I'm okay. What are you doing here?" I asked.

"It's okay. We have to get you out of here."

"Kimberly... I..." I was confused, distressed, and needed to hold her, all at the same time. "You'll have to find the keys to release my feet. They should be on that guy somewhere," I said, nodding toward the man whom Ward secured in plastic cuffs.

"Desmond, are you okay?" asked Ward.

"Yes, I'm okay."

"Your guy has the key to release him," Kimberly told Ward.

"Kim," said a feeble voice from behind Kimberly.

49

Desmond

36 Hours Later

I was relieved to be at home again. Moscow was an extraordinary experience. It would take me a while to sift through everything and get some perspective. I felt as if they had dragged me through a wormhole and I was catapulted out again. I'd been in freefall ever since. Kimberly and I were both drained. While I was being debriefed by national security authorities, Kimberly spent most of her time with her father somewhere in the nether regions of the American Embassy, where he was being held before transportation home and most likely to a federal prison for the rest of his life. I eased my body out of bed, leaving my sleeping wife. I disappeared into the bathroom before pulling on a pair of jeans and a t-shirt. William was going to school, and I needed to see him.

When I returned to our room from sending our son off to school, Kimberly was still sleeping. I removed my clothes, slipped back into bed, and engaged in a little coaxing while waiting for her to stir and turn to me. I needed her.

"You promised to take care of my needs," Kimberly whispered. We'd both been too exhausted to do more than kiss and hold the other close since finding me in that dank basement.

I chuckled. "You're awake."

"How are we going to talk to them about what happened in Moscow?"

"Shush," I said. "We have all day to figure it out. Right now, I'm only interested in you."

She turned her head in my direction and our lips met in a light kiss. "Turn over," I whispered. She did as she was told, and I immediately stroked her face, neck, and shoulder. I bent my head and my tongue flicked over each nipple until they turned into hard little peaks.

"Mmmm," she hummed. "I've missed you."

"I know, I've missed you too." My fingers moved to stroke her clit.

Kimberly moaned. "Desmond... I need more."

I loved the way she said my name with a low husky voice when the pleasure was building deep inside her. As my fingers moved to her entrance, I kissed the side of her neck and jaw. I bit her earlobe, pulling it between my lips and letting my tongue play with the soft skin.

"Desmond," she wailed. "Stop being mean to me." Her hand reached for my cock.

I chuckled and moved her hand away. "Is this what you want?" Two of my fingers slid into her, making her arch her back and moan louder. My fingers moved in and out, stroking the wetness inside while nibbling at her neck.

Kimberly was making a low, continuous moan. When she tightened around my fingers, I pressed my thumb on her clit. It was all she needed to be pushed over the edge. She stopped breathing as pleasure washed over her and she opened her mouth in a silent cry. I was watching her. She looked beautiful in these moments. I kept stroking her until she came.

Kimberly turned to me and nibbled along my stubbled jaw. "That was nice, but I'm not done with you, Mr. Renault. I'll be back," she whispered, slipping out of bed and heading toward the bathroom.

I lay with eyes closed and arms folded beneath my head, listening to the faint noises coming from the bathroom. Something was going on with her and she wasn't talking about it. I was sure it had to do with her father. I knew she was doing a lot of processing and I didn't press her after their marathon conversation. Except for the ninety minutes she'd spent with her dad while I was conversing with the security services, I didn't let Kimberly out of my sight since she found me in that basement. All she'd say was Angela didn't tell her the half of it.

I pressed for further information from the authorities about who was involved in the plot to kill my father. I asked a direct question about my mother's involvement, to which the answer was not as far as the FBI knew. Mark was a traitor who deceived me. Now I understood what Nolan meant by the comment about my ability to be an excellent judge of character. I shuddered at the thought of what might have been if Kimberly didn't track me and been able to find me before I disappeared.

When she returned to bed, I opened my eyes. I unfolded my arms to wrap them around her slight form. She sucked on the skin along the side of my neck while scratching my scruff. I loved it when she did that. She kissed me while slipping one hand over my chest and over my well-defined abs until her fingertips reached my already hardened cock. I moaned as she pumped. "Kimberly," I breathed, moving one hand up and down her spine. She straddled me, guiding my erection to her and looked deeply into my eyes, getting lost in the lust and desire reflected there. She smiled and sunk on me. I didn't move, allowing her to adjust to having me inside of her again for the first time since the morning I left her in our bed.

When she moved, I did too, meeting the downward movement of her hips with light, soft thrusts that made both of us moan. "Desmond," she whispered, sliding her arms around my neck while moving her hips, "I love you. I don't want to ever lose you."

I stared at her, taking her in. "You're never going to lose me. Never," I whispered back. My eyes rested on her pert breasts. I pushed my upper body up so I could take a nipple into my mouth and suck it hard. Kimberly shouted out her pleasure at the rough stimulation of a sensitive, erogenous zone. My hands moved to her hips, holding her in place as my thrusts became more forceful and reached deeper.

The shift in tempo caused her to cry out as her pleasure increased. I rolled us over and hooked one of her legs over my waist. I continued to plunge my cock deep into her until that familiar sensation was at the base of my spine. My fingers tightened on her soft skin and we both knew it wouldn't last much longer. It had been too long since I'd been inside of her, and we were both close.

"Kimberly," I breathed, "let go, baby. Come with me." My thrusts became a little harder. She placed both arms around me and bit my shoulder. I shouted her name when we both lost control as a powerful thrust pushed her to the limit and elicited a high-pitched scream. My seed spilled into her.

My body sank onto hers and we held each other, our breathing short and raspy. I rolled off her, but we remained locked in the other's arms, savoring our reunion. It was time to talk, or at least to begin the first phase.

"Do you remember the first time you and I were in here?" I asked.

"I'll never forget. You avoided me fucking your brains out, but this is not the time to reminisce. You need to tell me how I tell my mom that her former husband held mine captive in some foreign city and is now facing a life sentence in a federal penitentiary."

"Right after you tell me how I tell my mom and sister that their husband and father were murdered by my best friend's father and Leanne's business partner, in league with two vicious mob organizations."

Kimberly laughed hysterically. I knew this was a reaction to the forty-eight hours from hell we'd lived through. I took her hand and sat beside her. "I still can't believe that you put yourself and our poppy seed in danger," I said. "Lorna told me she insisted you remained in the car, and you agreed to do so. They could have killed you. What were you thinking?"

"I was thinking there's no way I was going to let my children grow up without a father like I did, and I wasn't ready to lose the man I love. I needed to be there, Desmond. Can't you see that? I needed to be in Moscow so I could direct Ward and Lorna to where you were. Let this go, Desmond. Nothing would have kept me from coming after you. I had to save you. I had to be there. We are married. We fight for and protect each other."

"But, Kimberly, that's—"

She interrupted me, saying, "No, Desmond, no buts. We are each other's strength. I need you to see it that way."

I sighed and nodded. I knew she was right. It would just take me a little while to get used to the idea. Her being in harm's way made me crazy. "You planned it and didn't tell me."

"Because you would've tried to talk me out of it. Desmond, I'm here, at home with you. Unharmed. Okay?"

"Okay, I still don't know how you gained that detailed map of the layout of Moscow, even the sewer system, and how you discovered the real name of the Pakhan. The FBI has been trying to uncover that for years."

There was a lot about my wife I still needed to discover.

50
Kimberly

THERE'S SO MUCH *you don't know and I'm not yet ready to tell you.*

I shrugged. "If I tell you, I'll have to kill you."

"I'm listening."

"Everyone has a talent. Mine is a geekish affinity for navigating my way around the web and gaining any information I need. Apparently, that skill runs in the family," I said with a slight break in my voice. "After all, I'm The Calculator's daughter and that is his legacy to me." It might be over the top to say, but it was true. He wanted me to have his skills. "To find anything I need, I write a piece of code that tells the world wide web depository what information I want to access. If it's archived digitally, I'll find it. The name and/or a specific identifying signature of almost everyone who lives on the planet will be stored digitally in some shape or form. I can triangulate four, eight, ten, one hundred different pieces of information to find what or who I'm looking for."

His eyes didn't leave mine, almost as if he was trying to figure out if I'm overexaggerating or not. "If I run a photograph through facial recognition software, the computer will search every camera within given parameters until it finds a match. The photo I found was too old and blurred. I'd have to access the entire country to find him."

The technique I used to locate Svetlana Gorev's bank account was top secret. By now, I redirected all her money to Russian orphanages as anonymous donations, and Lady Svetlana would have to jump through many hoops to reinstate her identity. It was no less than she deserved for endangering my husband's life.

It was more difficult to locate Voldemort's money. He'd been very smart about hiding his tracks, but not as smart as I was. I hadn't been mean. I left his checking account untouched but his three offshore accounts in different locations were drained and redistributed. Voldemort deserved a double surprise. Not only would he be several million dollars lighter, but the FBI would also find documentary evidence of his involvement with Bratva and the Shade in the 'erased' box on his computer hard drive. Retribution was complete and sweet.

"But, Kimberly, that means you would have to..."

"Do you ever want to have sex again?" I asked, interrupting him.

He grinned. "That's bribery."

"Shut up and kiss me."

He did as I asked, his tongue slipping between my lips. When we came up for air, I grasped his hand. "I need you inside me again." Desmond grinned and allowed me to lead him back into the house and upstairs. He must be enjoying my heightened sexual appetite.

About two hours later, Desmond and I led Madeline, Angela, and Leanne into the sitting room. There was a lot to talk about. It was time to tell some shocking truths. Four pairs of eyes were glued to our faces as we took turns telling the backdrop to our recent visit to Russia. Leanne broke when she found out the truth about her father's death.

Madeline Renault comforted her daughter, but there was a shuttered expression on her face as she looked at her son. Not in a million years did she suspect the Bratva tried to recruit her son as they'd done to her husband.

For my mom, the most shocking news of the evening was the revelation that Nolan kidnapped Desmond and was planning to seek a ransom, which would in effect destroy the Renault family business. Her ex-husband and my father turned out to be criminals. Angela raised tearful eyes to me. We broke into two smaller immediate family groups for deeper conversations.

"I'm so sorry that you found out this way, Kimberly," said Angela. "I tried to downplay his criminality to protect you."

"I know." I'd known about my father from the time with the FBI. Nothing would be gained by it. That part of my life would remain known only by Desmond and Barbara, who would never reveal the truth about my past.

"So, you went to Russia, not because you missed your husband, but because you felt he was in danger?"

"Yes, I'd met Svetlana Gorev just before Desmond and I went to Big Sur for the weekend and I didn't trust the whole situation. When she told Desmond to go to Russia, I knew I had to go too."

"But you didn't tell him? I bet he was upset about that, given your condition."

"I'm just pregnant. Not an invalid. And yes, he is still upset, but he'll get over it. He's overprotective."

"So, what will happen now, to your dad, I mean?" asked Angela.

"I expect there'll be a trial of some sort, probably not a public one, and Dad will spend the rest of his life in jail for treason," I said in a matter-of-fact voice. The recent revelations still numbed me. It would take time for my heart to thaw and for me to come to terms with what my father had done to Desmond, knowing who he was.

My father's involvement with it all was quite horrendous. He'd been on the Bratva hook because he owed them money for his gambling debts. They owned him. He persuaded the Pakhan to let him extort money from Renault Technologies as payback for Damien Renault's betrayal after the disappearance of Michael Morse.

Michael put him in touch with Svetlana and Mark. Having kept tabs on me from the time he left home and eventually the country, partly to protect me, he knew I'd been taken into FBI custody. The untrusting Michael gave the order to find out if I knew of my father's whereabouts. The biggest shock was when I married Desmond Renault. Nolan tried to modify the kidnap plan, but the Pakhan would have none of it. Eventually, the whole thing came to a head in a derelict house on the outskirts of Moscow. In the end, his own daughter orchestrated the downfall of The Calculator. The conversation with my father before we left Moscow ran through my brain. I sat in stoic silence as my dad relayed the story of his life. My father was a selfish, craven man. Everything was about him. He'd use his own child as a means to an end.

"Kimberly." Angela touched my arm. "Are you okay?"

I stared at my mother. I didn't know how to define 'okay.' At that moment, Desmond came over to us and knelt in front of me. He took my face between his hands. "It's okay, honey," he said. "We'll work through this, you and me together. Okay?"

"Okay," I whispered.

"Come," he said, "Leanne wants to talk about telling Johnny of Michael's role in Dad's death. She won't go to the club again until he knows. You too, Angela. I need your wise counsel here."

Leanne, Angela, and I thought Johnny should be told of his father's role in Damien's death, but Madeline was against it. She could see no merit in raking up the past. Why cause someone such excruciating pain and for what purpose? The truth would be devastating for Johnny and he was innocent.

I looked from my husband to his mother. "Desmond, there is authenticity in your relationship with Johnny. Can you and Madeline honestly say that over the years you haven't both carried secrets?"

Desmond shrugged. "I suppose, but I didn't think about it like that. I wanted to shield Johnny from hurt because he had nothing to do with his father's actions."

In the end, it was Leanne who called the shots. "Quite frankly, I'm going to find it impossible to work alongside Johnny for one day, never mind for however many years, knowing that his dad had a hand in the murder of mine. If you won't tell him, Des, I will."

"Okay, Lea," Desmond said with a sigh of resignation. "I'll do it."

"Do it tomorrow, Des. This can't wait."

51

Desmond

JOHNNY and I were in the summerhouse, and he was pacing. He didn't take the news well, but it wasn't unexpected. How did someone react to finding out their father was the reason mine was dead? His frustration with me was valid, but our friendship meant a lot to me. After this news, I wasn't sure that he would want to be in the same room as me because of the guilt that was already displaying on his face.

"How can you even look at me right now? Why does my family have to be so fucked up?" Johnny ran his fingers through his hair. He had never had a perfect life. Mostly, his family had always been dysfunctional, with one parent constantly cheating on the other and the whole world knew about it. When the door of the summerhouse flung open, Johnny turned around to stare at me like he was going to say something, but then he left.

Kimberly warned me that this conversation wasn't going to be good, but he deserved to know, and the longer I kept it from him, the better the chance he would find out from someone else.

"What happened? How is he?" Kimberly came in and sat on the love seat beside me and took both my hands in hers. "What do you need?"

"Let's go to the lodge. Get away from here for a bit," I said in a quiet voice.

We drove in silence to the Renault family's mountain lodge in the foothills. By the time I walked around the SUV to open the door for my wife, she was already out. I took her hand and headed onto the path that took us higher into the mountains.

"What happened? Please talk to me."

"It was not very pleasant. I watched my friend go from shock and disbelief, to accusing me of lying, to utter devastation and anger. In the end he just stared at me, then left."

Kimberly nodded. "I can imagine how hard that was for you."

"I've lost my best friend, and I expected it."

"Why? This is not your fault, and he deserves to know the truth."

"I know. Leanne is right. Now I'm waiting for the aftershock from the impact it will have on him. And then there is my mom. I have to confront her at some stage. It's something that has eaten away at me for years. I can live with the fact that she had an affair, given how Dad behaved, but with Michael, the man who plotted to kill him? That's the part I can't handle. Did she know and have a part in it too?"

"Desmond, don't let this eat away at you." She looked up at my grim face. "Hey." She nudged me. "You're not alone. You have me now, and William and Poppy Seed."

That brought a smile to my face. I took her in my arms and held her tight. "You have transformed my life, and I am so lucky. I love you, Kimberly Bennett-Renault."

"I love you too. The baby appointment is coming up," she said as my hands touched her belly.

My wife was gorgeous and soon we were going to have another child running through our house. Was it weird I was excited to see her as a mother? William wasn't an infant, so to see her with a small baby in her hands—perfection.

"You know you don't have to prove anything to me. You are not like Nolan. I see how you are with William and no child could have a better dad. No matter how tired you are, like you were when we got back from Russia, you insisted on waking him and having breakfast. I love that. I love you."

"You make me a better person; you save me from myself." I kissed her again.

"We save each other. Now, let's pick up our son and do something with him. Maybe take him to Big Belly Burger as a rare treat."

Spending time as a family was something I held dear to my heart, especially since William still didn't know about the other baby. We wanted to take our time and get things organized before we told him.

"Congratulations, mom and dad," said Dr. Daniels.

"So no longer a poppy seed," I said. "I rather like Poppy."

"Sorry, poppy is now a strawberry," said the doctor with a grin.

"He's only keen on Poppy because he wants a girl," said Kimberly.

"I'm afraid I don't enjoy doing an ultrasound under twelve weeks," said the doctor, you'll have to wait until sixteen weeks for the sex, but I can let you hear its heartbeat. Would you like to?"

"Yes, please," we said in unison.

"Okay. I'll just get my doppler. Kimberly, could you..." Kimberly hitched up the scrubs t-shirt and pushed her sweatpants to her pelvic bone. Dr. Daniels turned up the amplifier box and placed the listening device on her belly.

One of my eyebrows reached my hairline, and I looked at the doctor. "Is that—?"

"I think so." The doctor responded to my unfinished question.

"What? What is it?" asked Kimberly as Dr. Daniels put the doppler away and used her stethoscope. "Is everything okay, Dr. Daniels?"

"Yes, nothing to be concerned about. How have you been feeling?"

"Okay, except for morning sickness, and I sometimes feel bloated like I have a stone in my belly, especially once I've indulged my cravings."

Dr. Daniels smiled. "Yes, Desmond, you're correct. You heard a double heartbeat."

I reeled in my chair. "Twins? We're having twins? Fuck..."

The doctor's grin broadened. "You have two blessings. Congratulations. You can exhale now. That would be good. Desmond, please get your wife some water. There's a dispenser outside. You should have some, too."

When Desmond returned, she took the water. "Are you sure?" Kimberly choked out. "I... I... Desmond...?"

"It's fine honey. Everything will be fine."

"No, it won't," Kimberly whined. "It's okay for you. You're not the one carrying this, this... looking as big as a house. This is all your fault..."

"Yes, dear," I said, kissing her forehead. I grinned at the doctor.

Dr. Daniels smiled at us both. "Kimberly, there's nothing to worry about. You're young, fit, and healthy with your family around you. Enjoy your pregnancy. I prescribe plenty of back and foot rubs." She winked at her patient. "That's it for today, you two. See you in a month."

52
Kimberly

"Well, you generated a stir tonight," Desmond said as I came out of the bathroom in one of his white t-shirts which I had taken to sleeping in since my pregnancy. His eyes roamed my bare legs to my face. I was looking at him with a smile on my face. "It sure made the grandmas happy. I thought Angela was going to pass out. I can never read your mother, though."

"Oh, she is happy, I can tell. And so was auntie and big brother," said Desmond.

"William was so cute. He wants a little sister and a big brother." I laughed.

"Come here," said Desmond. "You're much more relaxed now than you were in the hospital."

"Well, it was a bit of a shock, even for you."

"Only for a minute. I love the idea of two poppies."

"They are not poppies any longer. They are strawberries and I hope at least one is a male."

Desmond chuckled as he reached for my hand and pulled me onto the bed beside him. "Nope, we have a Poppy and a Gina."

Desmond propped himself on one arm and angled his large body toward me. "Thank you."

"What for?" I asked, staring at him with smudged eyes.

"For agreeing to marry me, for bringing light and joy into my life, for giving me my very own family. I thank God Madeline went to AFC that day. She found you for me."

I stroked his face. "I'm the lucky one, and Dr. Daniels is right. I'm in good health. I have my family around me, including my handsome husband. Do you know, Desmond, when I moved back here from Boston I was used, abused, and angry? Just helpless. My whole life just collapsed. I was grieving for Cece and struggling to establish my business. I never imagined that in three years, I would become a wife and mother. Happiness was not what I expected to find. But I did find it and I never want to lose it. My greatest fear is that I will lose you, and all of this, William, our babies, our life together."

His finger traced the outline of my face. He bent and kissed my lips. "Put those thoughts out of your head. You will not lose me. And thank you for not putting any pressure on me around Madeline and what she knew about Dad's death. I will do it on my own time. There's just more upheaval at the moment."

In response, I ran my hand over his bare chest and then over the ridges of his abdomen to his hips. I hooked my fingers under the waistband of his boxers and pulled them. Desmond lay on his back and raised his butt off the bed so I could push them down his legs.

My eyes rested on his cock as I licked my lips. I moved down the bed and pushed his boxers off his body. Taking my time, I placed soft kisses along his lower body while running my nails over every inch of his skin. Desmond raised his head so he could watch me. I continued to kiss my way up Desmond's body until I reached his balls. They too got kisses as well as his cock. I grinned when the tremor in his body stirred.

When my lips closed over one of his nipples and my fingers tugged the other hard, Desmond could not stand any more. He pulled my body up and latched his mouth onto my breast and suckled it, rolling the nipple between his teeth, then gave the same treatment to my other breast. His hand found my clit and his fingers slicked between my lower lips. I flung my head back and moaned with pleasure.

His erection jerked hard against my belly, and my hand reached to stroke him. Desmond moaned. His mouth released my breast and his eyes begged me. I shifted my body until I was directly over his rock-hard cock, sliding onto him and my juices coated him until it fully wedged him inside. My hips rocked, and when Desmond rolled both my nipples, my movements picked up speed.

I closed my eyes and savored the sensations created by our rhythmic age-old dance. Soon my breathy little mewls and trembling thighs told him I was on the verge of letting go. He sat up and swung my body onto the bed, grabbing one of my thighs, angling it high over his hip, and pounded into me. He buried his face in my neck and breathed in my scent. Obscene noises filled the room as we enjoyed each other.

"Ahhh, Desmond, yes, baby, yes, yes, yes," I called out as I gave myself up fully to the pleasure my husband was giving me. It suffused my entire being, and my walls clamped around him. His response came in soft grunts. He knew he could not hold on to his control any longer. His hand found my sensitive little nub and his thumb pressed down. In that moment, ecstasy lifted us higher, higher, and then exploded, melding our two bodies and two souls.

Our bodies were damp and clammy; our breaths came in short sharp puffs.

My body went limp and Desmond rolled off me, not wanting to let his weight burden me and our two little poppy/strawberries. He lay beside me, breathing hard, the perspiration streaming off him.

He watched me in peaceful repose, serene. My lashes fluttered open, and my eyes homed in on his face. I gave him a soft dopey smile and my lashes shuttered again. Never had lovemaking been so satisfying.

Desmond got off the bed and he came back with a towel and a warm damp washcloth. He wiped, then dried me.

I smiled at him. "Will you marry me?"

He chuckled and kissed me. "I was going to ask you the same thing."

"I'm serious."

"So am I. I've been thinking about it for some time. We should have a proper wedding here at the mansion."

"Angela will want a Rabbi."

"Angela can have anything she wants. After all, she was on my side from the very beginning." He grinned.

"Yeah, I know. She was a traitor, but I'm not complaining. She told me you were a good man."

"And you scoffed, no doubt."

"Yeah, I did."

Desmond flung the cloth and towel into the bathroom and joined me. He gathered me up in his arms. "So, you think we can ditch our peculiar marriage and have a conventional one?"

"No, not conventional, never conventional, and we ditched that other one a long time ago. I suppose I'll have to let Leanne dress me up."

"We better take the whole family on our honeymoon, too. Then Leanne won't call when I'm making love to my wife."

I laughed. "To be fair, we were not making love."

"We were about to," he insisted.

"I think we should go back to Big Sur and just have a family holiday with William before the poppies arrive."

"I'd love that."

Epilogue
Desmond

THREE YEARS Later

The morning air was still cool and fresh against my skin as I woke. The sun just peeked over the horizon, and the birds chirped their morning song. I looked around our bedroom, at the walls covered in pictures of our twin girls, laughing and playing with each other. Kimberly started tossing and turning, and then she sat straight up.

"Good morning, Mrs. Renault. Sleep better last night?" I asked, touching her belly and then giving it a quick peck.

"This one is going to kill me if I don't start getting decent sleep. I'm just a zombie. One child is eating my insides. The twins are going through their 'no' stage, and William doesn't want to do anything but play video games."

"Listen, this pregnancy has not been easy for you, but just think of when you get to hold that sweet child in your arms..." I say, watching her face light up. "See, doesn't that make it all worth it?"

She nodded and sank into my embrace.

"We've come so far," I said, my voice filled with emotion. "How big of a family are we thinking? Five? Eight?"

Kimberly laughed. "Four. After this one, we are done. I love my babies but... yeah, we are done."

The new house we built from the ground up was gorgeous and spacious. We gave the Renault Mansion to my mother. With our family growing, it was necessary to get a place of our own. I smiled, my face full of love. "Now we just have to make sure our fourth baby is as healthy and happy as our first three," I said, squeezing her tight.

We came a long way in the last three years, and even though at first this was constructed as a marriage of convenience on her end, the love became real and she reciprocated my true feelings. Kimberly was the wife I dreamed of, and I tried to make her happy every day.

I leaned in, giving her a passionate kiss. We stayed like that until the twins woke early from their nap. I got them out of their playpen and hugged them to my chest. Being a father of such wonderful children made me the happiest I've ever been.

"Desmond, if this isn't a boy, I'm never having se—" Kimberly stopped in her tracks. I was lying on the sofa with the two-and-a-half-year-old identical twins Gina and Poppy, asleep on my chest.

"You know you should put the girls down in their playpens. You are spoiling them."

I grinned. "Only a little."

"Come on. Up," Kimberly said, taking one twin. I followed her upstairs to put the girls to bed.

"What's wrong?" I asked with a grin. "Having those pesky libidinal urges again? I can help with that."

"If this one isn't a boy, there'll be no more sex for you."

"Yes, honey," I said, drawing her to me to kiss her neck and stroke her twelve-week pregnant belly.

"I mean it."

"Mm-hmm," I hummed, walking her into our bedroom. Her arms slipped around my neck, and she gazed into my eyes.

My life was not full until William and Kimberly came into it. I knew now that I never knew the meaning of true love until I stepped into Kimberly's office that first fateful night. I couldn't imagine my life without her, and she was the most wonderful mother to our children.

"Thank you for showing me that men can stay. That my kids will have a father that will choose them over anything else," Kimberly whispered into my ear before dropping her lips to mine.

After breaking the kiss, I whispered in her ear, "It's us against the world, baby."

About the Author

Ashley Zakrzewski is known for her captivating storytelling, sultry plots, and dynamic protagonists. Hailing from Arkansas, her affinity for the written word began early on, and she has been relentlessly chasing after her dreams ever since. She also writes under the Pen Name Kaci Bell for clean romance.

Her favorite thing is to hear from readers - so if you loved a book, hit the contact button and shoot her an email to make her day!

She has made the switch to being on all major ebook retailers and also giving her readers the option to buy eBooks and paperbacks directly from her website.

If you like to save money and support the author, she offers Buy One Get One Free eBooks on her website and bundles that save you even more $$$. No coupon code needed. All discounts will be applied in the cart. Just visit www.ashleyzakrzewski.com

If you would like to sign up for her newsletter to hear the latest news and get an email when she releases something new, then you can sign up for that here: https://view.flodesk.com/pages/638f846544fd43768982b30a

Made in the USA
Coppell, TX
05 March 2026

72944091R00204